FLIRTING WITH FIRE

PIPER RAYNE

Cover Design: Angela Haddon

Line Editor: Gray Ink Editing

Proofreader: Shawna Gavas, Behind the Writer

Everyone knows that if you play with fire you'll end up getting burned...

What happens when you attend a first responder's bachelor auction with your best friends? Well, if your name is Madison Kelly like me, your friends end up bidding on a date for you with your high school crush.

That's right. Even back when I was 'Fatty Maddie' to all my classmates, I had eyes for the quarterback of our football team. Not like I was the only one.

Mauro Bianco may fight fires for a living, but he still sets my heart ablaze. One look at the rugged, muscular man he's turned into and I want to slide down his pole.

One date. That's all I'm committed to. A few hours and I can tuck him back into that tattered old shoebox in my closet.

As always, the universe has other plans. I never would've predicted that in a matter of days he'd turn from my dream guy into my business partner-***and that's when things got interesting.***

Flirting with Fire

PROLOGUE

Nine years ago…Highschool—AKA Hell

Madison

"I don't want to go," I whine for the hundredth time tonight.

"Get out of the car." Lauren stands on the driver's side of my dad's beat up Wrangler that he gave me last week for my sixteenth birthday.

I push up my glasses. "It's a *senior* party. I'll let you pick the movie if we can please go back to my house. I'll even let you sneak into my dad's liquor cabinet."

Since this is my dad's weekend, I get a tad more freedom with the newfound single life he's embracing. It's meant either late night or early morning arrivals back home depending on how easy the women are.

Lauren grabs my hand, yanking me out of the truck. "I'm not sitting around watching some dumbass romantic comedy again."

I stumble out, my feet landing right in a puddle. My white

trainers are now caked with brown mud. "Great. My mom's going to kill me."

"It's fine." Lauren looks cool as usual. Lucky for her, the style of baggy pants and t-shirts are in, although she's sported the same look since we were in kindergarten. Tonight, when her mom dropped her off, I knew there was trouble on the agenda when I noticed she had on a sheer layer of lip gloss.

"Says you, who won't be spending the next couple hours with her soaked socks squishing in her shoes."

She rolls her eyes. "If you would have let me dress you," she singsongs.

"Yeah, well my stomach doesn't look like that in a tight t-shirt." I point to her lean waist. "My back fat would be squeezing out the sides."

Lauren and I have been friends forever, but we're completely different. After school, Lauren's day is filled with soccer, softball or volleyball depending on the season. Mine is spent at home with the exception of the theater club where I'm a set designer. Did you think I have the leading role? Think again. Girls like me don't get center stage.

"Shut up. You're perfect." She swats at my shoulder like she usually does.

I let the topic go because I don't want to be the friend who brings other people down.

The bonfire is roaring and a bunch of kids from our high school are sitting around on logs. Fall came early to Illinois this year.

Some couples are making out and I glance away quickly. Other kids are enthralled in Keeten Berkshire's telling of some urban myth about a girl who ventured into the woods years ago and was found cut up in pieces the next morning. We've all heard it a million times, but he adds his own spin to the story about how no one missed her because she was such an ugly loser.

My stomach rumbles with nerves. I don't belong here. Hell, Lauren only half belongs herself. The seniors from her soccer team invited her after she made the winning goal last week in a clincher. At least she actually talks to some of these people. Me, on the other hand, I'm way out of my comfort zone.

"Let's grab a beer first." Lauren drags me the opposite way of the bonfire and part of me suspects she heard Keeten telling the story and she's worried I'm going to run off scared and be the one found cut up into little pieces tomorrow morning.

All the liquor is stashed in the woods so that if the cops come to break up the party, they won't find any evidence of underage drinking.

Sometimes I wonder about the intelligence of the police force. Don't get me wrong, my classmates go to great lengths to cover it up. There's a garbage can spray painted in camouflage that covers the keg. Different liquor bottles are set on opposite sides of the log with a green and brown tarp that someone took the time to sew together. But if I know this, how do the cops not?

"I'm driving," I say.

She stops at the back of the line for the keg. Intrigued eyes scan over the two of us, probably wondering why the hell I'm here.

"Oh yeah, well, hold a cup to look like you're drinking." She tosses me a red Solo cup.

I hold it in my hands.

"Not upside down." She snatches it away and turns it over, shoving it back into my hand.

"Jeez, calm down," I grumble.

I push my lips out over my braces because they've been more irritating than usual lately. I kind of wish I had that wax stuff so I won't cut my lip again. Another six months and I'll be free of these train tracks.

My cheap-ass dad refused to get them for me when I was in middle school. His lame excuse was that I wasn't responsible enough. Maybe he should be the one to visit the bonfire tonight and feel like an outcast compared to the others my age.

The line takes forever to move, mostly because of a few girls at the front complaining about how their beer has too much head and the guys joking about wanting head themselves.

I roll my eyes while Lauren interjects into their conversation with some crude comment of her own making them all laugh. The girl can fit in anywhere. It's a constant reminder that I'm holding her back from being a 'cool kid.'

The other kids disperse, heading back to the bonfire with their filled Solo cups. A few giggling cheerleaders stumble over some branches, but their strong football player boyfriends come to their rescue.

My heart aches to be one of those girls, but when babies in utero were handed the traits of a homecoming queen, I must've been missed.

Sure, my mom is always rambling on about how people peak at different times in their lives. I keep telling myself that I'm smart and I'm going to get into a good college. I just need to believe once my braces are off and I convince my dad that he's not wasting money on contacts, things will improve.

Okay, and maybe get my act together by running with Lauren when she asks. Maybe then I won't have to wait until my hormones finally wake up and let me peak.

"Maddie!" Lauren hollers and I'm dragged from my thoughts.

I stare down at my cup overflowing with beer under the tap. "Sorry." I take my cup from her but stay in place.

Why is she filling my cup?

"The tap is fucked up and it won't stop. No one wants to miss out, so move along." Lauren motions with her hand and my brain finally processes the sighs behind me.

"Sorry," I say, stepping out of the way, my beer sloshing over the side of the cup. I push my glasses up on my nose.

"Let's head back to the fire." Lauren slides her arm through mine, leading the way. Her athletic and coordinated stride means she doesn't trip over a single branch in the dark but saves me from falling on my face twice.

———

The fire grows larger. I know this because I've been studying it for the past half hour since Lauren said she was going to head back to refill her cup and never returned. Not in the mood to risk my ankle again, I chose to stay in place.

The night is going fine. Lauren introduced me to her senior soccer teammates who smiled politely and carried on talking about the team they're playing next week. I'm not standing alone and the other people around aren't mean so I can't complain.

Then Lauren asked if I wanted a refill. I'd dumped half my beer in the grass and pretended to sip on the rest.

"Nah, I'm good."

"Well, I'll be right back." Lauren tightened her hand over my forearm to assure me she wouldn't be long.

I took a spot across from the make-out couples. Somewhere between the mesmerizing orange and yellow flames I forgot where I was, letting my mind drift to a time in my life when I wouldn't be the awkward loser. It was hard sometimes to believe that there ever would be such a time. Why wasn't I born gorgeous? Why were my hips so wide and why didn't the skinny gene run in my family? Having a cheap-ass father only added to my problems.

Something caught my eye and I glanced up over the flames. My heart leaped in my chest right before it lodged in my throat.

Mauro Bianco.

He's staring back at me.

I look away but sneak a glance back a second later. That's when I realize that he isn't staring at me, he's mesmerized by the fire as well.

I study his face. The way the fire reflects in his blue eyes transfixes me so that I don't notice right away when liquid is pouring down my back.

"Ugh!" I stand up, grabbing the fabric from the back of my dress.

"Oh shit, sorry," Kami whoever from my physics class says. "Good thing the dress is ugly as fuck."

The other girls in her group all laugh, remarking how funny her comment is and confirming how ugly my dress is.

My shoulders slump and though I wish I could stand up to them, I only turn around. Mauro is gone.

I search the area for Lauren, but she's nowhere in sight. At this point, I'm cutting my losses and leaving this bonfire with the hopes that she never drags me anywhere like this again. I've been meaning to read the hot new dystopian series everyone is raving about anyway.

Wandering around, I try to ignore the feeling that everyone is staring at me, whispering to their friends with wonderment as to why I'm here. Once I reach the treeline, I contemplate if I want to chance heading back by the drinks. Lauren's been gone for forty-five minutes now and I've reached the conclusion that she's lip-locked with a jock somewhere.

Squinting—as if that ever helped anyone see better in the

dark—I peer through the trees, not seeing anyone. Not the keg, not the alcohol and not the line of kids. Could they have moved it?

Pulling out my phone, I shine it through the trees to see if my usual sense of direction is playing tricks on me.

"Mind not blinding me?" a deep voice asks, and I can only make out a large guy shielding his eyes as he walks out of the foliage.

"Sorry," I mumble, feeling like an idiot.

The closer he gets the clearer the person becomes. His letterman jacket. The worn jeans that cover big brown boots. His backward baseball cap and the scruff along his face that a high school senior shouldn't have.

"Hey." He snaps his fingers and points to me, as if he's trying to remember my name.

Of course, I've daydreamed about our wedding and he doesn't even know my name.

"Maddie," I say.

His hand lands on the tree behind my head and my stomach tingles with anticipation until the rancid smell of alcohol surrounds me when he breathes.

He's drunk.

"Right. Maddie. Never seen you at one of these things."

I push up my glasses for the millionth time. "Yeah, uh. Hopefully you didn't rub against any toxicodendron radicans." I point to the forest behind him as my face heats.

I finally get the chance to talk to him and *this* is what I come up with?

"What?" He shakes his head like he didn't understand me. "I'm having a bad night. I don't usually drink but..." His words trail off and I'm not sure if he lost his train of thought or is just choosing not to continue.

"It happens." I nod at the woods. "Did you see anyone else in there?"

He looks back toward the woods like he doesn't remember coming out of there.

"I try not to check out other people while they're taking a piss." He chuckles and his eyes light up in that aqua color that makes me tongue-tied.

"Oh, I thought the alcohol was back there."

He chuckles a deep rumble and an energy charges between my thighs. The sensation is one I'm not familiar with.

"This is the piss stop, that's the refill station." He points to the other side of the woods past the bonfire.

Shit.

"Okay, thanks." I head in the other direction to look for Lauren, praying to God he doesn't remember this encounter tomorrow.

His hand grabs mine before I get far enough away, igniting a rush of goose bumps along my skin. "You seem sober."

"And you could tell that how?"

One side of his lips tick up into a smirk. "Funny and smart, huh?"

"How do you know I'm smart?"

"Those two fancy words you said earlier. Why not just say poison ivy?"

I can't help the smile that spreads across my face and I'm sure that if someone snapped a picture right now, I'd be looking up at him in adoration. "How do you know they mean poison ivy?"

His smirk grows and turns wildly attractive and has me involuntarily clenching my thighs. "What else could I rub against that would cause me harm in a forest? Not all jocks are dumb."

My head snaps back in surprise. "I never said that."

"You stereotype I'm sure." His tone has done a one-eighty from moments before.

I stare down at his hand on my arm and he follows my vision, retracting it.

"Sorry."

"I am sober, so what do you want?" I ask, happy to change the subject.

"A ride home? I need to sleep this shit off."

In a car alone with my crush? I glance around for a camera crew to charge out of the woods and tell me I'm on Punk'd. Jocks only fall for the geeks in the movies. That's not real life, but that doesn't mean I'm going to say no. I didn't get my 4.0 grade point average for nothing.

"Let me grab my friend and I can drive you."

"Cool." He walks alongside me toward the bonfire and I can't help but wonder what everyone else here is going to think when they see us together.

———

I should've known things would not go as smoothly as I hoped.

After tracking Lauren down with Jay Hewitt, the captain of the varsity soccer team, it confirmed my earlier thought that I truly am holding her back. Even worse was that Jay said he'd drive her back to my house after the bonfire died down and Lauren agreed.

This leaves me alone with Mauro. I can't be trusted not to make a complete ass of myself. I don't know what it is about him. When he's around, it's like I'm incapable of forming a complete thought.

He decided he didn't want to walk around the party with me on a wild goose chase, so I gave him directions to meet me at my Wrangler. I told myself it wasn't because he didn't want to be seen walking around with *me*, and that it's probably just because he's so drunk.

I'm still wondering if he'll be there when I make it back to where I parked.

Hightailing it back the other way through the muddy grass area, I find Mauro leaning against the truck.

"It's locked." He wears the most bored expression on his face.

"Sorry."

Since my Wrangler is old as hell, I have to actually insert the key into the passenger door before heading to my side.

"Don't go thinking you're getting lucky," he jokes, sliding his large form into my car.

He sure takes up a lot more space than Lauren.

"Don't worry, I won't take advantage of you," I say in response.

Wow! Did I just flirt with Mauro Bianco?

I start the car with shaking hands. Other than a shoulder brush near his locker that sent my heartbeat in a tailspin my freshman year, I've never been this close to him. I'm trying my best to concentrate on the road and not the fact that my entire body feels like I just ran a triathlon.

"Tell me about yourself." He reaches down, grabbing the lever of the seat and adjusting it so he's leaning farther back.

"There's not much to say. I'm a sophomore."

"You must know my brother then. Luca Bianco?"

Um...he can't be that naive to think that the Bianco brothers aren't known by every female between the ages of fourteen and eighteen within a fifty-mile radius. I mean they're three attractive Italian brothers, each a year apart from each other. All of them accomplished athletes and gorgeous as hell.

"I think I have PE with him." I think I pulled off a casual vibe with my response which is hard when almost every girl in school tries to get her schedule changed to have PE with any one of the brothers.

"He's cocky and arrogant, right? We're not all alike." His voice is fading like he's growing tired. "Take me, I'm going to graduate this year and have no clue what the fuck I want to do with my life. No football scholarship doesn't leave me with a ton of options. I'm thinking about joining the army."

I'm hoping he ignores the fact I'm driving to his house without any directions from him, but everyone knows where the Bianco brothers live.

"That's very...heroic." I'm sure my voice betrays my worry.

"You don't make it sound that way. My mama is pissed. Like beat me with a frying pan pissed for even thinking about joining. Not that she's against me serving my country, she worries about me not coming back. You know moms." He runs his hand through his hair.

The thought of something happening to him overseas and not coming back sends a chill through me.

"What makes you want to join?"

A low stream of air flows out of his mouth and I'm reminded once again that he probably wouldn't be speaking this freely with me if he weren't drunk.

"All I know is I don't want to run a sandwich shop when I'm older." He shrugs.

The Sandwich Place is the Bianco family business and is located downtown across from the courthouse. I'm sure as the oldest son in an Italian family the pressure to take over the shop is immense, but he doesn't seem like someone who would shave meat for a living.

"Nothing else has ever piqued your interest? No classes?" I put my blinker on to make a right-hand turn, looking in all directions before I finally push down on the gas pedal.

"I've lived through high school one party at a time. My future seemed like something so far off in the distance...like it would never actually come." The melancholy in his voice suggests that thought haunts him. "What do you want to do?"

"Well, I have a little longer than you, but no way my dad won't make me go to college. I'm not sure what I want to do with my life either. Does that make you feel any better?"

One corner of his lip tips up. "A little. I figured you'd spit out doctor or some shit where you'll be in school for the next ten years."

"So are you relieved that I'm as indecisive as you?"

He chuckles again, turning the radio up a notch. "Chasing Cars" by Snow Patrol plays and Mauro sings softly along to the lyrics. "I know it's selfish, but it does relieve me."

I turn down Irving Park Road to head to his house.

"You're easy to talk to." His forearm flexes as he rolls down my window. The cool fall air flows into the car. "Sorry, I feel like I'm gonna puke."

My fingers wrap around the steering wheel even tighter. "Tell me and I'll pull over."

My dad would kill me if someone puked in my car.

He leans back again and as the song continues to play, his voice fades. I chance a look to find his eyes closed.

A few minutes later, I pull up to the curb of his bungalow. Three football helmet signs dot the yard with Bianco at the bottom and each of the siblings' numbers.

The residential street is dark and vacant when I climb out of the Wrangler. I open the passenger side door and nudge Mauro.

His eyes snap open, wide and blue. "Shit. I'm sorry." He bolts up.

"Hold on, be careful." I step back.

"I'm good." He gets out—a little wobbly, but able to walk. "Want to go to the park?"

He poses it as a question, but he's already heading into the darkness, halfway across the street.

"I think you should probably go lay down."

"Nah." He waves me off. "Come on. Let your hair down a little."

I follow him because when you're a girl like me and a guy like Mauro invites you along, you go.

The park is barely lit with a yellow tint from the street lamps along the path.

"Remember the days when everything was so simple? The hardest decision was the slide or the swings."

He bypasses the swings for the slide.

"I was a monkey bars girl."

"Probably because you're determined. I bet you worked forever to master those things." He lifts his eyebrows.

For being drunk, he's intuitive. Then again, I've never been drunk. Maybe that comes with the alcohol.

"A month. It was the first and last physical thing I ever beat Lauren at."

He turns from climbing the ladder and points to me. "That's why you look so familiar, you're friends with Lauren Hunt."

I mentally chastise myself. We already established he didn't really know me.

"We've been best friends since kindergarten."

"But you're so different."

Yeah, she's hot and I'm homely looking.

"Yeah, she's super athletic and I can't run without tripping over my own feet," I say instead.

He stops, sitting at the top of the slide, his long legs leaving him almost halfway down already. "I was going to say because Lauren is a ball buster and you're...sweet." He slides down the metal slide while my heart flips in my chest. "I was a slide guy. Anything to get me up high. I only did the swings if Cristian or Luca dared me they could jump farther."

He skips over the part where he kind of complimented me, but I know it's something I'll never forget.

Wandering some more, he heads toward the outfield of the baseball field and collapses on his back.

"Lay with me." He pats the spot next to him.

"I should really get home." I wind my dress in my fingers until I realize that's pulling my dress higher.

"Come on. We're just getting to know one another."

I sit down next to him and he grabs the back of my dress, pulling me down.

"You ever wonder the point of this is? Life. Why we're here? Like we both go to Catholic school. Don't you ever wonder about God's plan for you?"

"Yeah."

Suddenly, he leans on his side, holding his head up with his hand.

"I feel like I'm meant to do something meaningful. Not sit in an office, or worse, inventory and order sandwich meats. I want to live, knowing that tomorrow isn't guaranteed so I don't look back on my life and wonder what the hell I did with it, you know? I get how it is with my parents. They each came here for a better life and the sandwich place is their life." He laughs. "And me, Cristian, and Luca. It makes them happy."

"So you just want to be happy?" I continue to stare up at the sky, attempting to ignore the proximity of his body heat so close to me.

He's just a boy, he's just a boy.

I see him shrug from the corner of my eye. "That's where I'm fucked up. I want it all. The family, the house, the career. I don't want to settle, but no one gets the trifecta."

A pinch in my heart has me turning my head to look at him. How can this jock, who I never really thought much of except for his hot body and beautiful face now, break off a piece of my heart?

"What about you? Do you believe in love?" he asks.

I look away, gazing back up at the stars and trying to keep my breathing even. "I used to, but after my parents' divorce, I kind of agree with you. You can't have it all, so I'd rather choose career and screw the family."

"You don't want to get hurt?" Mauro is much more intuitive than I would have thought.

"I suppose. Both my parents hurt after the divorce." I press my lips together, remembering that time in my life.

"My parents fight like crazy, but usually their bedroom door is shut hours later. My brothers and I flee the house while they're making up."

He slides his hand down between us, running his fingers up and down my arm.

"Will you look at me?" he asks in a gentle voice.

I turn my head and lock gazes with him. His hand is suddenly on my cheek, and he's leaning over.

I squeal inside when his eyes fixate on my lips.

"Can I kiss you?"

"Okay," I practically whisper.

Lame, Maddie. Lame.

"Relax and close your eyes."

Does he know this is my first time being kissed? Is that why he asked permission and is directing my body how to respond?

As my mind is swimming with a million simultaneous thoughts, he presses his lips to mine and all those worries vanish as his tongue slowly slides into my mouth.

I've long imagined what it would feel like to be kissed at all, but the fact that my first kiss is from Mauro Bianco feels like I'm in a movie or something.

Every nerve in my body fires and he moans softly, his body weight starting to press into me as he deepens the kiss. My breasts press against his chest now and though the sensation is new and unfamiliar, I understand now why girls want to do this. I open my mouth some more, loving the sensation of our tongues brushing together.

"Shit." He pulls back, sitting up and pressing his hand to his lips. "Your braces."

Blood leaks from his lip.

"I'm sorry." My eyes are wide and my heart races as my cheeks heat.

He picks up his t-shirt, blotting his lip. "It's okay." He stands up, working to find his balance for a second. "Want to ride the slide?"

Just like that, the kiss is forgotten and he's wandering away.

"Mauro, what the fuck are you doing?" someone yells as they cross the street. "Fuck. Ma's going to kill you."

"Cris, I might have had too many, but I got a ride. Do you know....?" He glances back to where I'm unceremoniously getting myself up off the grass, his arm stretched out toward me.

I step out of the darkness and Cristian's eyes widen for a second.

"Hey, Maddie." He disregards his brother beelining it over to me. "Everything okay?"

"Um...yeah. I just gave your brother a ride."

The blood on Mauro's lip is pooling now but isn't streaming down.

"Nothing else?" Cristian dips down to see my eyes. I can barely form a coherent sentence, let alone assure him I'm good.

I just had my first kiss with the boy of my dreams and my braces cut his lip. I do live in a movie, but not a romance, rather a horror film.

"Yeah, everything's good. You can make sure he gets inside?"

"Yeah." Cristian heads over to his brother, hooking his arm over his shoulder. "Thanks a lot, Maddie."

"MADDIE!" Mauro starts singing the Barry Manilow song using my name.

"The song says Mandy, fucktard," Cristian says.

Mauro laughs for a second before dead silence fills the air. "I'm gonna puke."

I hop in my Wrangler and glance over to the park where I see Mauro's head in the trashcan and Cristian waving goodbye to me.

My phone rings in the center console and I pick it up.

"Where the hell are you?" Lauren screams when I answer.

"Sorry, I got lost," I lie and start my truck, getting the hell away from the Bianco house.

————

The rest of the weekend felt like it crawled by. I played our kiss over and over again in my head—both the amazing part and the embarrassment of his bleeding lip.

Even still by the time Monday rolled around I can't help that hope that blooms inside me like a fragile flower. It's right before homeroom that I first spot him walking down the hallway.

I feel half nauseous, half excited and more than anything anxious to get speaking to each other at school over with.

I pause as he approaches and smile wide at him so he'll know that it's okay to say hello. Instead, he walks right by me with nothing but a polite smile.

Mortification is swift and complete, even if no one else is the wiser.

I run to the girl's bathroom, passing Lauren on the way and hearing her call my name, but I ignore her. I don't want to be near anyone right now.

When I reach the bathroom, I race into the stall and let the waterworks loose.

I can't believe that I actually believed, even for a second, that he could have feelings for me. What a joke.

I should have known I was the only one who felt something that night.

CHAPTER ONE

Present Day

Madison

"One thousand!" Lauren stands, her paddle high in the air like she's the damn Statue of Liberty. Actually, strike that, the paddle in her hand isn't *hers*, it's mine.

"Lauren!" I scold, rising from my chair.

Whose idea was it to switch our paddles and bid on a hot bachelor for the other? Not mine, that's for sure. More importantly, why did I go along with the idea that Lauren could pick a guy for me to date at this First Responders Fallen Hero Bachelor Auction? I was out of my mind to think she'd make the right pick for me.

That's how she snuck the first couple of bids by me because when Mauro Bianco stepped foot on that stage, the multi-tasking function in my brain turned off.

He still looks like a real life model. The spotlight glows over his head, giving the appearance that his dark hair holds streaks of natural highlights. His chiseled jaw is more defined than his boyish one at eighteen.

My entire body heats with flames only he can extinguish.

It's not his broad shoulders and tight waist, the dimples in his cheeks or his luscious pink lips that undo me. It's his eyes. The way they transform from aqua to the deepest blue of the ocean depending on what feeling is spiraling around inside him. Mix those with the bronzed skin of his Italian heritage and I'm done for.

The MC goes back and forth between Lauren and another woman who wants a piece of Mauro. I'm not sure whether I want her or Lauren to win.

The gavel lands on the podium and my muscles tense as he points to Lauren and yells, "Sold!"

She drops the paddle in the middle of the table as though it's a generous bundle of hundred dollar bills.

"You can thank me at your wedding." She smirks.

Lauren saw me through my Mauro Bianco fangirl phase. I never told her what happened that fateful night I drove my drunk crush home—I was too embarrassed to tell even her.

"I don't want Mauro," I protest even though my body is literally giddy to think about another night alone with him. One where I'm not in braces and glasses. We may not be on equal footing now, but the gap is shortening.

Don't get too cocky, my inner voice warns.

"I need to be filled in." Vanessa's blonde hair swings side to side as her head swivels between Lauren and myself.

Vanessa didn't make us a trio until college after we got thrown into a quad without a fourth. She never met the Maddie who turns into a babbling mess when Mauro's within a twenty-foot perimeter. And she won't know her now. I refuse to morph back into the insecure girl who propped him up on a pedestal.

"Later," I whisper, not wanting to rehash history in this moment.

"If this is the way we're going to play it." She turns to face the MC who is now introducing Mauro's little brother, Luca. "Then game on."

At the end of the auction, once we've all pissed each other off by selecting one another's dates, somehow, we each ended up with a Bianco brother. Lauren practically tackled Vanessa to prevent her from bidding on Luca for her and Vanessa has told me that she will not be going out with Cristian, who's a police officer.

Good times all around.

After we pay for our dates, I feel a little better about things since the money is going to help such a wonderful charity. Then I spot Mauro across the room and decide I'd feel a helluva lot better if my date wasn't flirting with some blonde who won't stop touching his bicep. The two are entranced in a moment. Is she the other woman who was bidding? I narrow my eyes, but I can't be sure.

I might as well see what the action is about in the banquet room since there are more hot firefighter, police officers, and EMTs around. I leave my two roommates to fight it out with their designated dates.

Hell, maybe Mauro will have some insanely busy schedule and be unable to go on the date. Ever.

You don't really wish that.

Or maybe he'll shuck the responsibility. It's not like in high school he was one to follow the rules. Rules never seemed to apply to the prom king and quarterback. When others were being stopped for sneaking off school property for lunch, Mauro was waving his goodbye and peeling off around the corner. Everyone else had to carry around passes to be in the hallways during class time, but Mauro acted as though the hallways were his kingdom. We didn't have any classes together, but word was he was usually asleep in the back row.

A callused hand lands softly on my forearm. "Excuse me," a deep voice says.

I stop and circle around. My entire body shuts down for a second as Mauro Bianco stands front and center only a couple of feet away from me, his eyes just as transfixing as years before.

"I heard you were my winning bidder. Well, not for me, but a date. Which I guess is technically still me." He shakes his head, chuckling to himself.

I giggle.

Like I'm still sixteen. Ugh.

He holds his hand out. "Let's start over." His smile is infectious, his eyes—alluring. His muscles, worth salivating over. I'm back to being a sophomore again. "I'm Mauro Bianco. Thanks for coming out to support such a good cause."

"Hi. I'm... Ma...Ma...Mad...ison Kelly."

His smile grows and my gut twists. My palms sweat while my heart pounds against my chest like a bass drum in a rock band as I wait with baited breath.

"Nice to meet you," he says, ignoring my stutter.

My insides deflate like a balloon with a slow leak, hope streaming out with a slow hiss.

Of course, he doesn't remember me.

I was always invisible to him.

CHAPTER TWO

Mauro

Great, I get the drunk girl. I'll be calling Luca later to give her mouth-to-mouth. She's a little unstable like she can't decide if she wants to pass out or throw up.

Add on the fact she's staring at me like I approached her at a bar while she was partying with her friends, and I'm thinking either she's not the girl who bid on me or she's regretting it now.

"You know we don't have to go out. I mean if you think it was a mistake," I say, offering her an easy out.

Her eyes scrunch and her lips dip. She's cute. More than cute. The girl next door type, but there's a sexiness under her forties garb that hides her curves.

"Do you not want to go out with me?" she asks.

The weakness in her voice pulls my eyes away from her heart-shaped lips to her eyes. Gray with small specks of blue. Like a cloudy day right before a storm.

I shrug my jacket on, glancing at my watch. "Sorry, I'm due on shift in an hour."

"Oh."

"Are you free tomorrow? Maybe lunch?" I offer since she didn't take the out.

Again, her lips dip but she quickly sips from her straw. "Sunday?"

It's then I realize my days are all fucked up.

"Shit." My fingers thread through my hair. "I covered for a guy last night and we had five calls from two to four. I'm lagging. Monday then?"

"I work."

"Of course you do."

Could I be blowing this anymore? She's nice enough to bid good money on me, the least I can do is a weekend night. Let's see...I work tonight, and then Wednesday.

"I can do Friday night."

She continues to sip her drink, the liquid slowly lowering in her glass.

"So, is Friday okay?" I draw out my sentence to make sure she's understanding me. I'm starting to wonder if she'll remember this tomorrow.

She nods and her eyes pop open again. "Yes. Friday's good."

I pull out my phone. "Can I have your number? That way we can text later in the week. I can pick you up or we can meet. Whatever you're comfortable with."

Her lips stay on the straw, her eyes glued to my chest. I want to wave my hand and say 'eyes up here.'

Girls becoming tongue-tied and googly-eyed used to make me feel like king of the fucking world. Now it's a major turn off.

She swallows and places her drink on the nearby table.

"Oh." She pulls out her phone from her purse. Except

with her phone comes the entire contents of her purse. We both watch as everything falls to the floor.

Instead of bending down, her eyes fix to mine and her cheeks flush. Something oddly familiar tugs in my gut but I can't place it.

I bend down and she quickly follows suit. I scoop up the lipstick, her wallet, a pill case. Holding her checkbook up in the air, I decide to lighten this meeting up. "Plan on winning tonight no matter the cost?"

I smile.

She doesn't.

I hand it over to her and mumble, "I'm kidding."

She tucks it back into her purse along with the tampons which I ignored. "Thanks," she murmurs.

Once we're standing again, she slides her purse under her arm. Her dress reveals nothing. Not her tits or her waist or her ass. The thing hides all the goods.

She holds her phone in her hands for a moment, not asking for my number to text me hers. Instead, I pluck it from her grasp.

"Do you mind?" I ask.

Her face pales. "No."

I text myself and my phone goes off, the sound of a girl moaning and a slapping sound coming from my pocket.

"Fuck!" I hand over her phone and dig for my own. Grabbing it after all the heads in a twenty-foot perimeter turn in my direction, I press to view it before it does it again.

She giggles across from me, her eyes casting down to her phone.

"My brothers think this shit is funny."

Looking up at me through her long eyelashes, there's a brightness that wasn't there moments ago. "It kind of is."

"So, you're cool if I keep that as your text notification

ring?" I raise my eyebrows and the flush deepens to a coral across her cheeks.

"I didn't say that."

I quickly change the ringtone before I forget and she texts me when my mom's around. No need to deepen the permanent bruise from where she slaps me on the back of the head already.

Tucking the phone back into my pocket, I rock back on my heels. "I'll call you midweek and we'll set something up then."

"Sure." She's a little more alive now and I feel a small amount of hope at the prospect of our upcoming date.

I nod, the awkwardness wrapping around us like a roll of cellophane.

"Okay, talk to you then," I say and smile.

"Okay."

Finally, I walk out of the banquet center, not even bothering to say goodbye to my brothers. They can go blow themselves after putting that notification tone on my phone.

Heading to the firehouse to work my shift, I can't help but feel like that girl seemed familiar in some way, but I don't know a Madison Kelly. I really hope I didn't pull her from a burning building at some point and she's got some hero complex because I am not a hero by anyone's standards.

———

Walking into the fire station, the aroma of curry masks the scent of testosterone.

"Fuck Patel, that shit messed up my stomach last week." Donovan breezes through the kitchen area to the weight room.

"Then make your own dinner," Patel spits back and glances over at me as I sit down at the big table. "So, how did it go? I didn't hear SWAT being called to the Hilton on the scanner, so the ladies weren't fighting over you?"

I chuckle. "Nope. Just two bidders and the one gave up quick."

"You disappointed?" he asks before he turns his back to me to return something to the fridge.

"Please. Standing on stage being bid on based on how attractive the audience finds you? It's for a good cause though and one date isn't going to kill me." I play with the napkins in the center of the giant table.

"You expect me to feel sorry for you? You posed in the Chicago Firefighters Calendar three years in a row. I don't remember anyone knocking on my door." He moves around the kitchen like he's a professional chef. I guess in some ways he is since he's the only one willing to cook for us during our rotation.

"I'm not asking for pity." I stand to help him out as much as I can although my culinary skills are not existent. I was raised by a traditional Italian mama—you get the idea. It might be a little sexist, but it doesn't make it untrue.

"What's going on with you?" Patel asks.

"What do you mean?"

He glances over his shoulder at me while chopping up chicken. "You look like your mama just scolded you."

"First off, I'm twenty-nine, my mom doesn't scold me. Second, I'm fine, just tired of the same old routine."

Patel stops what he's doing, washing his hands and then drying them on a dishtowel before throwing it over his shoulder. "Maybe you need to speak to the shrink."

I shake my head. "This isn't about Hunter. This is just me approaching thirty and being stuck in the same damn routine."

Patel is about ten years older than me. Married, three kids, a happy life. I think he's had his shit together since he was eighteen. Whereas I still feel like I'm trying to get my shit together as I approach thirty. Ever since we lost Hunter at a fire, my life has felt less appealing, less meaningful.

Leaning against the counter, his gaze digs into mine.

"Shouldn't you be finishing the dinner?" I eye the uncooked chicken.

"They eat when they eat. What's the routine?"

I'm embarrassed to admit I brought this conversation on myself. I could've easily headed to the weight room with Donovan or sat and watched whatever the other guys are in the television room. It's like a silent plea for help when you go to Patel with a problem. Everyone knows that.

"All the shift work and then doing jack all with the other forty-eight hours. I fill it up, but something is missing. I'll spend some time with Cailin and Devin, but the labor jobs have been few and far between since I took some time after Hunter died."

Cailin is Hunter's widow. He was my best buddy in the firehouse and we ran a contracting business on the side together. After Hunter died six months ago, I've been trying to make an effort to go around her place and see if she or her son need anything. It has to be a hard adjustment for them and I want to help however I can.

Patel quirks an eyebrow at me.

"It's not like that." I know there's more bite to my tone than he deserves, but I want to make it perfectly clear so that there's no uncertainty.

"I think you don't want it to be like that, but she's sad and the baby needs a father and—"

"And nothing is going on. I'm just helping her out."

He tips his head back, letting the subject go even if it looks like I didn't convince him that I would never go there.

"Hunter and I were just getting our business off the ground. We'd planned to flip houses and now..."

I put the chicken in the frying pan, but Patel snatches the spoon away from me.

"You'll burn it."

"I was trying to help you." I wash my hands at the sink.

He laughs because we both know he doesn't want anyone's help. "If your mind is on other things it won't work out."

I lean on the counter next to him because the firehouse can be like a sorority house at times, there are ears everywhere.

"Start it yourself." He shrugs.

"What?"

"Start the flipping houses thing yourself. I've seen your work. What you did at my place was top notch. We get compliments all the time."

I shrug and he knocks me in the shoulder.

"It was just flooring."

"Yeah, and if I would've done it, it'd already be busting up at the seams." He pours the curry in with the chicken, adding a few more spices to the mix while taking the lid off the pot of rice. "I'm serious though. You don't give yourself enough credit. I get that Hunter was your partner, but you can do it by yourself, or find another partner if you have to."

The flickers of late night talks Hunter and I had in this very kitchen during a shift come to mind. The business that was going to put money in our pockets so we could live well and keep on being firefighters. God knows the pay is crap, but we loved it. We're both adrenaline junkies who never wanted to sacrifice our flexible schedule for some nine to five office job. He worried with Cailin and Devin that his salary wasn't going to be enough and he'd ultimately have no choice.

"He was the numbers guy. The guy who was going to find and make the deals, keep us on budget. I was the hands."

Patel eyes me again and shakes his head. "I never pegged you for a weakling."

"Do I have to remind you of the beating your team took last week on the court even with home team advantage?" I smirk and he chuckles to himself.

"You underestimate yourself. Start small. Find a cheap house and go at your own pace." Patel puts the rice in a huge bowl to feed anyone who's sticking around. "You need my help to invest?"

"Nah. I'm good." I wave him off.

"Are you sure because…"

I step away from the counter, digging in my pocket for my phone as it vibrates with a call. "I'm sure. Thanks, Patel."

"Think about the shrink thing." He uses his dad voice on me, but I look away, pulling my phone out as a distraction.

Cailin.

"Hey, Cailin," I answer, purposely upping the happiness vibe in my voice.

"Devin and I were wondering if you'd like to come by Friday for dinner and a movie?"

I head up the stairs into the sleeping quarters of our house with my bag over my shoulder. Every time she calls me here, it topples on another layer of guilt and grief. Probably because this is where Hunter's and my friendship was born. This is where he told me he met Cailin and that there was something different about her to him. Where we planned the flash mob for his proposal. Where I saw his eyes fill with water when he announced that he was going to be a dad.

"Sorry, that's the night I'm going out with the lucky woman who won me tonight."

There's silence on the other end and I hate the fact that she's upset.

"Maybe I can stop by after," I offer.

"Nah. If all goes well, you'll be lucky, too." I can tell she doesn't mean what she's saying, but I'm not calling bullshit on it. Patel's warning is ringing through my head and I can't say I haven't worried myself that she's looking for something I can't and won't offer. The loss is still fresh and she's clinging to anything and anyone she sees as security right now.

I promised Hunter that if anything ever happened to him that I'd make sure she and Devin were good, and I don't go back on promises.

The brunette from the charity event flashes through my head again. I'm not sure why. If I'm honest, her shyness and timidness annoyed me. I'm not sure what my type is, but someone who agrees with every fucking thing I do and say sure isn't the one for me. Lately, that's all I've been getting.

"I can give you a call," I say.

"Okay."

The alarms go off in the building.

"A fire?" she asks. "Be careful," she says before I answer. She knows the drill.

"I will. Talk to you soon."

"Text me after?" Her voice lowers and I know she's remembering the night Hunter was no longer able to do so.

"Will do."

I click the phone off and head down the stairs to put on my pants.

As I jump on the truck and we race out of the station, I push all my concerns to the back of my mind. Safety is number one when we're on a job and I can't afford to be distracted.

CHAPTER THREE

Madison

I sit in my car outside my childhood home. The weeds are as tall as the broken windows that are now replaced with plywood. The cement stairs are crumbling and slanted, making it a danger just to step foot in the house.

The need to make this a home others will love burns inside of me. One that a family will cherish and a neighborhood will smile upon. It wasn't my happily ever after, but it will be someone else's.

A black sedan pulls up right behind me so I turn off the ignition and step out of my car with my legal pad in hand.

"Miss Kelly, I'm thinking I deserve an extra percent on my commission for getting us in here so fast."

My Realtor, a man in his fifties with a heavy gold chain around his neck, his wrists and his pinky finger adorned with the same, is good at what he does and he's negotiated some amazing deals for me in the past. Especially when I'm going up against some of the most bullheaded developers in the area. Small fish in a little pond doesn't even cut it when it comes to describing me. They want the buck and I want to pull out the beauty.

"Hey, George and I've told you to call me, Madison."

He holds out short and stubby fingers for me to shake.

We do some quick small talk and then it's on to business as usual as he walks up the sidewalk I used to play childhood games on like Step on a Crack and Break Your Mother's Back.

"As you know, it's a three bedroom, one and a half bath. Basement, small kitchen. Yard is decent. It's up for auction next Tuesday."

"The last thing I need is a bidding war."

George opens the door and the foulest smell has us using the collars of our shirts to cover our noses. Staring down at the junk filled floor has me thankful I wore my boots.

"I have to say the commission checks are nice but looking at houses with you always makes me want to shower after." George stays by the front door.

He always does and it doesn't bother me. The first time he showed me a house there was a rat that had drowned in one of the toilets. It was already decomposing and explained the smell, but he was fighting his gag reflex that entire showing.

"Call the fire department if I don't come back in fifteen minutes." I put on my face mask and head through the front area to the back.

I dig through the massive amounts of newspaper and magazines on top of an old dining room table. Stepping through more floor rugs that are wet and soggy doesn't leave a lot of hope for the floorboards.

When my parents and I lived here, everything was bright and cheery. My mom would grow plants on the ledge by the front door. Herbs in small planters in the bay window of the kitchen. The smells of freshly baked cookies or pot roast were second nature while I was out playing in the yard.

Then the bad start to seep into the good. The days my mom never got out of her bed. Or the fights in the kitchen where spaghetti sauce ended up splattered all over the wall.

The bones are good in this house and has loads of potential. I refuse to let it be the ugliest house on the block.

Heading back to the front door after one quick pass through the top floor, I find George typing away on his phone, still as a statue.

"This is it," I say when he glances up at me.

"Are you sure? I think this might be the worst you've ever taken on."

He's right. I'll be digging into my savings and probably won't make nearly the profit I usually do, but I remember why I turned to flipping houses to begin with. The money at the end is nice, but it's about bringing out the best of what's already there, not building something shiny and new like a developer would.

"I'm sure. I just have to beat out Oswald. They'd cut corners and make a steal on this property."

"Yeah, I always steer my clients clear of his places."

We exit the house and I stand on the porch that I fear could cave in at any moment. I take a moment to look around my old neighborhood, staring at the houses up and down the street.

I don't understand.

"How can it be just this house in such disrepair? They have flowerbeds." I point to the house directly across from us. "They have a gate surrounding their front lawn." I point to two houses down.

George shrugs. "You know the city. There's no rhyme or reason. Sometimes someone elderly dies and they have no family to take care of their assets or their families want to hang on to it until the market goes up, but they don't main-tain it." He takes the steps down and turns on the sidewalk, staring back up at the house.

"Yeah, I suppose so." We continue down the walkway and he moves to shake my hand but turns it into a fist bump instead.

"Let me know when you're ready to list."

I fist bump him, laughing out loud. "Thanks, George."

———

I arrive home and open the door to my house to find Lauren flying down the stairs. She puts her finger to her lips and sneaks into the hall closet.

A second later, a half-dressed Vanessa stomps down from upstairs. There's no urgency in her steps, but her eyes are bouncing all around as she descends.

"What is going on?" I ask.

"Lauren gave that Bianco guy my number." She raises a hairbrush in her hand. "Now I'm going to beat her to death."

I raise both eyebrows. The two fight like sisters and I think I'm the middle child.

"You might want to reconsider. Cristian could be the one to answer the 911 call."

She pretend swats at me with the hairbrush but I just laugh at her.

"I'm starving." I head to the kitchen, cringing at the sound of furniture sliding on the hardwood floors. "Do I need to remind you that I still need to sell this place at some point?"

"Don't worry. Those nifty felt pads you bought are doing the trick," Vanessa calls out.

I open the door and investigate what's in the fridge.

"Come out, come out wherever you are," Vanessa says in a singsong voice from the other room.

Did I say I was the middle child? I meant the mother. I'm like the damn guardian of these two women.

"Put the hairbrush down and we'll talk," Lauren says, and Vanessa must try to follow the sound of her voice because I can hear her running toward the foyer.

Lauren's small enough to hide behind the vacuum in the closet and Vanessa would miss her.

Cracking open a soda, I pour it into a glass and raise my voice so she'll hear me. "I don't get what the big deal is," I say to Vanessa. "Go on one date with the guy. I can't say enough good things about Cristian." I sit on the stool at the breakfast bar so I have a bird's eye view into the entryway and watch her continue to play this childish game of hide and seek.

"He's got two strikes against him. One, he wears a badge. Two, he honors the badge."

"Wouldn't that be the point of his job...to do it well?" I sip my drink.

Vanessa crinkles her brows. "It's admirable and I'm sure the girl he ends up with will love that about him. I'm not that girl."

"No one said anything about marriage. It's a date. For charity."

Vanessa opens up the hall closet, jumps in front of the opening and pushes back all our coats. "Hah!"

Lauren's not there, which means she's snuck off to a different hiding spot now.

"Damn you!" Vanessa hits the back of the brush on her palm.

"Back to you being upset that he has your phone number..." I say, trying to understand her issue.

"He called me today. He didn't text, he *called*."

"The nerve of the man." I sip my drink, grabbing a banana from the counter.

"Who calls anymore? It's desperate if you ask me."

"Or considerate," I offer.

She rolls her eyes, moving to the bathroom doorway now. "You date him then." She raises both eyebrows before stepping into the bathroom.

If only my heart didn't skip a beat when I look at his brother.

"Oh, that's right." She peeks her head out. "You love his brother."

"No, I don't."

She heads back into the bathroom and I can hear her opening and closing the cupboard doors. Meanwhile, a crawling Lauren still dressed in her scrubs finds refuge behind our kitchen island. Again she puts her finger to her lips like we're six and this game actually means anything.

"I saw the twinkle in your eye." Vanessa enters the kitchen, her long blonde hair half curled and half straight, and I realize she must've been in the middle of getting ready for her night. She either has a date or she's off to her mystery job. I really hope the two aren't combined together.

"There was no twinkle. Sure I had a crush on him in high school, but hello, I'm nine years older and wiser now."

"Wiser how?" Vanessa sits down at the stool next to me because this is Vanessa. She's grown bored with the game whereas Lauren would play for the rest of the night—she's *that* competitive.

"Wise to the fact that my life is not a movie where the ugly duckling turns into a swan and gets the handsome prince. This is reality and you date within your level."

"Level?" Vanessa grabs my soda and takes a sip.

"You know fives with fives, eights with eights. Sure maybe there's a seven and six somewhere together. Tens only go with sixes when they want something from them."

Vanessa's face falls to a frown. "And what do you think you are?"

It's a test. I'm sure of it. "A six."

"A six?" Her mouth hangs open.

"Is there an echo in here?"

Vanessa slides off the stool and stands in front of me. "Stand up," she demands, using her authoritative voice she inherited from her father.

"I'm eating."

She cocks her head to the side.

I roll my eyes and stand.

"Go stand in front of the mirror." She points to the gold-framed mirror I found at a flea market and re-finished into an antique looking mirror someone would pay hundreds for at Pottery Barn.

"I'm not playing this game. Yeah, yeah, you and Lauren think I'm beautiful. I'm not saying I'm a two. A six is completely respectable."

"Just go stand in front of it." She pushes lightly on my shoulders.

I drag my feet, chomping on my banana the whole time. "Okay, what now?" I look at my reflection.

"Your eyes are stunning. Your hair is silky and smooth. Your figure is spank bank material if you'd stop hiding it. Can you honestly say you're only a six?"

I shrug. "I feel more comfortable dating in my division." Turning back around, I grab my soda and head to the couch, leaving Lauren hiding behind the island.

"Oh, Maddie, you're impossible sometimes." Vanessa follows behind me. "Ouch!"

I turn around before I can sit down to find Lauren with the brush in her hand and Vanessa's clutching her ass with a pained look on her face. "Damn you!"

Lauren runs up the stairs laughing maniacally as though she's ready for round two, but Vanessa sits down next to me rather than follow.

"How do I blow off this guy nicely?" she asks. "I can't have him going around telling the district what a bitch the Commander's daughter is. My dad would kill me."

"Just tell him you have work. Speaking of—" I straighten my back and turn to face her, wanting to broach the subject of exactly where she's earning money since she's been so cryptic, but she stands quickly.

"Good idea. I'll just say I have no idea what my schedule is going to be like." She leans forward, kissing my cheek. "You're so smart and beautiful, you little eleven you." She winks and runs up the stairs.

A few seconds later I hear her scream, "Lauren, grow the fuck up!" A door slams.

The joys of living with my two best friends.

My phone dings next to me and when I glance at the name, my stomach flips.

Mauro: Are we still on for Friday night?

Me: Yeah. I was thinking Dice and Spins. It's a cafe. Maybe around seven?

Mauro: Sure, I've never heard of it.

Because you're not a dork who loves board games.

Me: I'll text you the address.

Mauro: Perfect. See you then.

My thumbs hover over the phone. Should I respond? Is he expecting something more back from me or is that the end of our conversation?

God, I'm so terrible at this stuff.

I press the thumbs up emoji and no three dots appear. I'm

ashamed to admit that I watched for them for a whole two minutes.

I have no idea how I'm going to get through our date without making a fool of myself like I did before. Maybe I should consider myself lucky that I'm the only one who remembers the first time around.

CHAPTER FOUR

Mauro

I'm leaning against my truck, waiting for my slow-ass brothers to make an appearance along with a Realtor who was nice enough to agree to show me the house.

Patel's words definitely got to me and that's why I'm outside a house Hunter and I had our eye on as it went into foreclosure. The bank owns it now and I'm hoping the fact that it's going up for auction means that not a lot of people are interested.

Cristian runs around the corner, his earbuds in, wearing his man leggings, shorts, and a skin-tight shirt. Looking about as unmanly as you can while working out.

His pace slows to a walk when he rounds the corner and he pulls his earbuds out of his ears.

"Hey," he says, leaning over with his hands on his knees, catching his breath.

"You're an embarrassment to the Bianco name." I push off my truck with my foot, open the door and grab a water, tossing it in his direction.

"An embarrassment? Hello." He pulls up his shirt to reveal his eight pack. "And I don't have the cushy twenty-four on, forty-eight off schedule. My ass sits in a patrol car for eight fucking hours straight." He gulps down half the bottle. "Thanks for this." He raises the bottle he asked me to bring him into the air.

"Whatever happened to old t-shirts and basketball shorts?"

He looks down at his attire, clearly confused over my question. "This is climate control. I sweat less and it dries fast. Hate to break it to you, brother, but no one wants sweat rings around their neck and pits that don't dry for hours anymore."

"I know what dri-fit is, I also know what size I am. Not sure you can say the same." I eye his erect nipples poking through the thin fabric.

"You're objectifying me." He covers his nipples with his hands.

I roll my eyes just as my other brother pulls his motorcycle into the four-by-four space between me and the car in front of me. Luca takes off his helmet.

"One downside to you working in the city is that you must not see many motorcycle accidents."

He puts the helmet on the bench of his bike. "I've seen plenty, but thanks, Dad."

Luca saunters up to us in his jeans and the t-shirt my mom gave him for his birthday, *I fix stupid* with a cartoon of an ambulance on it.

My youngest brother is a paramedic. He's good at his job, which is surprising once you get to know him.

"Nice shirt," I say.

He glances down. "Well, it's a hell of a lot better than *Christine* over there." He nods to Cristian.

"They're compression pants," Cristian argues.

"They're man leggings," Luca and I say in unison.

Cristian rolls his eyes and unplugs his earbuds.

"You know you're probably going to be the first of us to go down with a heart attack," Luca says. "It's always the guy with picture perfect health. 'No way Cristian had a heart attack, the man ran five miles a day, ate nothing but vegetables, he was so disciplined.'" Luca laughs.

Cristian shakes his head at him.

"This is the house." I motion toward it with my hand.

The three of us stand outside of it, just staring for a moment.

"It's a shit hole," Luca says.

"Or a treasure," I say.

I feel both their eyes on me. They think I'm delusional and they might be right. I should find a house that only needs a few upgrades, not a complete overhaul, but the return on this will be bigger if I can pull it off.

"You think you have the skill to do this?" Cristian, always the sensible one, asks the type of question I assumed he would.

"I think between me and the people we know, yes."

Luca places his hand on my shoulder. "Even I can't revive this house." He moves forward, driven by his natural curiosity toward anything that seems too big to conquer. He rarely accepts defeat.

Having brothers like Luca and Cristian is like having the angel and the devil always weighing in on a decision, which is why I invited them over.

"I hate to be the jackass here, but..." Cristian joins Luca, pretending to tiptoe up the front steps, steps that appear as if they might sink into the ground.

"Nice neighborhood though." Luca stands on the porch, tucking his sunglasses into the neckline of his t-shirt. "How much again?"

I stand there envisioning a nice fence in the front, a walkway lined with flowers and hydrangeas along the ground in front of the porch. "Twenty K to start."

"It's going to be auctioned?" Luca asks.

"Yes, it is," a female voice says behind me. "Which means you need to make sure all your finances are in order and ready by Monday. My feeling is that you won't be the only one who's looking for a steal in a nice neighborhood."

All three of us turn around and find a woman in heels and a short skirt standing on the sidewalk. Her eyes bulge out of her head and her gaze flows up and down each one of us.

"Hi, I'm Mauro, the one you talked to on the phone." I step forward and hold my hand out. She takes it while still examining Luca.

"I'm Greer and I'll be waiting outside while you guys take a look."

She wiggles between Cristian and Luca, bending over to punch the code into the lockbox for the key. One quirked eyebrow from Luca as he checks out her ass and the door opens.

Once we're inside, Cristian strips his shirt off and uses it to cover his nose and mouth. "This is horrible." His voice is muffled as he tiptoes around the room like a little girl.

"Man up." Luca kicks a rug out of the way between the dining room and kitchen. "I know I'm the optimistic one, but Mauro, this is a kick me in the nuts project." He disappears through an archway.

"This smell is almost as bad as a decomposing body." Cristian circles around, staying in the same spot.

"Afraid to get your new running shoes dirty?" I cock an eyebrow.

He ties the shirt around his face like a bandana so it's still covering his nose and mouth. "Fuck off." He heads toward the stairs, his back to the wall as he slowly moves up them like he's clearing a house. I guess none of us are ever too far removed from our day jobs.

"The backyard is killer," Luca hollers and I leave Cristian to examine the top floor and head Luca's way.

"Big? It didn't look that way from outside."

"No, I meant you're actually going to get killed. Rose bush thorns galore." He's staring out the kitchen window. "You're on your own there." He claps me on the shoulder. "Where's pretty boy?" Luca glances at the open stairway to the basement. "Let's make him be the first one to go down there."

It's dark and the stench wafting from the open door doesn't make it appealing in any way. "Please. I thought you were a man?" I slide by him.

"I'm not gonna get murdered. We all have our roles in this family. Cristian's is to beat up the perps. Mine is to save lives."

"I run into burning buildings without knowing the layout. I can handle a basement." I take one at a time, gingerly placing my foot down in case the boards won't hold and pushing cobwebs away from my face.

"Okay, but if there's some junkie down there high as a kite thinking he's Batman, remember how I told you to wait for Cristian." Luca's footsteps follow mine.

"I'm running into a building when everyone else is running out. I think I can handle a little danger. Unlike you who can't go anywhere until the scene is safe. You're hiding in your ambulance while we do the hard work."

"You chose that career," he says.

"Damn right I did."

I wouldn't change that—ever. I just need to supplement my income and since I've always been good with my hands, here I am.

"I understood that career, this one not so much." Luca stays on the bottom step glancing around the basement that looks like it's always been dirty and dingy with creepy crawlers lurking in every dark corner.

"It's a great way to make some money on my two days off between shifts."

"I have no problem filling in my off days." Luca waggles his eyebrows.

I roll my eyes. "Yeah, but you'll have a family to support one day." I direct my flashlight into the crawl space.

"Did hell freeze over?" He finally joins me, kicking a few boxes to the side with his black boots.

"No, but don't you ever think about it? I mean, I'm twenty-nine—"

"And I'm twenty-seven. You can forget about me getting married anytime soon."

"Upstairs is secure!" Cristian yells down from the top of the stairs.

"Thanks, pig!" Luca yells back.

"Real original." Cristian's footsteps barrel down the steps. "Can we get the fuck out of this nightmare now?"

I turn around, pointing the flashlight at him. "Shut the fuck up. This is gonna be someone's dream house when I'm done with it."

"If you say so." The t-shirt still tied over his nose.

"Did you know Mauro's looking for a wife?" Luca says.

I punch him in the shoulder.

"I didn't say that."

Cristian says nothing, just glancing between Luca and myself.

"Why aren't you surprised?" Luca asks. "Are you two shit-heads having meaningful conversations without me? You know if you two get sucked into the whole marriage thing, Mama's gonna double down the pressure on me."

"First of all, stop giving girls you want to blow off the number to the deli," I say. "It's getting old and it only advertises the fact to Mama that you're with a different girl every week."

"Week?" Luca asks, a smirk saying 'if you only knew' on his lips.

Cristian rolls his eyes and heads up the stairs.

"Did you hear about the girl who bought him?" Luca follows Cristian, but he's already cleared the stairs by the time we get to the first step.

Hell, he's probably out the front door.

"Can we please concentrate on the house?" I ask, exasperated.

"It's a lot of work, but I'll help you out depending on what you'll pay me." He waggles those damn eyebrows again. A move he thinks is cute, but I'm not some chick he's trying to pick up. One day he'll meet his match and I'll have a bowl of popcorn ready to watch the show.

"I have to get the house first," I say.

He picks up a dead plant on the windowsill in the kitchen and it falls to the counter in one big hunk of dried dirt.

"So, you're doing it then?" Luca asks.

"I've seen some other houses and they're not feasible. This is the only place I can afford and still make a decent return on."

He nods. "All right, I'm in. I can squeeze in a day or two."

"Don't do me any favors."

He laughs and we leave the house, the Realtor shutting and locking the door behind us.

"So the auction is next Tuesday at the courthouse," she says. "Get your funding or bring your checkbook. I doubt that many people want this house, but you never know."

She holds out her hand. "And if this is successful, maybe we can continue to do business." Her smile tips up a notch.

I shake her hand. "Thanks."

She gives one more inspection to the three of us and then heads down the stairs.

"Maybe she'll drop the commission rate if you sleep with her." Luca elbows me.

I shake my head. "Not interested right now."

"Sometimes I think I'm the mailman's kid around the two of you fucking saints." Luca jogs down the stairs heading to his bike.

Cristian and I follow. "Luca was saying something about your date from the auction?" I ask him.

His shoulders sag. "It's the fucking Commander's daughter. Out of all the luck, I get the one girl where if I don't go on the date, the Commander will be pissed and if I do go out he'll be pissed. I'm screwed either way."

"Is she good looking?" I ask.

"Does it matter?"

"Is she worth risking your job to get laid?" Luca chimes in as usual.

"She's a fucking knockout, but you guys know her," Cristian says.

Luca and I look at one another. "Who?" I ask.

"She's friends with Madison and Lauren."

"Who?" I ask again, my forehead scrunched.

"Oh that's right. They weren't cheerleaders." Cristian shakes his head and gives a wry laugh.

"What does that mean?" I ask, crossing my arms in defense.

"Lauren and Maddie went to our high school, but they weren't in *your* crowd." Luca laughs.

"Whatever. So the Commander's daughter went to St. George, too?"

"No. I don't know how she knows them, but it was Maddie who bid on me for Vanessa."

What is he talking about? Maddie, Lauren, and now Vanessa. None of the names ring a bell.

"Why would someone bid for someone else?" I ask.

"Lauren said they thought it would be fun," Luca chimes in again and I'm wondering how they're in the loop, but I'm not.

"Sucks for you two," I say with a laugh.

They both widen their stances, share a look of amusement and cock their eyebrows at me.

"Hate to break it to you, but Maddie didn't bid on you. Lauren did." Luca laughs while Cristian chuckles.

"I'm going out with a Madison and she didn't go to our high school. Which reminds me." I pull out my phone.

"Maddie is Madison, you idiot," Luca says. "Her and Lauren were my year."

"I went to high school with Madison?" I try to let her face come back to me, and though I can picture her bright blue eyes and long chestnut hair, nothing about her is familiar from high school.

"Yes, but she definitely wasn't hanging out at the bonfires and football pep rallies." Luca grabs his helmet off his bike. The only responsible thing I've seen him do in the last few years.

"Well, shit and she doesn't even want to go out with me? Her friend bid on me?"

Luca straddles his bike with a grin. I look over to Cristian, but he's putting his shirt back on and starts fiddling with his earbuds. They obviously think this conversation is over.

"Yeah, but we're all in the same boat." Cristian's thumb moves over his phone screen. "Maddie's awesome and I think you'll have a good time with her."

"She seemed pretty quiet and way too accommodating," I say.

Luca kicks his stand up, letting the bike rock a little under him.

Cristian's hands freeze on the screen of his phone. "And that's bad?" he asks.

"I want a woman who knows what she wants. Has her own damn opinions. Doesn't just agree with everything I say."

Cristian peeks over his shoulder, a look of amusement that matches Luca's. "You want a girl to come up and grab your nuts?"

"I want a girl who knows what her favorite food is, has an opinion about where she wants to go for dinner, likes whatever sports team she likes and doesn't default to my favorites." I stuff my hands into my pockets, digging out my keys for my truck.

"Well then, Maddie might not be the one. Like I said, she's nice." Cristian slaps me on the shoulder. "Treat her good though, okay?" He inserts one earbud.

"What do you think I'm going to do, leave her in Garfield Park?"

He puts his other earbud in. "That's not even funny man. I have a friend in that district and the shit that goes down there..." He shakes his head.

Cristian loses the entire point of my statement—the fact I'm not a jackass. I'm not Luca.

"It's one date," I say. "And who knows, maybe she's nice but still has a wild streak."

Christian again glances over to Luca who's smiling like he's fucking Mickey Mouse.

"Well, good luck on your date," he says.

Cristian jogs away and Luca's bike starts up.

I head to my truck.

The conversation is over, but I'm curious now.

Where's my damn yearbook?

CHAPTER FIVE

Madison

*S*peek through the window of Dice and Spins before deciding to wait outside. My habit of arriving ten minutes early is making me feel awkward while I wait for Mauro to show up. Maybe I should round the corner and wait to make a dramatic entrance like a woman who is fashionably late—one who struts across the pavement, her legs elegantly stepping one in front of the other as she unbuttons her coat and lets it slide down her arms behind her for the mystery man to take while she shakes out her hair. All while the man who's been waiting on pins and needles for her to show is mesmerized thinking how blessed he is to have this gorgeous woman walking toward him.

Ding.

Ding.

Ding.

"Lady!" a man yells and I look up to see a bicycle barreling right toward me. The guy seems to be about my age with a satchel over his back, a long stream of blonde hair coming out from under his helmet and a nasty 'get the fuck out of my way' look on his face.

"Sorry." I sidestep, only to run into another pedestrian on the street.

That person puts their hands on my shoulders to right me and keeps on walking without a word.

Heat scorches my cheeks and I step forward thinking I'll just wait inside and look like the girl who has no life and has been crossing days off on her calendar with big red Xs until today.

Not that I did that.

Okay, I did. But I do that every day though. It had nothing to do with Mauro.

A large hand grabs the door handle of the cafe before I can.

"Hey, Madison," Mauro says, opening the door with a polite smile.

He wore cologne. It's the first thought that comes to my head. The woodsy cedarwood scent makes the city vibe disappear behind me. That and the way his dark jeans hug his strong thighs in just the right way and the way his grey Henley shirt makes his eyes look a dusty shade of blue.

"Hi, thanks," I mumble, stepping into the cute café. One that Lauren and I have spent hours in competing with each other over Scrabble, Monopoly, or my personal favorite, Life.

The door shuts with a swoosh behind us and we stand on the welcome mat. A lot of booths are already taken with families and teenagers alike enthralled in their games, appetizers, and drinks sitting forgotten at the edge of their tables.

"I've never been here," Mauro says, extending his arm forward, allowing me to lead.

"It's fun. We pick a game, order some food and then play." I guide us to the back of the room to the ordering station.

"What game is your favorite?" he asks, his gaze roaming over the bookcases of board games to our left.

"You pick." I'm not really sure what Mauro would want to play, if anything. Maybe this was a bad idea. Maybe I should have suggested a quick tapas place. Somewhere where our date would go quickly and he wouldn't figure out what a nerd I am. He probably thinks this place is totally juvenile.

Oh, God. Sweat is starting to gather at my temples. I don't know if I can do this.

"Lady's choice," he winks and my stomach does a triple backflip worthy of an Olympic gold medal.

"How about...Boggle?"

He doesn't smile, but nods. "Sure." There's an uneasiness on his face I can't help but notice.

I should've picked something else, but Boggle doesn't take long to play. I don't think he'd enjoy being tormented with a three hour game of Monopoly.

"We can always play something else," I say.

He grabs the box from the bookcase. "No. It's your night."

The reminder that he's only here because I paid for him to be here is like a bucket of cold water on my face. He'll amuse me by playing a few games, making small talk and having a bite to eat before he disappears forever this time.

I should be happy. He's not in my sector of the dating pool. Maybe after tonight, I can finally put my childhood crush to rest.

After the mental pep talk, I order a trio of hummus with vegetables and pita bread along with a berry and pecan salad.

Mauro's still dissecting the menu as me and the girl behind the register admire him. His Adam's apple is prominent while his neck is stretched out to read the menu above us. His strong forearms that have probably axed down thousands of doors are crossed over his chest. I can't even fault the girl for staring at him like he's the latest Hollywood heartthrob because he looks exactly like that.

His head tips back down and the two of us try to act like we weren't just fantasizing about what he'd be like in bed. If he noticed or felt our stares, he ignores them.

"I'll have the combo platter with wings, moz sticks, and potato skins. And a Miller."

I guess I should order a drink. If anything, it will make me feel less intimidated by him. Liquid courage, right?

"Can you add a glass of Riesling to our order?" I ask.

The girl smiles and hands us a number.

I open my purse to grab my wallet, but Mauro hands her a card before I have a chance.

"Hey, I'm supposed to pay," I complain.

He signs his name on the electronic device. "You paid enough. My treat." He winks, but it comes across as more playful than seductive.

She hands him back his card and he puts his wallet in his back pocket.

"Thank you," I say.

He holds up the box in his hands. "Lead the way."

The girl behind the register smiles at us, though it's probably mostly to Mauro. I grab the order number which is at the top of a long metal stick and head farther back to where there are still a few empty tables.

Don't think about how he's walking right behind me.

Good thing I wore my 'bounce a quarter off my ass' jeans.

I slide into one side of the booth and his large body folds into the bench across from me.

"Would you rather a table?" I ask, wondering if this will be uncomfortable for a man his size.

"No. I'm good. But thank you."

The Boggle box sits in the middle of the table and we both stare at it for a minute.

"Would you rather eat before we play?" I ask—anything to fill the awkward silence.

He leans back in the booth. "Whatever you want."

Again a reminder that I paid for his time tonight. I could kill Lauren for this.

"You decide."

He shakes his head. "No, please."

"Well, they're usually fast with the food orders, but we can probably get one game in." I grab two notepads and two pens from the stand on the table that includes extra timers and dice in case the ones that are supposed to be in the box are missing.

"I think my brother Luca would love this place." He looks around, taking the cap off the pen.

"He is pretty competitive, right?" I ask. I can talk about Luca. I don't know a ton about him other than that he played four sports in high school and still graduated in the top five percent of our class.

"Competitive is an understatement. He's like the idiot who would challenge Hulk Hogan to an arm wrestling match and expect to win. Everything is a competition to him." Mauro's lips curl and my stomach decides it's time for some gymnastic moves again.

"I do remember him being sure of himself." *Shit. I shouldn't have said that.*

He snaps his fingers and points. That flipping in my stomach quickly stops and starts churning instead.

"Luca told me you went to St. George?" The fact he states it as a question is like a knife in my back.

Our school wasn't that big and I know he was two years older than me, and I wasn't close to his social hierarchy, but we did share that one night.

It's probably a good thing he doesn't remember me, I remind myself.

"I did."

"I don't remember you." His face doesn't hold any arrogance with his comment. It looks more like he doesn't understand how I don't ring a bell to him.

"Well, people can change a lot in nine years."

His lips tip up into a half smile. "I hope you're right. I was a little self-centered then I guess, but who isn't in high school?" He shrugs.

Me. I want to raise my hand. I wasn't.

Wanting to veer as far away from this conversation as possible, I pry the box open and shake up the pieces in the plastic container.

"Do you know how to play?" I ask.

"I think so."

"Just try to come up with as many words as you can. The letters have to touch and you can't use a letter twice in one word."

He nods and poises his pen over top of the paper.

I place the plastic container in the middle of the table, taking off the cover and flipping over the timer at the same time.

Barely able to concentrate, I come up with a few five letter words but mostly three and four ones. My eyes flicker to the timer because this whole game thing was a bad, bad idea. The silence is excruciating and the late realization that I made our date somehow educational instead of fun sets in.

"Time's up," I say.

Mauro's sheet is filled, but I can't read a lot of the words because of his bad handwriting.

He leans back, propping his paper up so I can't see his answers.

"If you want to go first." I hold my hand out and he doesn't argue.

"Okay." He rambles off his list and I pretend I don't have some of the words.

Don't ask me why. Maybe because I don't want to castrate him with the first game we play. He seems bored and losing would probably make him even less interested in being here. I feel like we're both mentally checked out from the date.

I guess it just confirms my belief that Mauro might be nice to look at and a great hero in my dreams, but in real life on a real date, we aren't compatible.

I lie, allowing him to win because I made him come on this date. I don't even bother to read off my five letter words.

Thankfully, I can tuck my notepad away and repackage the game when the waitress comes over with our food. The bartender is there as soon as she's done, placing our drinks down on the table.

Mauro eyes my food and seems to grimace. I ignore the look and spread my hummus over my pita bread while my mouth really waters for the potato skins he's piling sour cream on.

We eat mostly in silence and though I haven't been on a ton of dates, this is by far the worst.

"How is it being a firefighter?" I ask, wiping my mouth with my napkin.

He chews faster, taking a sip of his beer to wash the food down his throat.

Way to go, Maddie, you're really hitting this one out of the park.

"It's great. I love it."

"That's good. I'm glad you found something you enjoy."

He examines me for a second and then dips a mozzarella stick into the marinara sauce.

"What about you? What do you do?" he asks before taking another bite and after I've sipped my wine.

"I own my own company."

His eyes widen and a soft, genuine smile appears. "That's awesome."

He doesn't ask what exactly I do and I don't volunteer any information.

"You have a good schedule, right?" I ask, attempting another round of conversation.

"Yeah, but if we're out all day and night, it's like the first day off is recovery time. I can't complain though." He drinks from his beer. "What do you want to play after this?"

"Whatever you want," I answer.

I swear I catch a sour expression cross his face, but it disappears quickly.

His phone rings.

Here we go. The "friend" who needs him.

He presses the ignore button and places the phone face down on the table. "Sorry."

"No problem." I'm a little shocked he didn't take the out when he could.

"What brought you out to the bachelor auction?" he asks.

"My roommate's dad is a widow and she was hoping that if he gets involved with someone, he'd spend less time up in her business."

He chuckles softly.

"I understand, having a mom who doesn't understand privacy. That's how you ended up on a date with me, right? Your other friends are going out with my brothers?"

Is it possible that guys gossip just like girls?

"Um...yeah. Lauren Hunt?" I leave it open because maybe he remembers her from high school.

His lips purse, but he shakes his head. I'm about to continue, but the recollection of her crosses his face. "Soccer team?"

"Yeah." My tone might hold a tad of bitterness now that he remembers her and not me.

"She bid on you for me. I bid on Cristian for Vanessa and Vanessa bid on Luca for Lauren. It was really stupid. I have no idea why we agreed to it." I push my plate away, uncomfortable eating in front of him.

"So you didn't want to go on a date with me?"

"NO!" A few people at the tables around us glance our way so I lower my voice. "I wasn't against it."

He shakes his head. "Don't try to sweet talk me." The smile that consumes his face suggests he's just joking. "So you knew who I was when we met that night?"

The flush heats my face. "I did." I take a large sip of my wine.

"Why didn't you say anything?" He seems genuinely perplexed.

His plate is clear except for the green lettuce and ramekins with half used sauce. He picks up his beer, holding the glass to his lips.

"I don't know." I shrug.

"Do I scare you?"

"What?" His question throws me for a loop. "Why would you say that?"

"That's the loudest I've heard you speak since we met. Figure it has to be something." He leans back in the booth, a pleased smile on his face.

"And?"

"And nothing. You're a people pleaser." He finishes his beer.

"A people pleaser?" My forehead creases.

"Yah. A people pleaser. You haven't once picked anything you wanted to do this entire date."

"We're here because I chose this place. I chose Boggle."

"Where you let me win." He raises an eyebrow.

My eyes glance down at the paper. "No, I didn't."

He eyes the paper. My hands move, but he's faster,

swiping it up before I can grab it. His eyes scan the paper, his smile growing wider.

"You beat me."

I tear the sheet from his hands. "I was being polite."

"You were being accommodating. Did you think I'd get pissed off if you won? Or that it would wound my self-esteem?"

Okay, seems we've moved past the awkwardness now.

"I was just being nice."

He nods like I just confirmed something he already believes.

"I'm sick of nice." He says the word nice like it's bad.

My back straightens. "Well I'm sorry, I'm a *nice* person."

"I think you're confusing nice with a people pleaser. You didn't have to lie and pretend that you lost. You could've thrown the piece of paper in my face and told me to suck it."

At this point, I think that my jaw is hanging open. Is that the kind of girl he wants?

"That's not me."

"You sure about that?" The grin on his face makes me want to smack it off him or kiss it off him—I'm not entirely sure which.

I narrow my eyes and cross my arms over my chest. "Yes, I'm certain."

"It's too bad because you're gorgeous. I had high hopes coming into this date that I pegged you wrong." The cocky smirk on his lips might look delectable, but I'm ignoring the tug at my lady bits especially over the fact that he called me gorgeous.

"Sorry to disappoint you. I think suffice it to say this date is over."

"We could do another round of Boggle. You could just pretend that you don't spot the words again."

I throw my napkin on my plate, down the rest of my wine and slide out of the booth. "I'm done."

He catches my wrist before I can step away.

I wrench it back. "What?"

"Now this, I like." His gaze flows up and down over me.

A million swear words go off in my head, but I keep them to myself.

"Have a nice life."

I stomp away, ignoring the blatant stares from onlookers questioning why a girl would dare leave a man like Mauro Bianco in such a fashion.

Needless to say, I think I'm over my persistent high school crush.

CHAPTER SIX

Mauro

*H*er strawberry scent lingers after she flees from my unwarranted wrath, the crumpled up Boggle sheet still lay on top of her barely touched salad and hummus.

I tried to ignore the signs.

I let it go when she sheepishly looked at me when I opened the door for her.

Like I didn't hear her mumbled thank you.

I kept throwing the decisions her way when we had to pick a game.

The food she ordered was bird scraps at best.

And then when she wouldn't eat in front of me.

But when she let me win, I couldn't help but call her out on acting like she didn't find the word *ate*. She's way smarter than me. I realized that the minute I found her in my old yearbook.

She was the president of the Honor Society her sopho-more year. I saw her picture with the glasses and braces, more meat on her bones. I'm fairly sure that's why she chose to keep her identity a secret from me. And if we were in high school again, I wouldn't have blamed her, but we're adults now. And when I called her out on it, I had high hopes she'd own who she was. Say 'yeah, I was a nerd back then but so what?' I'm still amazing and look at me now.

Hell, I'd respected her if she shot out some cocky comment that I could've had her in high school but I was too shallow so I'm not getting a piece of her now. I would've made sure to prove her wrong.

But she sat there all timid, eyes cast down and shy body language. After years of dating the same kind of woman and the fact that my ex-girlfriend Jenna screwed me over, the dam broke.

Sliding from the bench, I pocket her Boggle sheet and grab the game to place it back on the shelf on my way out. Some other poor sap can get schooled by his date.

Once I'm back outside, I walk close to the storefront windows, trying to find shelter from the light mist falling out of the dark sky.

Glancing at my phone, I see it was Luca calling me earlier. I dial him back.

"Where are you? We're heading to Rush Street tonight, want to join?" he asks.

Another night at a club? No thank you.

"Nah. Thanks though."

"When did both my brothers go pussy on me?" He doesn't bother to hide the displeasure in his tone.

Luca parties every night he isn't on shift. Never did I think two years difference would feel more like six.

"I just finished with a date." I stop at the light, waiting to cross.

"Didn't go well, huh?"

"How'd you know?"

A bachelorette party files out of a limo parked by the curb. The poor bride who has dicks glued on every inch of her clothing stumbles into the pizza place. Yeah, she's not making it to the bar.

"Because you're talking to me. You should be on your way to your apartment, or better yet have her pressed against a brick wall in the alley. The last place you should be is on the phone with me."

I can't argue with him, he's right. The date was a bust especially when I morphed into an asshole at the end.

"I'm heading home."

"Perfect. That's where I am."

My mood sours further. Luca tends to travel in packs. Him and his freeloader pack of wolves probably drank the last of my beer.

"Why?"

"Oh, sweet brother. You gave me a key, remember?"

I step onto the red line train. The doors shut behind me. "That was for emergencies."

"I was out of beer. That *is* an emergency." One of his jackass friends laughs in the background.

"Leave my apartment and don't take the key with you," I warn, tapping end call.

I slink down into an available seat. It's too early for the train to be filled with young nightlife people like Luca but too late for commuters. Two couples sit on opposites sides of the train—one with limbs entwined and faces close. The other with backs straight and faces forward. The woman with her head in her phone and the man staring out the window. It's like seeing the before and after effects of the infatuation phase of a relationship.

Either the beer or exhaustion sets in and my eyes close as I rest my head against the glass of the window. Madison's temper those last few seconds together overtake my thoughts. The way her cheeks flushed with anger and not arousal. How her sulking shoulders straightened and her jaw jutted out. The fire that glinted in her eye of all the things I could tell she wanted to say to me.

All of it made me so rock hard, I almost pulled her into my lap and kissed her. Luckily, I refrained because I'm pretty sure she would've smacked me across the face. No matter how hot her fight got me, I realize now that it was wrong of me to take out my own frustrations on her.

I exit the train at my stop and by the time I'm walking up the steps to my apartment I can hear the music inside blaring. Of course since my day has been a suckfest, Mrs. Peterman opens up her door just as I hit the landing, her wig half-cocked on her head, Mr. Wiggles in her arms as she stares at me with a pointed glare.

"I can't hear Survivor," she tells me.

"Sorry, Mrs. Peterman. It's my brother."

"I saw him leave two hours ago." She sucks her false teeth back into place.

"Yeah, my other brother. The paramedic. Luca?"

She looks at me like I'm speaking a language she doesn't understand.

"I can't miss anything on the show. I'm trying to be nice here since you boys do so much for the city, but my show is important."

I put up my hand in apology. The last thing I need is her calling the landlord. "I know, I know. I'm sorry, Mrs. Peterman."

She nods and steps back into her apartment, shutting the door behind her. The echo of five different locks following her departure. You'd think a woman so scared wouldn't mind a little music when it meant that a cop and firefighter lived across the hall.

I open my door because unlike Mrs. Peterman's door, my

brother believes he's invincible. Or that he can take any burglar who wants to rob us.

"Turn down the music." I don't wait for him to oblige because Luca and his buddies are all out on our small porch that overlooks...nothing spectacular.

I press off on the stereo and Luca whips his head around, his attention inside the apartment immediately.

"Mrs. Peterman complained." I raise my hand before he can make some remark about what a pussy I am.

"You'd think after that time I carried her down two flights of stairs and got her to the emergency room she'd stop giving us shit," Luca says, coming in from the patio.

I open the fridge, grabbing a beer and twisting it open.

"First of all, you don't live here." I point at him with the neck of the beer.

He shrugs, propping himself up on the kitchen counter, grabbing a tortilla chip from a bag he opened from our pantry. Forever the little brother.

"We're family." He holds his arms out, inviting me into a hug I want no part of.

"There's a reason we don't live together." I inspect the kitchen, the empty beer bottles all over the table and chips and salsa strewn about the counter. "Cris is going to freak. Thanks for leaving me a Friday night of clean up."

I leave my beer on the counter and organize the beer bottles so after Luca and his dimwit friends leave, I can at least chill out and watch television.

"Cris needs to lighten up. So tell me about your date?" He hops down and tosses his empty into the recycle bin before lining up a row of four shot glasses.

"I'm not taking a shot," I say.

"Then I'll take two." He pours Jim Beam into the glasses but doesn't call his friends in. "Come on, I'm your brother and panty melter extraordinaire."

I toss the paper towel in the trash. "I was an asshole and now I have to apologize."

"You were an asshole to Maddie?" His jaw hangs open. "She was always the sweetest girl."

"Not so sweet when you piss her off." I snag my beer and tip it back. The shot is looking more appealing now when I think of how I have to make it right with her.

"How'd you piss her off? I mean after high school, jeez, you really are an asshole."

I pause with my beer halfway lifted to my lips. "Excuse me?"

"Come on. You aren't that dense, are you?" Luca's friends come in, all saying their hellos and fist bumping me. Half of them I've known just as long as my own friends. I figure this is good. Luca will leave and I don't have to hear him tell me off for how I treated her. Instead he says, "Hey guys, I'll meet you down at the club."

They all look at one another like their leader gave them a confusing order.

"Luca, go. I'm gonna clean up so I don't have to hear Cristian's bitching when he gets home. After that, I'm hitting the sheets."

Luca shakes his head and nods toward the door so his friends leave.

After the door shuts, Luca grabs a shot and hands it to me. I down it without argument and he downs another one.

"You looked her up in the yearbook, right?" Luca's eyes narrow to slits, curious to what the fuck I did. I'm not sure why he cares. It's not like he's friends with her. He's never mentioned her or her friend until the auction.

"Yeah, I looked her up."

"And?"

"And what? She looks different, I noticed that. I get what you guys were saying...that we didn't travel in the same circles and that I was a dick in high school, but none of that has anything to do with her."

He blows out a breath and lets out a cocky chuckle, suggesting I truly am the stupidest person he's ever met.

"Madison Kelly loved you, man. I mean head over heels for you. Hunt probably bid on you because she wanted to give her best friend the date she's been waiting a decade for."

"Hunt?" I have no idea who he's talking about.

"Her friend, Lauren Hunt."

"You refer to her by her last name?"

Luca shakes his head. "I don't want to talk about her. You really don't remember Maddie?"

I swig down a few more mouthfuls of beer. "She looked kind of familiar in the pictures. But I was a senior and she was a sophomore. I didn't know a ton of sophomores." I shrug and then throw my empty beer bottle into the recycling.

"You didn't know a lot of nerds." Luca tilts his head and gives me a challenging stare.

"High school was eleven years ago. I wasn't an asshole to her tonight because she wore glasses and had braces. I was an asshole because she was all shy and timid." I throw my hands in the air. "I have no fucking clue why I'm still talking to you about this."

Going out to my balcony, I pick up after Luca and his destruction crew.

His footsteps follow behind me like I assumed they would. "You're talking to me because it bothers you that you hurt that poor girl's feelings." He frowns and sticks out his bottom lip. "You came to your more knowledgeable brother for advice." He extends his arms and uses his hands to motion me in for a hug. "Come, Luca will make it all better."

I throw a cheeseball at him and it pings off his forehead. "You should probably get going to meet your friends."

He chuckles. "Tell me what's wrong with shy and timid? They're usually the kinky ones in bed."

I stop to stare at him, unamused.

"What?" He raises his hands up in a placating fashion. "It's not stereotyping if it's fact."

I plop down on one of the two chairs we have on the small outdoor space. Propping my feet up on the metal railing, I stare out at the sliver of skyline view we have before the next building blocks it. I notice a party full of girls in the condo building across the street, and it's clear what Luca and his friends were doing out here.

"Nice." I shift my eyes from Luca to the girls.

He sits down in the empty chair. "You can't blame us, they were having a sex toy party." He pushes his own long legs against the metal railing.

"I don't know why I did it, okay?" I don't turn to him, but I feel his eyes on me. "I just... I'm done with girls who try to mold themselves into a version of a woman they think I'll like. I knew she was different from the moment I met her at the auction. I mean it's nice she doesn't flaunt her amazing body. Truth is, before I approached her at the auction, I was excited that she bid on me. I can't even describe my first impression of her other than that she was out of my league. Then I approach her and she can barely say a word or keep eye contact."

"Hard life when you turn women into babbling messes."

Luca doesn't understand my dilemma or why I acted the way I did to Madison. He's still in the 'you're hot, come home with me' stage. The only thing he needs to know about her is that she's of age and that one of them has a condom. It doesn't matter if he knows whether she has siblings or not. He doesn't care what her favorite travel destination is, or if she's an early riser. Actually, he usually hopes she is an early riser so she wakes up and gets the hell out of his bed without expecting breakfast.

"Stop judging me." He points at me, like he could actually telepathically listen to my thoughts.

"Just go find your Friday night girl."

He sits up, resting his elbows on his knees and stares over at me. "I get what you're saying. You're getting older and looking for a wife."

"I'm not looking for a wife, just a girl who will be herself and has a backbone and isn't afraid to show it."

Luca just stares at me, confusion laced in his features. "Then I'd say the girl who used to write your name in her binder in high school probably isn't your girl. But you still need to apologize for no other reason than the fact that I have to go on a date with her best friend and I don't want your fuck up ruining what is already going to be a horrible night for me." With that cryptic comment, he rises out of the chair and puts his hand on my shoulder. "Your fighting girl is out there somewhere."

I let him leave and enjoy his night as my mind stays in flux. Like usual, I disagree with my brother. Madison Kelly might just be my fighting girl.

CHAPTER SEVEN

Madison

The anxiety of coming home early after my date crashed and burned like an Indy 500 car that hit the wall straight-on sets in when the dark windows of my place greet me. Vanessa must be at her mystery job and Lauren is either on a date herself or just out. Of course, I wouldn't put it past her to be doing PI work on Vanessa. She's way too worked up about Vanessa's comings and goings.

After I've driven up the alleyway and parked in the garage, I make my way through the backyard toward the house. The back door opens before I reach it and Lauren softly closes it shut behind her.

"Lauren," I say in a calm voice.

Her hand covers my mouth, and my back ends up hitting the banister of our porch. That's going to leave a bruise. Sometimes her quick reflexes make me think she was an assassin in her prior life.

Without any explanation, and with her hand still covering

my mouth, she turns me around and pushes me forward to lead me to where I just came from—our detached garage.

She doesn't remove her hand from my mouth until she callously shoves me into the backseat of her yellow Fiat which is parked in the garage.

"What the hell?"

She ignores me, throwing a blanket over us so we're concealed while peering out the back window.

We watch as Vanessa steps through the outside entrance of the garage, her heels clicking on the new cement I poured a month ago in preparation of selling this property. She doesn't give a glance to the Fiat when she presses the garage button and the large door rises.

A black town car waits idle for her in front of us and she presses the code on our keypad, making the garage door lower, leaving us with a view of her climbing into the back-seat, unable to tell if there's anyone already in there.

Lauren, the little acrobat, jumps into the front seat and thrusts the keys into the ignition and hits the button on the remote for the garage door opener. The tires squeal and she peels out of the garage.

"Hello! What the hell are we doing?" I climb awkwardly into the front seat, the seatbelt my first priority.

"We're going to follow her." Her small foot presses on the gas pedal and we round the corner of the alley into the street.

"I'd like to not die tonight." I grasp for the door handle, anything to hold on to.

"Please. I know Chicago roads like a cardiologist knows the heart."

I don't even try to argue with the deranged line of think-ing. Instead, I close my eyes. After a minute, I peek out of one eye because it's good to test your heart under stressful situations, right?

"Tell me about your date." Lauren tries to spur a conversation as she speeds past a biker on the right.

"Later."

"What?" She brakes hard, almost rear-ending the car between us and the town car. Her eyes stay focused on me as the red light illuminates her face through the windshield. "Maddie?"

"Nothing. We'll talk about it after this little PI move you've kidnapped me for."

She doesn't press the gas and I notice she's still in her scrubs from the physical therapist's office. "Did he treat you bad? Because I'll find him and nut check him." The pissed off expression on her face says she's serious.

"No. I mean...well...I took him to Dice and Spins."

A green light replaces the red one streaming into the car and I slam into the back of the seat when she guns it.

"Why would you take him there?" she asks.

"Because I thought it would be fun."

The town car stops at a light to turn left forcing Lauren to piss off the person beside us as she presses on the gas, squeezes in and slams on her brakes. Horns honk and I sink down in the seat.

"Seriously, you'd never be able to be a real PI person. The driver is probably on to you."

"Don't change the conversation. How did Mauro enjoy playing Life?" Her condescending tone confirms what I figured out mid-date—that it was the worst date idea ever.

"He didn't seem to care until I...lost."

"You didn't?"

The town car is moving and Lauren follows the car toward the lakefront.

"What? Women do it all the time," I insist, but even I can hear the lack of confidence in my voice.

"Not you, Maddie." She shakes her head. "I have to say

though, I'm surprised he noticed. He always seemed so self-centered."

I stare ahead as the car slows down due to the traffic around Lakeview and the masses of young people heading out for the night.

I'm not sure I want to stick up for Mauro, but if we hadn't had that small fight at the end, I never would have realized that he noticed everything about me. In truth, that might be what scared me the most. Like he could see inside me...how messed up I was from high school...how my beliefs about myself didn't catch up with my outward appearance. Lauren may believe that Mauro is all about himself, but he nailed me in one night. I can be a people pleaser and whether that had anything to do with having a mom who fell to pieces when my dad divorced her or a dad who moved miles away after the divorce so that I only saw him for a few days in the summer and maybe on holidays, I don't know. Or maybe it came from trying to make up for my lack of beauty at a time in my life when everyone is judged on how attractive they are. Regardless, his words sunk into me like tattoo ink on bare skin.

I might be a confident woman in my job, but when it comes to social situations, I am and probably always will be a people pleaser at heart.

"Duck!" Lauren says as the car comes to an abrupt stop.

She sinks down low in the car and I mimic her incognito behavior.

"I think this is a little extreme. Vanessa will tell us when she's ready," I say.

Lauren pays no attention to me, her eyes trained on the town car pulling around the front entrance to a condo building none of us would be able to afford a simple studio apartment in.

The town car driver exits the car, rounding the front until he opens up the back passenger one. A doorman heads out at the same time, holding the front door open of the condo building.

Vanessa steps out first, a raincoat I never knew she owned cinched tight around her waist, leaving only fishnet stockings and stiletto heels visible.

"It's so cliché I'm nauseous," Lauren says.

I jab her in the shoulder. "This proves nothing."

I'm fully in defense mode until a man emerges out of the town car. No suit, no tie, no clean-cut hairstyle that would suggest that he's a successful businessman. Instead, he's sporting a scruffy unkept beard and shaggy haircut with a plaid shirt untucked over a pair of jeans.

"It's so much worse than I thought," Lauren says.

"We don't know anything for sure."

Lauren's judgmental gaze flickers to mine. She's cast her verdict already.

I'm not so sure. Maybe it was my night with Mauro, that he wasn't who I pegged him for, but I'm not convinced that Vanessa is an escort.

The doorman tips his head toward Vanessa in a familiar way to suggest that this isn't her first time here. They disappear through the doors a second later, leaving the silence in the car thick like the fog on an early spring morning.

"It's worse than I thought. She's not even like Julia Roberts. There's no Edward...what was his last name?" She doesn't wait for me to answer. "I mean did you see that guy? She's going to sleep with *him* for money? Why wouldn't she just come to us? God knows I don't have a ton of extra cash because of my student loans, but I'd give her every extra penny I could."

Lauren's hand goes to the door handle.

"No!" I yell, reaching forward to stop her.

"We have to save her. If we catch her red-handed, she'll

confess. The three us can figure this out. Surely you'll give her a pass on rent."

I love Lauren, but she's wrong. "If we go in there guns blazing, Vanessa will flee. She'll move out of the house. She'll refuse to have anything to do with us."

"No, she'd never."

"Vanessa is hard-headed and after having a father who dictated her every move her entire life, she's not about to swap him out for two best friends who are going to treat her the same way. She has to come to us for help."

I don't inform Lauren that I've already told Vanessa not to pay me, but on the first of every month, there's always an envelope under my pillow stacked with small bills. It pains me each time, but Vanessa would never let either one of us flip a bill for her. She's too proud, a trait she inherited from her father, although she'd deny the accusation.

"She can't sell her body." Her tone has turned defeated.

"We don't know for sure that she is."

Lauren's fingers weave around the steering wheel, her fingernails digging into the indentations. "She's in a town car with fishnets and heels."

"Maybe it's her date. He's older. She could be embarrassed to tell us."

I'm not sure I believe the words coming out of my mouth. Vanessa has a type and the man that followed her into that condo building isn't him. She might have daddy issues, but she's not looking for another one.

"Come on. I'll buy you ice cream." My hand lands on Lauren's arm. "She's a smart girl. If she was into something bad, she'd tell us."

Lauren glances at the building again, the town car now gone, the doors closed.

"Okay," she agrees reluctantly.

Ten minutes later Lauren has processed my words about

Vanessa and although she'll never tell me I'm right, we both know that I probably am.

"If you're buying, we're going to George's."

"Then you better hit the gas if you want to make it before they close," I say.

Lauren listens to me and although she's back to her sane self, no longer weaving in and out of traffic and almost hitting parked cars, there were a few close calls with pedestrians. Lauren's justifies her near misses with the theory that it's Friday night and people shouldn't come down to the city if they don't know how to follow the traffic signals.

Twenty minutes later, the glass doors of George's are shut and locked behind us. I have my typical cookie dough ice cream bowl in hand, while Lauren opted for cookies 'n cream. Instead of hopping back in the car, we walk down the street. We pass a few couples strolling along after dinner and I'd be lying if I didn't yearn for what they have.

"Tell me what happened on your date," Lauren says, finding a park bench and sitting down.

"I made a fool of myself, but what's new about that?" I take a seat beside her.

Her shoulder knocks mine and I sway before righting myself. "I'm sure you didn't."

"I thought I was over the high school crush, you know. That I could go in there and be all 'look at me now.' But the minute he was inches away, my voice locked up and I was that girl again. The one who thought he'd never go for a girl like me."

"Is that what you were looking for? For him to want to date you?"

I shrug. "I don't know. Maybe. Probably. I at least wanted to be asked." I bury my head in my ice cream. "I know it's stupid."

"Why is that stupid? He's the one for you. Why do you think I bid on him?"

I glare at her from the corner of my eye. "Thanks for that by the way."

She giggles, spooning a big heap of the cookie into her mouth. "So you let him win and then what happened?" she mumbles over the giant cookie lodged in her mouth.

"He was angry. Called me out. Said I was a people pleaser."

"You're nice," she counters, sounding as affronted as I was at the time.

"See!" I point my spoon at her. "That's what I said, but he said I was confusing the two."

"You're not a people pleaser when it comes to me. If that was the case, Vanessa would be sitting on this bench with us."

Point proven.

"But when it comes to people you don't know, you do tend to give in too easily." Her eyes cast down and I think she's afraid of how I'll take her criticism.

"No, I'm not."

"You are," she insists.

"Sometimes I really just don't care when presented with two options." I shove a spoonful of ice cream into my mouth.

"I get that, Maddie. I probably care too much about getting my way which is why we've been best friends forever. I can take advantage of you by always getting my way."

"Hey."

She leans into me, placing her head on my shoulder. "I'm kidding. I throw you a bone every now and then." Her eyes flutter in a 'forgive me I'm beautiful' motion.

"We were only together for like two hours. I can't be that transparent to a guy who didn't even remember I existed until his brothers told him we went to high school together."

The ache from that jab returns like scar tissue under the surface of my skin.

"Maybe Mauro has changed."

"Well, I'll never find out because I told him to—"

A smirk crosses Lauren's face. "Told him to what?"

"I told him to have a nice life." Mimicking the conviction in my tone I had with Mauro hours earlier.

"Oh Mad, you are too nice. I'm not exactly shaking in my boots over here." She laughs and I join her.

"What should I have said?"

"You should have said even if I see you in my next life it's too soon."

"That's mean." I toss my empty cup of ice cream in the trashcan beside the bench then stand up.

"Yes, Maddie. Mean is the exact opposite of nice," she says with a smile on her face. "See where we're going here?" She throws away her cup and swings her arm around my shoulders. "I'll have an effect on you yet." Her hip hits mine. "It's okay to be nice, I wouldn't want you any other way. Hopefully Mauro will be in your rearview mirror now."

"Not when you marry his brother." I don't even bother to look at her because she's probably planning my death based on the glare I feel on the side of my face.

"Never."

"Stranger things have happened." I steal a glance and her eyes are narrowed to slits.

"Pigs would be flying, a snowball would not melt in hell, you'd be holding your breath and the Cubs would win the World Series and still I would never walk down the aisle with Luca Bianco."

"I hate to remind you, but the Cubs did win the World Series."

"Again!" she yells. "They'd have to win it again. Damn it."

We're laughing as we climb back into her yellow Fiat to go

home and I realize this was just what I needed after my disastrous date. But one day we won't live together anymore and no one will be around to help pick up the pieces. An ache starts up in my chest. I'm not in any rush for that day to come.

CHAPTER EIGHT

Madison

The room in the courthouse is pretty packed when I arrive, which never ends up in my favor. I'm definitely not the only one bidding on Property 1731. I go over the figures in my head again while more people file in, mentally calculating how high I can bid for my old house. I rationalize the lower than normal return I'm willing to take, telling myself that the emotional aspect of this project outweighs the profit.

To know that a family lives there whose love will saturate into the grain of the wood support beams will give me immeasurable pleasure. Yes, I know. Cheesy as hell, but my family crumbled under that roof and I'm determined to smack a new roof on that baby to bring a shelter of happiness to a new family.

Lucky for me, no one seems to want to sit in the front row. The room is filled other than a sprinkle of empty seats in the rows behind me, my row is vacant except for a man at the end who took the second seat in. Weird, why he would take the second? Maybe he's waiting for someone.

A minute later the auctioneer approaches the podium.

I straighten my back, thankful that the Oswald's have yet to make an appearance. They'd be my biggest competition for this property. Already giddiness starts to flutter my insides, thinking that maybe I'll get away with a low bid.

"Good morning, ladies and gentlemen. Are we all ready to get this auction started? I'll go over the rules for you newbies." Rachel smiles down at me. "For you regulars, be patient with the new people in town."

I smile back, my eyes on her until the door opens at the back of the room.

Tardiness is unacceptable and if it's Oscar Oswald, I hope Rachel tells him he's two minutes late so he can fly a kite. All the eyes shift in the direction of the door, but as Mauro Bianco strolls across the room, it's only my breath that's lodged in my throat. This cannot be happening to me. I close my eyes and peek out of one like he could be a figment of my imagination.

"Sir, the auction starts at ten on the dot."

Throw him out, Rachel.

Please.

"I do apologize, ma'am, but I just got off shift. We had a late call and I got here as soon as I could."

"You're a firefighter?" she asks.

I roll my eyes over the fact that he'd wear his fatigues like a fanatic fan of a sports team just to get an advantage at the auction.

"Yes, ma'am. Engine Fifty-Five."

Rachel smiles and holds out her hand for him to enter the room. "Next time try to be on time."

Try? I want to scream. Anyone else who didn't have that sexy panty-melting smile would be out on their ass.

It's bad enough that I have to share oxygen with the man, but his enticing scent hits me full force as his weight lands in the seat next to me.

"Hey," he whispers.

"Hi." I keep my eyes poised on Rachel who seems more enthralled in watching our interaction than performing her job.

"What are you doing here?" he asks, continuing the conversation even after I didn't make eye contact.

"Same as you I suppose."

"You're bidding on a property?"

"No. I thought this was people pleasers anonymous," I deadpan.

A huge boisterous laugh erupts out of him, echoing through the silent room. Rachel glances up from the papers her assistant is explaining to her.

Kick him out, Rachel.

She smiles instead because his laugh is like an aphrodisiac.

"You're funny." He leans back in the chair, his shoulder touching mine, his thigh brushing my thigh before I swing my leg over and cross them, effectively relieving some of the awareness of how close he was.

"Thanks. I'll add that to my credentials. Can be funny when I'm not busy putting other's needs before my own."

My eyes zone in on Rachel who is taking her sweet time with the paperwork, her and her assistant in the deep throes of conversation, papers shuffling. Something is going on up there.

"I meant to message you, but my schedule…"

I wonder how many times he uses his schedule or the fact he's a firefighter as an excuse or to gain an advantage.

"Will you look at me?" He asks the one thing I cannot imagine doing in this moment.

"Yes." I look over his shoulder instead of meeting his eyes. He won't be able to tell the difference.

His forefinger lands under my chin and he urges my face forward.

And there they are. Those gorgeous blue eyes staring right back at me.

His hand drops to his lap.

"I wanted to apologize. I never should've acted like that to you."

"It's fine."

"Don't do that." The kind voice he was using a moment ago now holds a tinge of irritation.

"Stop telling me what to do." I look away from him to Rachel once again.

Come on. Is this property really worth this?

"I'm sorry it's just—"

"What Mauro? I'm sorry if I'm not the girl you want me to be. If I'm not perfect enough for you. Well, guess what? I don't care."

The man at the end of our row looks beyond Mauro's squared shoulders in my direction. If I was Lauren, I'd flip him off. Say some crude comment about minding his own business in her Laurenesque way. But I'm not her. I'm Madison Kelly, the one who smiles like nothing is going on between me and the firefighter.

"Perfect? Enough for me?" He sounds more as though he's not asking me, but himself.

Whatever.

"Yes. Would you like it if I was telling you how to act?"

A smile tips his lips. "Please do."

I roll my eyes.

"Come on." He eggs me on.

I stand and head over to Rachel.

"Hey, Rachel, can you let me know how much longer until we start?"

Her vision shifts from her assistant to me. "Sorry, Madison. There are five properties that were taken out of auction and we're waiting on word before we start. Gives you more time with the hottie over there." She smiles conspiratorially at me.

"Thanks." I give her a tight smile.

Mauro's smile is wide and annoying when I sit back down in my seat. "What's the word?"

"It's going to be awhile. Some properties are coming off auction."

"What? Did she say which ones?"

His easy-going casual persona morphs into an anxiety ridden one like that.

"No. She can't tell us."

"That sucks, I hope it isn't mine," he says, rubbing his hands up and down his thighs.

"Yours? You haven't won anything. What property are you here for?" I ask, knowing a newbie would never take on the house I want. He's probably here for a condo that needs a few light fixture changes.

"I'm not saying."

I chuckle. "What? You think I'm going to want it?"

"You never know." He shrugs.

"That would go against my people pleasing efforts, don't you think?"

Again with the chuckle that's an on switch for the heat between the legs.

"Shit, Maddie, I wish I would've known you better in high school. You're funny."

"Only with you, apparently."

His hand covers his heart and his head falls back. "I'm honored."

I roll my eyes for the fiftieth time since he sat down next to me.

"So, your business, is it flipping houses?" he asks.

"Yes."

"Impressive. I'm just about to start my first redo."

"Good luck. Hope you're handy."

"I'm good with my hands."

I don't miss the sexual innuendo in his tone, but I don't react.

We wait in silence for another few seconds before he stretches—his arms high above his head, his torso rising. If I dared to sneak a peek I bet his shirt is rising, too.

I wonder if he has a happy trail?

No. No, you don't.

"So you think what? That this is a way to make a quick buck by flipping a house?"

"Whoa, never saw that jab coming." He laughs again.

Why is everything so damn humorous to him?

"Everyone thinks it's so easy. Buy it on the cheap, cut a few corners and double your money. I'm going to warn you, it's hard work."

"Thanks. I'll take it into consideration."

He crosses his arms in front of him, checking his watch and yawns. "I need a bed."

Can I join you?

Bad Maddie.

Rachel approaches the microphone. "I'm sorry ladies and gentlemen. Two more minutes. We're about done."

"What are you into flipping for if not for the money?" he asks, though his eyes stay trained on the wall ahead of us.

"To take something everyone thinks is ugly and past its prime and pull the beauty out of it so that people will love it again."

He says nothing but his eyes are burning a hole in the side of my head now.

"I didn't expect that," he says.

"What?"

"An explanation so, I don't know...profound?"

"Just do me a favor and if you are going to take the time to redo a house, think outside the box. Don't just go with whatever the latest trends are. Picture a family living there and do quality renovations, imagine what their life will be like while they're enjoying each and every decision you made along the way."

"Man, you're just full of advice today."

Rachel approaches the podium again, her assistant finding her spot right next to her with a stack of papers.

"Sorry." I cringe once the word leaves my lips.

"I don't offend easily, no need for apologies."

The fact he ignored the opportunity to take another jab at my people pleaser tendencies tells me he must have meant his earlier apology.

"Property 3902 is up for auction." A picture of the house comes up on the screen. "We'll begin the bidding at fifty-six thousand dollars." Rachel is all business as usual and I sit and wait for Property 1731 to be called.

The property doesn't get called until an hour later and though a lot of people have left, Mauro is still sitting right next to me.

Rachel eyes me, knowing my go-to property type. "Property 1731."

Mauro straightens in his chair, abandoning his phone to the vacant chair next to him.

No.

He looks over at me with the same expression of disbelief that's heating the blood in my veins. Forget the Oswald brothers. Mauro Bianco is my biggest threat?

Then he raises his eyebrows as though this is a challenge for him.

"Game on," I murmur.

"Don't play nice." He waggles his eyebrows and raises his hand. "Twenty thousand."

Narrowing my eyes, I put my own hand in the air. "Twenty-two thousand."

CHAPTER NINE

Mauro

If I could turn back time, I would. I'd go back to that board game cafe and keep my mouth shut about her letting me win because she has that fire in her eyes when she makes her 'game on' comment. You can tell this is her element, which probably means she's got the advantage here.

"Twenty-four," I raise my hand.

The auctioneer smirks at her assistant and points to me. We both know I won't have the winning bid for long.

"Twenty-six." The spitfire girl next to me raises her hand like an eager teacher's pet.

Was she?

With no one else coming in to bid, I figure it must be only us.

"How high?" I whisper to her. "Twenty-eight," I say.

"What? Why? I'm not telling you." Her head is twisting between me and the auctioneer, her hand already back in the air. "Thirty."

"Because we're just raising the price up for one of us."

"That's the point," she says out of the side of her mouth.

"We have thirty. Do we have thirty-one?" The auctioneer eyes me.

"If we go too high one of us isn't going to make a dime," I say.

"Then save me the trouble and bow out."

"Thirty-one going once." The gavel is in her hand, her eyes silently asking me.

"Fine. Have it your way." I shrug. "Thirty-three."

"There's no rule about going up two k." She sneers her arm extended. "Thirty-four."

"Sorry, newbie and all." I shrug.

Her blue eyes narrow and she bites her lip. I shift in my seat from the concentrated effort it takes for me not to lean in and take that lip of hers with my own teeth.

"Thirty-five."

She huffs, her shoulders deflating in defeat for the first time since the opening bid.

We're now way over the starting bid and if one of us wouldn't have come, the other would have had it for twenty thousand.

"What are you thinking?" she whispers.

I can't stop the cocky grin from forming on my lips. Not because I knew she'd bend to my way, but because she's open to listening to my idea.

"I'm thinking we partner up."

"WHAT?"

Now, this is the type of woman I could get under.

"I'm sure you plan on hiring a contractor."

"We have thirty-five on the table. Anyone else?" The auctioneer is not leaving me much time to convince her.

"Yeah, so?"

"I can be our contractor. I know a million guys from the

firehouses who are skilled at different trades. Not to mention, I told you I have good hands." I hold them up for her to see.

"Thirty-five going twice." The auctioneer is being nice and going a lot slower than she did with previous properties. She seems to have a soft spot for Madison.

"You'll listen to me when it comes to budget and decorating decisions?" she asks, her eyes shifting from the gavel about to slam down making me the winner of the property.

I hold out my hand. "Sure thing, but you show me the ropes. We're partners. Fifty, fifty."

She stares into my eyes, for the first time not looking away. The softness of her hand slides into mine and I grip her hand. "Partners." Her tone might not hold the declaration I was hoping for, but it's a start.

She may not realize it yet, but she didn't get the bad end of this agreement. I think she'll be surprised by my skills.

"Sold." The auctioneer points to me, smiling down at our entwined hands.

Madison retracts, and the air conditioning must have blasted on because goose bumps run up my spine.

CHAPTER TEN

Madison

"Did you just pinch yourself?" Mauro asks next to me while we wait for the paperwork to be processed after we each supplied a check for half the amount of Mauro's bid on my childhood home.

I wrap my palm around the spot that I did, in fact, pinch myself at.

Wouldn't you think it was a dream if you just decided to partner up with your high school crush putting him in your proximity for months on end? My sixteen-year-old self is throwing confetti in the air and dancing the cha-cha. My current self is wary as much as she is excited.

"I had an itch," I lie.

He smirks, his signature trademark that probably has women stripping their panties off, but I need to hold him back with titanium arms because he'll railroad this project from me if I let him.

"Congratulations you two. You're proud owners of Property 1731." Rachel holds the paperwork out and I snatch it from her hands.

Mauro looks over at me incredulously.

"I'll keep everything organized."

"What makes you think I'm not organized?" he asks.

Rachel shares a look with her assistant that reads more 'aren't they cute' rather than 'this property will be up for auction again in two months.'

"I have a system."

"I'm sure you do and now I'm part of that system. Can you send me copies tonight?" His voice isn't sweet and syrupy, instead, it's almost accusatory as if I'd screw him over.

"Do you think I'm going to cheat you? Your name is on here."

"Just making sure we're in this together." A dimness dulls his eyes for a split second before they sparkle again. "No fights where you lock me out of the house or anything." The one side of his lips tip and I can't help the way my body melts under his flirtatious nature.

"No worries." I shove the papers in my purse. "Thanks, Rachel and Tracy. See you soon I'm sure."

I head out the door, hearing Mauro speak his own good-byes and the ladies slight swoon back with we hope to see you soon, too. His footsteps loom behind me as I walk to the elevator.

"Let's go to breakfast, talk logistics."

"How about we pick up breakfast and go over to the house? The sooner we figure out our game plan, the better. I can have a dumpster there tomorrow to get all the crap out of the house."

He runs his fingers through his dark wavy hair.

Stop it, Maddie. Do not get sucked in.

"Okay. I'm off tomorrow and I can round up a crew."

"Hold up, stud. Let's go over plans before we start demolishing everything." I step into the elevator, the small box feeling even more claustrophobic with him sharing the space.

"Stud? I like it." His cocky grin appears—again.

"Don't take it as a compliment."

He steps forward, his hand landing on the silver railing at my side, his body so close to mine that my heart pounds in my chest as if it wants to reach out and touch him. "No?" he questions in a gravelly voice.

I shake my head, I haven't been this close to him since that night long ago and he still has the ability to paralyze my body.

"Stop messing around."

He chuckles and steps back out of my personal space.

Why would he even do that?

Running another hand through his hair, he stretches, bending and twisting in every direction.

"If you're tired..."

His gaze shifts to mine quickly. "No. We're in this together remember?"

"I know, but I slept eight hours last night and you... didn't."

"It's okay, I'm used to no sleep."

"If you say so." I shrug.

"Good, we should probably get some ground rules set," he says.

The elevator doors open. "Well, I'll pick up some break-fast and I'll meet you at the house. We can go over the business plan, talk about what we're going to do with improvements, so we know what walls to tear down."

"I'll grab the breakfast. What do you want?" he asks.

We exit the federal building and a man is walking toward us with a mass of media behind him. I freeze. We both shift our bodies to clear a path and it isn't until the suited man passes that I figure out who he is.

He doesn't see me, and just says "No comment" over his shoulder to the throng of reporters behind him before walking through the glass doors.

"That must be about that big fire. I know our Lieutenant said the investigation as to the cause is almost wrapped up and they're supposed to announce the findings soon," Mauro says next to me.

My gaze shifts to him because there's something about his voice...that's when I notice the flush that usually fills his cheeks is gone.

"Probably. The DA is my neighbor. That's him." I nod in the direction where Reed Warner finds solitude away from the cameras. He doesn't stop until he's through security and in the elevator.

"Good guy?" he asks, his eyes still on the media cluster that would make anyone think they're following a celebrity, not the district attorney.

"Really good guy. Did you know—"

He nods before I finish my question. "He was my buddy."

I'd read the articles six months earlier about a horrible fire where a firefighter lost his life. Even saw the funeral procession on the news with shots of a blonde woman with a son in her arms crying as they walked behind the firetruck.

My hand lands on his forearm, finding his skin cold and clammy and I don't think it has anything to do with the start of fall in Chicago. "I'm so sorry."

My touch seems to shock him back to the present and his gaze darts up to meet my own. All I want to do is hug him to my body, he looks like a newly adopted puppy shaking with anxiety.

"Hazards of the job." His hand covers mine. "Thank you though."

I slide my hand from his arm realizing that I just touched Mauro Bianco and didn't freak out.

The cameramen disperse, some going back to their vans parked along the street, others set up shots for the reporters in front of the building.

Wherever Mauro's mind ventured off to must clear. "Breakfast, right? I know just the place," he says.

His attention moves across the street and I spot the sandwich shop before he even mentions it.

"No one makes a breakfast burrito like my mama." He nods in the direction of his family's shop.

I drag my feet. "Are you sure you want to introduce me to your mom?"

He stops and smiles which is a relief after the look on his face moments ago. "She'll love you." He shrugs.

"Gee, will she approve of our shotgun wedding?" I laugh which spurs Mauro's amusement.

"You really are funny." He stares down at me while we wait for the walk symbol to appear on the streetlight.

"Thanks."

His eyes don't leave mine and my breathing picks up under his scrutiny. "I think we're going to make great partners."

I turn away first because I need to get a grip. Thankfully the pedestrian walk sign appears and I step off the corner before a hand grabs my upper arm and pulls me back as a blur of yellow streaks by me.

My back presses against his chest. Firm and strong.

"Watch it, asshole!" he yells at the cab driver.

"Thank you." I untangle from his grip as much as my body protests.

"No problem." His hand takes mine and he leads me across the street lightly jogging when the yellow hand replaces the white walking symbol.

He doesn't release my hand once we reach the other side of the street, like I assumed he would. Instead, he opens up the door for me to his parents' sandwich shop and shifts his hand to the small of my back.

He's Italian, they're touchy, I remind myself.

"Ma!" he yells into the empty restaurant.

It's a typical deli where you order and wait for your number to be called. You can have a seat at the long tables with stools along the window or in the booths that line the back wall which is painted in thirds. One with the Chicago fire department symbol, one for the police and another for paramedic. It's clear to me and their customers that their sons are their life.

"Mauro?" A woman who is shorter in stature, a little plump with dark, wavy shoulder-length hair emerges from the back, wiping her hands on her white apron that says, *My favorite hood is motherhood.*

"Hey, Mama." He smiles then hugs her and kisses her cheek. She does the same, but her gaze is fixed on where I stand behind him.

"This a friend?" she asks him in the cutest Italian accent.

Mauro steps back from his mom, holding his arm out in my direction. "Ma, this is Madison Kelly. Madison, this is my mom, Maria."

A warm smile crosses his mom's lips and her head tilts in a 'I know you' gesture. She points her finger at me. "Valedictorian?"

A warm flush heats my cheeks and Mauro studies me.

"Luca's class, right?" she asks.

"Yes," I answer sheepishly.

Her finger moves to Mauro and then back to me. "You two?"

"No," I quickly refute.

Her smile dims. "Oh." Her eyes shift to Mauro who shrugs like they're having a conversation between them without words.

"We're going to be business partners," he says after confusion masks her face.

"Business?" she asks, sliding behind the deli case and sifting through some paperwork.

"Remember Hunter and I were going to buy a house, fix it up and then sell it?" Mauro approaches the counter, his forearms flexing under the weight of him leaning over so his mom hears him.

"Yes." She doesn't turn around. I can't help but notice her curt demeanor after I said we weren't a couple. She rambles something in Italian and Mauro looks over his shoulder at me for a moment.

He responds back in Italian and before I realize it, she's turned back around, her voice rising, her face red again.

"Enough Mama," Mauro says, his back rod iron straight.

She tilts her head and I don't need to understand Italian because her body language says it all. It's a warning for him to watch how he talks to her.

"I'm sorry, but this isn't the time," he says, slightly chagrined.

"What is going on?" A man comes out from the back, taking plastic gloves off his hands and throwing them into a trashcan behind the counter.

"Papa," Mauro says.

The man who bears Mauro's light eyes, Cristian's nose, and Luca's mouth seeks the source of the reason for the high voices. "Hello." He rounds the deli cabinet, his hand already extended to me. "Anthony."

"Madison," I say and shake his hand.

"I was just telling Mama that Madison and I are going into business together." Mauro steps to my side, his hand finding the small of my back like he's presenting me as a gift, or a girlfriend.

I swallow past the dryness in my mouth and force on a smile that probably looks as awkward as this moment feels.

"Business?" his dad asks, a crease between his brows.

"The flipping houses thing? With Hunter...well, Madison already has her own business and we're going to work together on a house." His dad smiles down at me. I recognize it as the same smile Luca has, but his eyes are just as mesmerizing as Mauro's.

"Congratulations. That's wonderful news."

The deli phone rings. Mauro runs over and answers it before his mom can. He whispers something and hangs up. Again, he and his mom have a silent conversation, their eyes move to me and then back to each other.

"We're here for breakfast," Mauro announces. "Burritos, Mama?"

She smiles, her hand landing on his cheek as she studies his eyes. With a pat on the cheek, she smiles. "Anything for you."

"Non vedo l'ora," Mauro says.

His mom smiles and heads to the back.

"Very nice to meet you, Madison," Anthony says and follows his wife to the back of the deli.

Mauro comes over to me, sliding a chair out. "Sorry about the Italian. She's usually really good about not speaking in Italian when others are around who don't speak the language, but just hearing Hunter's name sends her in a tizzy." Mauro sits in his own chair across from me, legs sprawled out in front of him.

"That's okay."

I want to ask why that is? Was the partnership bad before he died? Is the fact that he died what angers his mom? There are a million reasons it could be, but it's none of my business. We need to keep this relationship professional.

"Your parents are nice."

A proud grin forms, revealing a mouth full of sparkling white teeth. "They're the best." He taps his fingers on the table. "What about your parents? Do they still live around here?"

My heart stumbles over a beat when I remember that he didn't know one key piece of information before we agreed on the partnership. If I were him, I would want to know. I cringe.

"There's something I have to tell you."

CHAPTER ELEVEN

Mauro

I notice the panicked look on her face and hear the anxious tone in her voice and my brows draw together.

"The house we bought is my childhood home." She presses her lips together, watching me absorb the information.

My phone vibrates in my pocket before I can ask why she bought her childhood home. Or how it ended up looking like it was previously on an episode of Hoarders. All these questions float in my head while she sheepishly stares at me with her top teeth pressed into her luscious bottom lip.

God help me, ever since the true Madison Kelly has shown her face, I've been trying to talk my dick down from the salute it wants to give her. The teeth on the lip is the last straw.

Seeing Cailin's name on the screen causes some internal conflict inside me for the first time since Hunter's death.

Usually, I'd stop whatever I'm doing to answer her call, but even I've noticed that they're becoming more frequent.

"Hold on one second." I pull the phone out of my pocket and head over to the doors. "Hey," I answer.

"Are you sleeping? I'm sorry." Cailin sounds as depressed as she usually does.

"No. I'm actually…" My eyes wander to Madison who is piling her hair up in a ponytail on top of her head. My mouth waters as the movement exposes her long neck and my lips beg for me to hang up this phone and venture over there for one taste. "I'm at The Sandwich Shop."

"Oh, tell your parents I say hello. Devin has been begging to see your mom."

"I'm sure she'd like to see him, too." The small argument we had in front of Madison surfaces in my mind. My mom and what might come out of her mouth would be too unpredictable if I let Cailin and Devin be around her right now.

"Since you're out and about anyway, how about a trip to the park with us?" Her tone is more chipper than when I first answered.

My eyes stay glued on Madison who's now pulled out a pad of paper and is scrolling through her phone. Her pen zooming along the page at warp speed like her mind is going too fast and her hand can't keep up.

"I'm sorry. I've got…" I pause because I'm not sure I want Cailin to know what I'm doing. Which is ridiculous because she wouldn't be upset. She'd probably think it was good or she'd be sad because Hunter was supposed to be a part of this venture with me. "An appointment."

Madison's pen stops and the tension in her shoulders fall.

"Oh…okay. What about dinner?" Cailin asks.

I was hoping to sleep through dinner. The only reason I'm still standing is from the pure adrenaline of starting in on this project. For the first time since Hunter's death, excitement fills my veins. I could kiss Patel for giving me the extra push I needed.

"Sure. I'll pick something up on the way over," I say.

"No. You're always spending too much money on us. I'll make dinner. How about six?"

"Sure."

"Great. Devin will be so excited."

My mom comes out from the back, her eyes taking in the situation. The fact I'm on the phone and Madison's by herself causes Ma to frown, and she shakes her head at me.

"See you then. Bye." I click the phone off.

So what if I'm still a tad scared of my mom. Italian mamas are unpredictable and scary. Don't judge unless you've been raised by one yourself.

Stuffing my phone into my pocket, I walk to the counter to pick up the burritos, but my mom turns her back on me and walks past me over to the table.

"I hope you like prosciutto?" she asks Madison. "I wrapped them in foil to stay warm." Instead of handing them to me, she hands them to Madison.

"Thank you so much." Madison drops her pen and reaches to touch my mom's shoulder in a kind gesture of appreciation.

My mom's entire face lights up. "Come back for lunch sometime. What's your favorite sandwich?"

Madison looks up to the ceiling thinking. "Honestly, I'm not much of a sandwich person." She shrugs. "If I had to give you one, I guess turkey?" The way Madison phrases it like a question brings a warm sensation to my heart. She's honest to a fault. Who knows if she'll ever see my mom again. She could have said any deli meat, but she didn't.

"Anthony will make you a sandwich lover. Come back for lunch someday." My mom pats her hand and stands.

"Thank you, Mrs. Bianco." Madison shoves all her stuff back in her bag and rises from the chair.

I grab the brown paper bag. "Bye, Mama," I say.

"Conosco I miei pollo." She touches my face again, her thumb gently rubbing my cheek the way she did when I came to her on one of the worst days of my life.

"I know, Mama." I glance to Madison who's granted us privacy and stepped closer to the door. "Business." I remind her like I did minutes ago after Luca's one-night stand from this past week called the deli. The guy can't get his shit together to save his life.

Her hand falls off my face to my heart. Her fingers drum over the organ.

Sometimes I wonder if she'd marry us off to any woman as long as it got her closer to grandkids.

My hand covers hers and I nod. Non-verbally telling her I'll think about it.

Although I have no intention to. My body might want Madison Kelly, but she agreed to a business partnership just hours ago. She'll show me the ropes and I'm not going to jeopardize my future by letting my dick get a say. So, I'll appease my mama because it will help her sleep at night, but I have no intention of ever letting Madison into my heart. Actually, I may shut that organ down until I'm six feet under at this rate.

I lean down and kiss my mom's cheek. "I'll be by Sunday."

She kisses my cheek back.

"Bye," Madison says, waving at my mom.

"Ciao," she says, the permanent smile plastered to her face.

"Where are you parked?" I ask Madison.

"On Dearborn in a parking garage."

"I'll walk you to your car and then get my truck."

"I'm fully capable of walking to my car. I've done it daily. For years now."

I laugh because she's so much more than the girl I saw on that date. I wish I wouldn't have done to her what I did at the café, but I can't help to think that if I didn't, she would've remained quiet and hidden. Whether or not it was me calling her out for letting me win or that she's just grown more comfortable with me, I can't deny that her humor and self-confidence is sexy.

"Yeah, well that's before you met me. Much to the contrary of what you witnessed on our date, I'm actually a gentleman."

She glances at me briefly and rolls her eyes. "Fine. I'll drive you to your truck after."

"Look at that, we're already compromising. What all great partners do." I smile, wrapping my arm around her shoulders.

Her neck strains as her eyes meet mine. "You have no idea how much compromising you're going to have to do to cater to my ways."

"Keep talking dirty, I like it."

She jabs me in the ribs and though I may not ever sleep with Madison, I think she'd make a killer friend.

The word friend shouldn't leave a bitter taste on my tongue though. I don't need to have been valedictorian of my class to realize that.

CHAPTER TWELVE

Madison

*W*e arrive at my old childhood home but stay by Mauro's truck to eat our breakfast burritos since it's gross inside and I'm already fearful I'll lose the burrito minutes after walking in and dealing with the stench.

"So, you were saying...this is where you grew up?" he asks, glancing up and down the street instead of at the monstrosity in front of us.

"Yeah, when we were in high school...not that you knew me, so it's not really *we*, but you know what I mean."

"I knew you," he says probably out of obligation.

"You don't have to pretend you did. I'm fully aware of our differences."

He bites into his burrito, a low satisfactory moan leaking out of him. It makes me wish I pulled those sounds from him.

"I'm not sure I understand what you're talking about." He sips on the iced coffee he stopped to pick up on the way over.

"Mauro, you were captain of the football team and I was captain of the geek squad."

"There's a captain?" He winks.

"Hardy har har. If we're going into this, I need you to know a few things."

"You're the woman American Psycho and you're going to seek your revenge and kill me?" He devours half of his burrito when I'm only a quarter into mine.

"No. The night we saw each other at the auction, I might've been a little awestruck."

God, this is embarrassing, but I need him to know I am not some dork that he can push around.

"I thought maybe you saw me as Ogre and couldn't stand to look at my face."

He's smirking when I glance up from my burrito. If I'm going to tell him this I have to look him in the eyes, so he respects me.

"No, that's not why. A person like you is probably used to always having the advantage. Having people cower down and listen to you because...well...you're really attractive and attractive people usually get what they want fairly easily."

"You must be speaking from experience." He raises both eyebrows.

I roll my eyes at him, trying to act like we both aren't aware of where we stand.

"I just need you to know, I know what I'm doing here. This is my fifth house and I've learned from my mistakes, so I'd like it if you didn't try to intimidate me into getting your way. That you believe the decisions I suggest and make are what is best for us and come from a place of experience and knowledge."

"Did you think if I wanted a different molding stain I was going to strip off my shirt? Or if we didn't agree on what price to sell it at, I'd do a strip tease?" He hops off the back end of the truck, crumpling up his foil wrapper and tossing it in the bed. "If we're being so honest, than I'd like you to know that

I'm more than just brawn, I have some brains, too. So please respect any suggestions I make."

I've offended him.

I follow him to the passenger side of the truck. "I didn't mean—"

His head turns and his blue eyes are lit with anger. It's a side of him I've never seen before.

"You meant that you thought I'd use my looks and my charm to get my way with you. That I wouldn't respect you as an equal partner." He steps closer. I swallow down the small amount of saliva pooling in my mouth. "Let me tell you, Madison, you might think you know me, but you know nothing about the real me. I seem to remember you telling me something similar last week." His arm lands on top of the truck, effectively caging me in. "I'll tell you this, you might be hung up on what you looked like in high school, but I'm not. I'm sorry if I was an idiot and didn't notice you back then, but I could accuse you of using your looks to get what you want in our arrangement, too. "

I stare into his eyes, watching anger transform to heat.

"I would never disrespect you, Madison. We'll both get what we want out of this partnership." He winks and pushes himself off the truck, leaving me weak in the knees. "Now let's go get dirty."

God, I so want to get dirty with him right now, but not at all in the way that he means.

Two hours later, we're back to sitting on the lowered tailgate of Mauro's truck. I'm finishing up sketching what I'm imagining for the main living space after we knock down the wall between the kitchen and the dining room.

Mauro is lying next to me, his forearm over his eyes,

halfway to dreamland. Part of me wants to tell him to go home and sleep, but if we're going to start demolition tomorrow, then we have no choice but to figure this part out today.

"What do you think about the staircase?" I ask.

"It's dark and scary," he mumbles from underneath his arm.

I laugh. "When I was younger, it left a great space to eavesdrop on my parents."

A flashback of their composed conversation when they decided on a divorce overtakes the one about the Barbie dream house they put together on Christmas Eve during happier times.

"How long did you live here?" He sits up, his back slouched.

I laugh. "You can lay back down."

"Nah, I'll fall asleep on you."

"Do you want me to sketch this and send it over to you tonight?"

He slides closer to me, shifting his weight to the arm behind me. "No."

He leans in a bit more and he points to the top, where the stairway bends to go upstairs. "We could open this up. The light from the window will come through, but there's still room for a little girl to eavesdrop on her parents' conversation."

My gaze meets his and he smirks.

"I like it." I smile at him.

"You do?" The disbelief in his tone is surprising.

"I do. So…" I scribble away to show that we'll be taking out part of that wall. "That's gone."

I hop down, mostly to get away from his nearness before I drown in his scent which may only be soap and shampoo but is still intoxicating when it's on him.

"That's enough for now. It'll be a couple days of demo," I say.

He follows suit, his boots hitting the ground. "I have tomorrow off and then I'm back on shift for twenty-four hours." His fingers thread through his hair, stress lining his jaw.

"No worries. I'll hold down the fort when you're at the station. We do need to hire a crew."

"I already have guys coming tomorrow," he says, hands on his hips.

"Pretty sure you were going to get the house then?"

"Well, I didn't think there would be a lot of people vying for this much of a fixer-upper."

"Only me." I shrug.

He smiles, the one that melts my insides. "I'm glad that we're doing it together. I think it will be fun."

"Hmm...you are a newbie," I tease. "Remind me how much fun we're having in a month."

He chuckles, his hand pulling on his neck.

"Are you going to be okay to drive home?"

He nods before I finish the sentence. "I'm good. I'll probably be asleep until dinner. You've got my cell."

"Yep. We're all good. I need you rested for tomorrow. If you can tell your crew to come in at nine or so. I'll probably be here at seven, but don't feel like you have to join me. Nine is fine for you."

He quirks an eyebrow. "I'll be here at seven. Fifty-fifty, remember?"

I giggle and nod. "See you at seven."

He nods and I grab all my stuff off the bed of his truck, turning to head to my car.

"Enjoy the rest of your day, partner," he says, securing the tailgate and heading to the driver's side.

"Sweet dreams." I open my car door.

Why don't I want to leave him?

Because you're still infatuated with him.

"Probably won't even remember them if I have them. Bye, Madison."

"Bye, Mauro."

We both get into our vehicles and Mauro pulls away from the curb. Rather than follow suit, I open my purse and pull a few M&Ms from the bag I always have in there, then grab my phone and pull up Vanessa's contact. Lauren should be at work and besides, Vanessa will be more on board with the crazy decision I made to be business partners with Mauro on this project.

"What's up girlie?" Vanessa's huffing with labored breaths into the phone.

"What are you doing?" I check my blind spot and pull out onto the street.

"I'm running."

Vanessa and working out is about as common as seeing a leprechaun riding a unicorn skipping down Michigan Avenue.

"Um...why?"

"Oh, fuck it. Where are you? Can you pick me up on the way home?"

I laugh. "Where are you?"

"On the corner of Irving and Western."

"Van, that's like two blocks from home." I chuckle.

"Yeah, there's a Dunkin' Donuts, I'll be in there." There's a pause. "Large ice coffee... definitely cream and sugar."

"I'll be there in ten."

"Thanks. You're a lifesaver." Her tone sounds about as frazzled as I feel emotionally right now. "Wait, what's up? Why did you call?"

"I'll tell you when I get there." I brake at a stop light.

"No, distract me from the lack of oxygen going into my lungs."

My fingers tap the steering wheel while I wait for the light to turn green. "I got that house." I start with the really good news.

A loud screech echoes over the phone. "That's great news! I can't wait to see what you do with it."

The light changes and I accelerate through the intersection. "It is, but I decided to partner up with someone on it."

"Why? You don't need a partner. Please tell me it's not that sleazy Oswald ass you're always telling us about... Thanks." I hear her sipping through a straw so she must've just been handed her order. "Tell me it's some hot guy with a nine-inch dick."

"You do know you're in public?" I shake my head even though she can't see me and turn right at the next intersection.

"Yeah, the woman is kind of looking at me funny. I'll be waiting outside."

"You really need to be more aware, Vanessa."

She huffs. "It's not my fault if people are prudes. Like she wouldn't want a nine-inch dick. Who doesn't? Oh, crap."

"What?" I ask.

I can hear someone who's not Vanessa yelling on her end of the call.

"I'm really sorry, ma'am. I didn't see him. Yeah, I'm sorry."

"Van?"

"Hold on...I will. Promise. Yes, I will definitely try to act more like a lady. Sorry again." The phone sounds muffled for a second then she comes back on. "Okay, my lips are officially zipped."

"A mom and child?"

"Yeah." Her apologetic voice says she knows how wrong she was, but it's Vanessa and she tends to act before she thinks things completely through. "Let's get back to you. Who's the lucky partner?"

"Mauro Bianco." I bite my lip, waiting for her to either lecture me or tell me to find out if he's got a nine-inch dick.

"Really?" I get neither of those reactions. Her voice is one of concern and worry.

"Yeah. He was there and we were both bidding on the same property, increasing the cost for each other, so he proposed that we partner on it and I accepted. We're fifty-fifty."

Silence.

Deafening silence.

"And he put down half the money?"

I'm stuck behind some guy on a bike and though I know it's good for your physical health and the environment and all that, they are really annoying when you're in a car and can't get around them.

"Yeah. And he said he's good with his hands and has friends on the department who do side work."

Traffic eases in the opposite lane so I pull out and around the bike.

The lack of enthusiasm on the other end of the call is popping my balloon filled with excitement.

"Are you sure this is a good idea?" she asks after a moment.

"I am." Not entirely true, but glass half full and all that.

"But this guy is the guy you had a crush on all through high school, right?" she asks in a wary voice.

"I can handle myself, Vanessa. You would've been so proud of me. It's like after our date when he was annoyed with me, I'm not afraid to speak to him anymore."

"That's good, Mad. Has he done this before? Flipped a house?"

"No, but he wants me to show him everything there is to know."

I make a left onto the street where she's waiting.

"But don't you wonder why he wants to partner up?" she asks.

"I just told you. It just made sense for this project. I'm a big girl, Van."

"Of course you are."

"I'm excited. To have a contractor who is as invested as me can't be a bad thing. He'll want to get it flipped as quickly as I do. Time is money and since it's half his money, he won't be dragging his feet."

The more I work to convince Vanessa what a good idea this is, the more my own reservations at the back of my head ease. I could list a bunch more reasons, but I'm stopped at the light across from her. I spot her sitting on the cement block of a parking space, head in her hands.

"I just don't want you to get hurt. He could be...using you."

I don't respond right away because to be honest, I'm a little hurt that she thinks I'd let myself be manipulated like that.

"You think I'd just sit there with a smile on my face and let him fuck me over?" I ask.

"No." Her head picks up and she's shaking it. I watch her until the light turns green. "I just think this guy is your 'what if' guy and you might not even realize you're letting him take advantage of you until it's too late."

Vanessa comes from a place of caring and I have to remember that as I accelerate forward to pick her up. She doesn't think I'm weak, she just thinks my long-lasting crush on Mauro could cloud my judgment.

"I'm here," I say and she glances to her right and spots me.

Instantly, a smile overtakes her face. She slides into my car, her arms around my shoulders. "Congratulations, Maddie."

"Thanks." I pat her arms, sweaty from the two block walk. "Nice try with working out."

She falls back into my seat. "I'm done with that. It was a stupid idea."

I giggle, pushing back the deflated feeling she left me with admitting her worries with Mauro swindling me. "One day and you're calling it quits?"

She sips her pale iced coffee and shrugs.

Typical Vanessa, bored with something after two point two seconds.

CHAPTER THIRTEEN

Mauro

With two coffees in hand, praying that Madison takes her regular coffee like she does her iced coffee, I step up onto the porch, where she's already in a folding chair with her computer on her lap.

"Good morning." I hold up the coffees and danishes.

"Finally rested?" she asks, her hair in a high ponytail, exposing her neck that's like a spark to kindling.

It doesn't help that I had a dream last night about her naked wearing only a tool belt.

"Yeah. I slept, ate and then slept again."

If I wouldn't have had to go to Cailin's, I probably would've slept the entire time. Usually I function on small pockets of sleep, but I hit a wall yesterday.

"Great because you'll be using those good hands you mentioned today." She smiles. Her teeth all white and glowing. "You're going to think I'm a dork, but I drew up a list of responsibilities yesterday."

She stands up and meets me on the edge of the porch,

accepting her coffee and taking a sip before continuing. "Oh, you remembered. Thank you."

She's wearing a set of denim overalls with a white t-shirt underneath and she looks cute as hell. Not in the two-year-old sense. In the 'I wonder what she'd look like in just the overalls and no t-shirt underneath' way.

"You're welcome," I say. The stirring of happiness inside me over the fact that I got her coffee right needs to be squashed.

"I usually make my own, but of course having roommates, I came down this morning and we were out. Not a note on the chalkboard adding it to the list to buy or anything. Not that I should be surprised, I tend to be the mother hen of our trio."

"You're making me feel kind of bad for Cristian." I sip my coffee, my eyes transfixed on her dark ponytail swinging as she talks.

"You live with your brothers?"

"Just Cristian. Luca's on his own with his buddies. Partying is still everything to him so we kicked him out two years ago. Not that he doesn't use our place as his grocery store. Drives Cristian crazy, but he's still young."

"He's as old as me." She drops her pen, crossing her arms over her chest and resting her hip on the ledge.

Her eyes remain on mine. This is a nice change of pace.

"You're not in the same spectrum of maturity, I assure you."

She giggles, that curl at the end of her ponytail teasing me as it appears and disappears.

"Well, Vanessa is about the same. Can't hold a job to save her life. Scrapes by to pay the rent. Lauren is determined and has a drive like no other, but only when it comes to succeeding in her job or winning a sports game, not so much with her laundry or keeping food in the cabinet."

"I haven't even asked my brothers, have they gone on their dates yet?" I open the bag of danishes and hold them out in front of her.

"No, thank you." She might deny them, but I catch her licking her lips after seeing the cheese and strawberry pastries. "They haven't. Vanessa is delaying because her dad is the Commander of Cristian's district and Lauren is downright refusing to date Luca. What kind of brothers do you have?" She smirks, clearly joking with me.

"I wouldn't want to date them either. I'm the best of the lot in case you were wondering."

She quiets for a moment, her gaze moving down to the pad of paper.

"We really should finalize this before they get here. The dumpster should be here by ten." She turns away from me, and I take the opportunity to check her out while she isn't watching me.

Her overalls hug her ass perfectly. I just manage to move my eyes back up to her face before she spins around to say something.

"Here's the list I came up with. I'm totally flexible, but I think it gives us each multiple areas to work in. It wouldn't be fair if you did all the manual labor and I only took the decorating and redesign. I have dates down that I'd like us to go shopping for fixtures and tiles. I think I have your schedule right, but if not, we can change it up."

"I feel like I'm the slacker between us."

A frown crosses her lips before she raises the coffee to her lips and takes a sip. "I'm sure you'll be proving your worth this first week of demolition."

I wrap my hand around her bicep. "Let me feel. I bet you have biceps of steel."

Her arm lays limp.

"Come on."

Rolling her eyes but obliging, she raises her arm and flexes, showing off some serious guns for a girl her size. I press my four fingers on the top and my thumb on the bottom. More than her muscle, I notice how soft her skin is.

"I'm gonna call you Zena,"

"The warrior princess?" she asks, her eyebrow quirked so high it's near her hairline.

I laugh. "Yeah."

"I guess that's a compliment."

My hand leaves her bicep even though I don't want to pull away.

"It is."

She rolls her eyes again, but more playfully than the first time. I pick up the sheet to scan it over.

It's printed in two columns, one with my name and the other with hers, on the other side is a two month calendar of dates she'd like things to be done.

"Two months huh?"

"Well obviously there will be things out of our control, but this is the proposed schedule if everything goes smoothly. We need to talk budget. Figure out how much demolition and contracting is going to cost. If you're comfortable with it, I'm going to leave that up to you."

The piece of paper drops from my grip and floats to the ground. I scramble to pick it up.

"If you'd rather not, I can..." she rambles out quickly probably taken by my surprised response.

"No. I can do it."

She smiles and I straighten the piece of paper in my hand.

"Great. I can do the one with the new finishings once I get your figures."

Looking it over, she's right, everything is right down the middle. She didn't leave all the numbers and paperwork to her and leave me doing everything that required muscle.

"I did leave some permits for you to get because although I don't want you using that dreamy smile on me to get what you want, I figure it might work on the clerks at the city and get them pushed through faster."

I so badly want to call her out on her dreamy smile comment, but I let it slide.

"Done. If I get a male clerk, I might need your help though."

Her cheeks flush and damn it if I don't want to cage her between my arms and feel her body pressed against mine.

I fold the piece of paper and put it in my back pocket. "Oh, and you got my schedule right." I wink and the rosy blush in her cheeks deepen.

"Look at this dump you two decided to lose a shit load of money on." Cristian's voice behind me makes me curse him for always being early for everything. I would have liked a few more minutes with Madison to myself.

I turn around to see my younger brother in his damn man leggings again with earbuds hanging from his neck. "You don't look like you're ready to work."

He walks up the steps, his attention only on Madison. "I have to work in two hours. It's my weekend off, do you guys work on weekends?" He smirks in my direction and then his arms wrap around Madison, lifting her feet from the splintered wood porch. "Maddie, you look great. You really should discuss your business decisions with me first though." He chuckles into her neck, his lips in the exact place I want mine to be. "You and Mauro taking on the world together?"

Her feet fall back to the ground and she smiles up at my brother like he's a long lost friend. If they were so close, how come I never knew her? "One beat down house at a time." She laughs and he chuckles, his gaze still not leaving hers.

Finally he looks over at me. "I was on a run. Training for the marathon. Thought I'd drop by and give you guys hell."

"Thanks. You can go back to training now."

Madison playfully swats my stomach. "He's joking, Cristian. You're always welcome."

"Thanks, Maddie. You always were nice." Cristian doesn't know about the word nice and how offensive Madison finds it after the board game cafe.

"Some might say I'm a people pleaser," she says, her eyes lit with mischief glancing in my direction.

"Who? My dumbass brother?" Cristian slaps my stomach harder than I expected and I hit him right back. "Fucker."

"I carry hoses, you carry a gun."

Cristian looks up at me, shaking his head. "Let's do a quick sprint and see who's faster."

"Let's run up a flight of stairs with forty-five pounds strapped on our backs," I deadpan.

"Jump a fence holding your weight on one arm."

"Carry two hundred pounds of dead weight in your arms down a flight of stairs that's crumbling without a face mask because you gave it to the victim."

He crosses his arms. "Go into a dark building knowing some creep is there hiding, his only intent not to go back to jail and he'll do anything to make sure he achieves his goal."

"Run into a building that—"

Madison's hand covers my mouth. "I think we get the point boys. I can say that you both have extremely hard jobs."

Cristian laughs. "I like this. You're the only person I've seen able to shut him up."

I bite the inside of her palm lightly and she removes her hand, staring down at it and back to me.

"Did you just bite me?"

"Why didn't you silence him?" I nod to Cristian who I can see is enjoying whatever this is between me and Madison way too much.

"Because me and you have work to do." She opens a bag. "Do you want to come in and see the house, Cristian?"

"Cristian got sick the last time he went in." I give him a shit-eating grin. "Some tough police officer he is."

Cristian laughs, shaking his head. "You're such an ass."

Madison pulls out a hat and places it on her head, pulling her ponytail out of the back and then twisting her hair into a bun.

"Too bad you can't help, Cristian. Demolition is good for releasing aggression. You're welcome to stop by anytime, we can always use an extra set of hands." She smiles and heads to the front door. "I'll see you in there."

She disappears through the door, a groan echoing from the hinges as it opens and closes.

"What the fuck?" I whisper-yell to Cristian.

"What?" His head draws back like he has no idea what the fuck I'm talking about.

"You're flirting with her."

"No, I was saying hi to an old friend." A smirk emerges on his lips. "Oh, man." He shakes his head in disbelief.

"What?" I shift in place.

"Jealousy looks good on you."

"I'm not jealous." I peek in the door to see that she's at the back of the house in the kitchen, looking out a window. A laundry basket full of stuff sits on the dining room table.

"You are and you like her."

I look in the house again and set my narrowed gaze on Cristian. There's a good chance he'll see through my bullshit. I might have been able to pull it over on Luca, but Cristian is a tougher sell.

"I just want this to go smoothly and if you date her and fuck it up by breaking her heart, it'll screw up my chances of having something profitable outside of the department."

He crosses his arms. "Jealousy, lying, are you sure you're my brother Mauro?"

"Fine." I roll my eyes back in my sockets. "Do I want to sleep with her? Yes. Am I going to? No. We're business partners."

"Interesting." He smiles and rocks back on his new, too colorful running shoes.

"Stop it."

He holds his hands up in the air. "Stop what? I'm not doing anything."

"I can't do anything about my attraction to her and you know it."

"Yeah, I do." A small part of me thought, (hoped?) that maybe he'd tell me to go for it. "I stopped by the deli last night. Mama's already got the two of you living in this house with a kid on the way."

"Mama just wants a grandchild." I pull off my hat and run my hand through my hair.

"Keep doing that and you'll be the first bald Bianco."

I shake my head, placing my ball cap on backward. "I'm screwed."

He grips my shoulder. "Can I ask you a question? Are you into her just for her looks?"

I shouldn't be surprised by his question. Have I dated mostly tens? Sure. The fact Maddie has transformed into a ten plus is not lost on me, but it's more than that. "No. As sick as it sounds, I think it's because she sees me differently. Not at first, she didn't. But this morning she told me she'd like me to do the budget for the demolition and construction of the remodel."

My brother smiles, familiar with how people underestimated my intelligence and didn't think I was smart enough for anything other than throwing a football through high school and college. "I told you, Madison Kelly is good people."

I rock back on my own heels. "Yeah, she is." This time it isn't just my dick reacting, but my heart beats a little faster thinking about her being a permanent part of my life.

"You're right. You're screwed." He jogs down the steps. "Let me know about this weekend." Heading down the walk-way, I hear the soft words of Mauro and Maddie kissing in a tree fall from his lips.

Smiling, I open the door of the house and the first thing I see is Madison's ass as she bends over to pick something up off the floor. For the first time in my life, I'm jealous of Cristian's tenacious willpower.

CHAPTER FOURTEEN

Madison

A week later, the house is bare bones. We have effectively stripped it down to the studs. This is my favorite part of the process—when I can see the inside structure of a home that's carried the weight of not only the roof and all the supporting beams, but the people's lives who lived here. It's now a clean slate, ready for a fresh start.

The stench that lingered from the refrigerator that was never cleaned out has dissipated a bit and I'm hoping that with the help of a few candles I've lit, it will disappear completely.

I'm sitting in the middle of the living room, taking in the space when the screen door opens and a big body steps in.

"Are we having a seance?" Mauro sits down across from me, placing a bag of food between us.

"Well, we *do* have to try to get the dead to move on."

He chuckles, placing all his weight on his arms as he extends them behind him, leaning back.

"My profession means that I can't help but warn you about candles and wood."

"I didn't realize you were such a rule follower," I tease.

He straightens up, opening the bag, taking out the Chinese food containers. "I'm not."

"I didn't think so."

I rise up and go to my laundry basket of essentials we might need for meals. Yeah, call me uber-organized, but this isn't my first time being so hungry I could chew my arm off in a house with no kitchen. Pulling out two plates and two plastic forks and napkins, I sit back down across from him.

In the last week, Mauro has transformed from the guy I didn't really know and yet placed on a pedestal, to a guy I'm getting to know a lot about and am really starting to like for the right reasons.

He's funny, and I like his dry sense of humor and the way he never cracks a smile when he tells a joke. He treats the workers well and somehow gets them to do a little extra work each day. Once he makes a decision, that's it. He's committed. And he always makes the best of a situation. When a wall got knocked out that wasn't supposed to, he said that it would allow more light in instead of asking me where I was when it was happening since he was at work.

"Always prepared." He chuckles to himself and opens up the containers and I'm surprised to see that it's Thai food, not Chinese.

I shrug. "It's a curse."

The curse of not having a present mother.

"You should be proud of it. I bet you've never been late on a bill." He lets me get my dish before his.

I use the fork and pull the noodles from the container.

"No."

"It's an endearing quality. Don't be ashamed of it." His words warm me. Most people would probably find it geeky.

He's fixing his plate and my gaze wanders across his body. His strong shoulders and taut waist. The way his jeans are worn just the perfect amount and hug his firm thighs. The fact that his hair is never fully done, but more styled with his fingers because no matter how neat it looks when he gets here, by day's end he's got that just-fucked hair going on. The light stubble along his cheeks and his manly jaw.

"Is there something on my face?" He sits back, wiping his face with a napkin.

Oops. My eyes cast down, heat rising up my neck. "No."

He lets it go instead of calling me out on my gawking. Just as I did earlier today when I bent over to grab something and found his eyes glued to my ass when I turned around. Let's just say, the exhilaration I felt in that moment was pretty close to when I earned Summa Cum Laude in college.

"So, tell me why you don't have a boyfriend."

My head snaps up to meet his inquisitive eyes.

He's kidding. Right?

"You tell me first," I say.

"Don't even try it. Come on."

Every fiber inside of me says this is a horrible idea, but I sit up from my plate. "I've never had a serious relationship. I've dated a few guys, but the relationships never lasted longer than a month or two."

His forehead wrinkles. "Why do you think that is?"

I tip my head back down. "I tend to date guys similar to me. Guys who want career success before a romantic relationship. We'd both understand when the other said they have to study or that they had to go to this networking event or whatever it was. The relationship was never the priority. Does that make sense?"

"Yeah, that would be a problem. What about now? You still put your career first?"

His question is innocent enough. He asks casually, but the

way he's intently waiting for me to answer has me wondering if there's more to it.

"Um...I think I use it as a crutch now. Maybe it's an excuse not to get involved with someone."

I'm not sure I've been this honest with anyone else before. There's just something about Mauro that doesn't have me wanting to give him a glazed over answer you'd give just to move on to the next topic of conversation.

"I'm with you on that one. I think I use the fact my job is dangerous as a reason sometimes not to get serious."

I look up from my plate, chewing the last of my chicken. He forks large amounts of noodles and chicken into his mouth. I'm not sure I've seen Mauro go longer than an hour without food.

"You've never had a serious relationship?" I ask.

His eyes dip back to his plate. "No, I did, sort of, I guess. We were together for a year, but I found out it was all based on lies."

"I'm sorry." I frown. "Did you love her?"

He doesn't look up from his plate as he pushes the food around.

"I think I thought I did, but I'm not so sure now. Maybe when you find out someone didn't love you, maybe that strips everything you felt for them? I don't know. Let's just say it was the ultimate betrayal."

My heart squeezes for him. Whether he loved her or not doesn't mean it didn't hurt. Whatever happened obviously affected him.

"See, so maybe I'm better off continuing to put my work first." I try to lighten the vibe, but his solemn eyes say he's having none of it.

"I learned a lot from it."

"Like?"

He stands up, heading to the cooler he brought earlier

today to make sure the crew had water. Bringing two over, he wipes the water off with his t-shirt, opens the cap, and hands it to me.

"Thank you."

He sits down, closer than he was moments ago. Not that I'm complaining.

"This is going to sound a lot like some 'I am woman hear me roar' statement, but I deserved better. She had me using my two days off as her chauffeur and errand runner. I thought I was doing it because we loved each other and I was helping her out. I realize now that she didn't care if I needed to sleep. She never even called me when I was on shift." He shakes his head. "You're going to think I'm taking estrogen tablets at this rate."

I knock my shoulder to his. "I'm going to ignore the fact that you're saying women are overly emotional."

He smirks at me. "You know that's not what I'm suggesting."

I raise my eyebrows. "Who knows if you are."

He holds up his hand with two fingers. "Scout's honor."

"You weren't a Boy Scout, were you?"

He chuckles. "For two weeks. Until all three of us got kicked out for wrestling. The leader told my mom that we'd have to be split into three different troops. That was the end of scouts for the Bianco brothers."

I lower his hand. "Then sorry, you can't use the honor salute."

"Were you a Girl Scout?" he asks, his smile already suggesting he knows the answer.

"Yes, and before you make fun of me, I did go all the way to Ambassador. It looked good on my college application."

"Ever think that's where those people pleaser skills were bred?"

"Hey." I shoot him a warning glare.

He chuckles, resting his weight on his hand. "I'm kidding. I know I've apologized, but I need to again. I should've never made fun of you because if you weren't nice, I'm pretty sure we wouldn't be sitting in this house. You wouldn't have given me this chance."

I straighten my back. "Do you think I gave you a bone? Like I agreed to be your partner as a handout?"

He straightens as well, pouring a big gulp of water down his throat while staring at me through squinted eyes. "Well, I'm the newbie and you're pretty established."

I shake my head. "Mauro, that's not true and I don't want you to think that. I agreed to this because this house means something to me and so that I'd have a partner who was just as invested as me. I'm sick of doing it alone. I thought it'd be fun, but it's been good having someone to bounce ideas off of. The fact you're good with your hands was just a bonus." I attempt to wink, but as usual, both eyes fall closed.

"Try that again?" he asks, pointing to my eyes.

"No. I can't do it." I pull my legs up and bury my head down into my knees, my long chestnut hair falling in a veil around my face.

He sweeps it back and my stomach flutters when his fingertips brush my cheek. "It's me. Come on."

"It's me? That's your explanation? That it's okay to embarrass myself. You're Mauro Bianco."

I shake my head and he tucks my hair behind my ear.

"You say that like I'm Bradley Cooper."

"To me you are," I mumble, half praying he didn't hear me, half hoping he did.

His finger lands under my chin, slowly raising my face until our eyes lock. "I'm just a firefighter from Chicago. I'm the oldest of three brothers from an immigrant father and mother who came to this country for the American dream. There's nothing special about that."

I swallow down the saliva pooling in my mouth.

Our faces inch closer.

"Don't pin me as a hero, Mad," he says in a low, gravelly voice.

My heart pitter-patters at the way he shortened my name.

"You're so much more than you realize. You're kind and sweet and generous and hardworking. The package you come in is nice eye candy, sure, and I'm ashamed to say that's all I knew about you at one time. Over the last week though, I've discovered that you're so much more."

Our faces inch closer again and I can feel his breath on my face.

"We can't do this," I murmur. "It could destroy everything we're building."

His eyes transfix on my lips. "I've been denying myself for days. Just one taste."

Another inch closer and my breathing grows shallow as my heart thumps an unsteady beat against my rib cage.

His hand molds to my cheek and I lean into his strong, callused palm.

"Mauro," I whisper. I'm not even sure if it's a plea to kiss me or to stop.

"Madison." My name rolling off his lips with so much need undoes any self-control I had left and my eyes flutter closed as I lean in.

"Mauro," a woman's voice says from outside the screen door.

We reel back from each other, my water spilling onto one of the candles. How fitting.

"Cailin?" he asks, standing to his feet.

A blonde woman walks in wearing tight skinny jeans and a top snug enough to show off some nice cleavage. She's wearing a gold necklace that draws your eyes down to her breasts just in case you didn't happen to notice them. Her hair is down—loose and curled in those waves I never seemed to master with my straight iron.

"You must be Madison." She disregards a flustered Mauro and beelines it over to me, holding her hand out. "I'm Cailin."

I wrack my brain for any recognition the name should bring me. She's definitely not the contractor we hired for the landscaping.

"Hi." I shake her dainty hand, watching her eyes wander up and down my body.

I've never been the woman other women are jealous of, so I'm not certain why she's sizing me up.

"Madison, this is Cailin Zaxby, she was the wife of my buddy, Hunter." Mauro takes up the space at our sides.

I nod hello.

"This place doesn't look very appealing." She cringes at me, a smear of lipstick on her glowing white teeth. She must be just off a whitening treatment.

"Consider this her natural look." My hand caresses a beam that separates the living room and dining room.

"Oh how cute, you refer to it like a person. Did you name her like those people who name beat up ugly cars?" I try to hide my disgust and Mauro should be thankful I'm a nice person right about now because I feel like taking her head and knocking it into a four by four.

"No, I don't." I move over to the table and pack up my computer and notebooks, shoving them in my bag. "I'll leave you two alone."

"That's not necessary." Mauro steps closer to me.

"Sorry, did I interrupt a meeting? It's just Mauro's been going on and on about this project of his and I drove by and saw his truck. Figured I'd stop in." She's lying. Not that I think she didn't just drive by and see his truck, but she's here for a reason other than to see the house.

"No worries, we were just finally taking a break after a week of demolition." I swing my bag over my shoulder.

Mauro's hands are tucked into his pockets, his eyes on the ground.

Upset that he got caught almost kissing the hermit?

"So, I know you work tomorrow, but we have that meeting the day after with the tile guy. We need to decide on stain and cabinetry so that we make sure it all flows. Just Pinterest anything you really like, okay?"

His hand touches my arm and I desperately want to lean into him. I want to finish what we started in front of Cailin and show her he's mine. But that's not me. And he's not mine. I'd do well to remember that.

"You Pinterest?" Cailin's voice bounces off the empty walls.

Mauro stares at me, his eyes conveying the apology he's yet to verbalize.

"Sounds good. Crossing fingers for a slow day tomorrow." He smiles and my belly lights up like a rocket's about to take off.

I step away from Mauro before I do something foolish like kiss him goodbye. "Very nice to meet you Cailin." I wave.

She's busy looking around like she'd rather be anywhere but here. "You too, Madison." She waves, not bothering to turn and actually look at me.

"Bye, Mad," Mauro says and I walk out the front door feeling about as empty as the house I'm leaving.

The candles. Shit.

I peek my head back in and see Cailin's hands on Mauro's shoulders giving him a massage.

Wow. They waste no time.

"I just wanted to remind you not to forget to put the candles out." I shake my head. "That seems stupid now. You're a firefighter. Of course you'll know to blow them out."

I glance at the floor to see that they're already blown out.

"I'm one step ahead of you." Mauro smiles, dislodging his shoulders from Cailin's hands.

"Have a good night." I wave and let the screen door fall closed behind me.

This time I head down the stairs to the solitude of my car.

Once I'm inside, I reach into my purse grabbing my bag of M&Ms, pour out a palm full and stuff them in my mouth.

CHAPTER FIFTEEN

Mauro

"What are you doing?" I side-step away from Cailin, still wondering why the hell she surprised me here. "Why are you acting like some jealous girlfriend?"

I keep my voice even, but anger boils inside of me. Anger I haven't seen surface since I cleaned out Hunter's locker at the firehouse.

"What are you talking about?" She plays off my question with a laugh and picks up the candles, placing them on the dining room table, familiar with fire safety.

The candles had made me uneasy, but Madison liked them, and I couldn't take my eyes off of her in the candle-light. I already installed two fire extinguishers, so I knew I'd get to it quickly should the unthinkable happen.

"Where's Devin?"

She stops and turns to me. Her lips dipping. "I was out for dinner with my girlfriends. My mom has Devin. It was my first night out."

Thank God, I was just misreading things. For a second there I thought Patel was right—that Cailin wanted to replace Hunter with me.

"I'm sorry." My hand runs along the back of my neck. "I'm just—"

"You like her?" she interrupts.

I shrug. My ability to lie is shit. Cailin wouldn't catch me like Cristian might, but she caught me about to kiss Madison so I think she knows the answer without me answering.

"We're partners. Come on, I'll show you around."

We head through the dining room to the kitchen.

"Don't lie to me, Mauro. I saw you a millisecond before you were about to kiss her."

"And yet you decided to interrupt?" I turn and cock an eyebrow at her.

Her cheeks flush. "I thought maybe she was taking advantage of you. You know you're so gorgeous women can't resist."

She pinches my bicep and I've never wanted to be away from Cailin more than right now. Even when she was knee-deep in snot and soaking my t-shirt after Hunter's death, I was good with it. She needed someone and I was willing to be that person she could lean on. Now...I don't know if that was such a good idea.

"She wasn't taking advantage of me." I stop at the stairs to the basement. It's dark and still looks haunted even with the new lighting we've put in.

"I'm not going down there. Show me the upstairs. Is there a bed?" she asks.

I squint my eyes, annoyed with her. "No."

"So you were just going to lay her down on the plywood and give her splinters in her ass? How romantic, Mauro." She laughs and the sound grates on me.

"I wasn't going to sleep with her," I bite out my words.

"Come on, you must find her attractive if you were going

to kiss her." She's smiling at me trying to play it off like she's teasing, but behind her smile there's insincerity.

"Who wouldn't?" I ask.

"Some wouldn't. I mean she has that cute, smart girl vibe, but her sense of style is a little lacking."

I've heard Cailin make fun of girl's I've gone out with. Hell, she tore Jenna apart after we broke up, but I figured she was in the grieving stage of anger at that point.

"I wasn't aware jeans and t-shirts were somehow out of style." I remind myself that she's been through hell these last few months and that I need to cut her some slack, so I walk up the stairs first, Cailin's heeled boots sounding on the stairs behind me.

"I think it was a guy's shirt."

My patience snaps. "Enough Cailin. She's my partner and yes, I find her attractive. Yes, I want to kiss her. Yes, I want to screw her. Am I screwing her? No. So put the claws away."

She draws back at the top of the stairs. "I was only suggesting..."

I raise my hand. "No. You were judging. She's a great person. Enough of the prom queen judging."

Her eyes fall to the floorboard. "I just want to protect you. After Jenna..."

"I can protect myself but thank you." I place my hand on her upper arm and squeeze. "I'm sorry, it's just..." I shake my head not wanting Cailin to know more than Madison because that's not fair. My conflicted feelings about Madison shouldn't be discussed with anyone but her. "Anyway, there are three bedrooms up here."

I flick the flashlight on since the sun has started to descend already with autumn upon us. "This will be one bedroom that shares a bathroom with this one." We head to the next bedroom before turning down a small hallway. "This is the master."

She steps into the space, eyeing the skylight. You can see right through the structure to what will be the bathroom.

"It's a nice space." She twirls around. "Hunter would have loved this." A tear slips down her cheek.

"Cailin." I sigh. "Don't."

It's the whole reason I was never really up on her coming here. This was my dream with Hunter and now I'm living it out with Madison. That has to be tough for her.

"He always told me that he'd give me the modern luxuries we'd see on the DIY channels. A house we'd be proud to host cookouts and parties at. A pool for Devin and his younger brother or sister."

Another tear spills down her cheek and I do what I've done the other hundred times I've been in this position with her. I wrap her in my arms, her head falling to my shirt, her arms tight around my middle.

"It's okay. I know it hurts, but eventually the pain will fade a bit and you'll find someone else to share your life with. I promise. And you'll be happy again. Hell, he might even be better than Hunter for you."

She pulls back, her eyes launching daggers into me. "How could you say that? He was your best friend."

Shit. Sometimes it's hard, knowing what I know, not to let my true feelings slip out around her.

I step back. "I'm just saying you'll find happiness again."

Shaking her head, she brushes the tears from her face. "Hunter was my everything."

She says it like I don't already know that little fact. She lived and breathed Hunter, practically suffocated him. Nothing was ever good enough for her. I was with him the nights he'd be exhausted on shift after being up the night before because they were fighting and Cailin wouldn't allow him to go to bed until it was settled.

"I know. I know," I say.

"If I'd had him for longer. Our time together was so short."

She cries into my chest again and I lightly rub her back.

"HA!" a voice yells into the room.

Cailin steps back, startled, but I have no chance to move before there's a body strapped to my back.

"You son of a bitch. I knew you were a loser like your brother." Little hands pull at the strands of my hair and the more I twist to remove whoever it is, the higher she climbs up me.

"Who the hell are you?" Cailin asks.

"His worst nightmare," she says, jabbing her knee in my armpit.

My t-shirt is choking me and though I could easily toss this girl off me I have no idea what the fuck is going on and it's not in my nature to launch a woman across the room, doing who knows how much damage to her.

Cailin backs up closer to the corner of the room, afraid.

"Jesus, Lauren, get off of him!" Madison runs into the room, unpeeling her arms from my throat.

The person on my back falls down to her feet, and I straighten my shirt, turning to look at the culprit of my attack.

"We are so sorry." Madison grabs Lauren's hand and tries to drag her out of the room.

"I can't stand to look at you. If you want to have some fling with some tart then go to your own apartment, don't do it here!"

Madison's cheeks flush the deepest red I've seen yet.

"Excuse me?" Cailin steps up, towering over Lauren. Not that it seems to intimidate Lauren.

"You heard me. This is theirs." She points to Madison and me. "He should have the decency not to fuck someone in their shared space."

"This is all really unnecessary." Madison pulls at Lauren, but she yanks her arm back.

"Is that what you think is happening?" I ask Madison.

"No. I mean...I didn't think she was here to you know...it's not exactly very romantic."

I want to remind her that it was a half hour ago when the two of us were surrounded with candles and Thai food declaring how much we've come to enjoy each other's company in the past week.

"Lauren drove by and decided to stop in. She saw what was going on and called me. I sped back over here as quick as I could so this wouldn't happen."

Lauren jabs me in the chest. "Do you know how great she is?"

My gaze flickers to Madison. "I'm well aware, yes."

"Well let me tell you...wait, what?" She stops talking, her eyes searching for Madison.

"Cailin isn't some girl I brought here to show off this place to. Not that it's really any of your business." I take a step in her direction, squaring off with her.

The sheepish look I expected doesn't appear on Lauren's face. Instead, she crosses her arms waiting for a better explanation.

"She's the wife of a fellow firefighter who died."

Lauren's arms fall. "Oh." She bites the inside of her cheek. "But you were pretty cozy in here." Lauren juts out her chin.

If Luca ever does go on his date with her, he's going to have his hands full. I can't fucking wait.

"Are you going to apologize now?" Cailin snarls.

"Lauren," Madison pushes and Lauren rolls her eyes.

"I'm sorry okay, but you know she's my girl and..."

"So she likes Mauro?" Cailin interjects.

"NO!" Madison screeches. "Lauren's just protective."

My eyes lock with Madison's.

"Yeah, I'm just protective of her. You know she's a hard worker and I don't want some guy taking advantage of her. This has nothing to do with personal feelings." Lauren walks backward toward the door. "Please carry on." She steps out of the room.

"I'm really super sorry for the misunderstanding." Madison follows and the sound of their footsteps trampling down the stairs echoes throughout the house.

I want to go after Madison, but I know mixing business and pleasure is a bad idea. The war inside of me rages on and I'm not sure which side will end up the victor.

"What a head case." Cailin slides her arm through mine. "I mean sending her friend here to attack you? Make sure she doesn't go all Fatal Attraction on you."

I blow out a breath and step away, letting Cailin's arm fall. "I have to go. I have work in the morning."

"Oh, okay. I should get back to Devin anyway."

We walk down the steps and I lock up, noticing that Madison's car is gone from the curb. I say goodbye to Cailin, see her drive off and climb into my truck.

My life was much simpler a week ago.

CHAPTER SIXTEEN

Madison

"Lauren, what the fuck?" I ask as we step out of each of our cars in the garage.

"What? I thought he was disrespecting you."

"I told you already, I don't look at him like that anymore."

We head into the house, void of Vanessa because it's after seven o'clock. Whatever job she's working, she's always gone by seven.

"That's bullshit, Maddie. At least be straight with *me*." Lauren sheds the shirt of her scrubs, kicks off her shoes, and heads up the stairs.

I follow her because I need to shower, too, to get a day of being at a work site off me.

"I'd be lying if I said he's not hot as hell, but I have to respect that we're partners. I'm not going to ruin that."

She strips off her pants and heads into her bathroom.

"Just be careful. I saw the way he was looking at you and I don't care what he says about that Cailin, she wants him."

Lauren shuts the door to the bathroom and I head into my bedroom to take a shower as well.

As much as Lauren can be on the impulsive side, I agree with her. Cailin's intentions don't seem pure. I'm surprised Mauro doesn't see the signs that his friend's widow is falling for him.

The water cascades over my skin, the warmth soothing muscles that have been working hard this week. I soap up my body, my mind wandering to our almost kiss.

The almost kiss I'll remember for the rest of my life. The heat between us was searing. The way his gaze dipped to my lips and then met my eyes. How his tongue slid out to lick his lips in expectation of them being on mine.

Damn that Cailin.

When he said, 'one taste' like he was begging for one drop of water in the Sierra Desert.

I drop my loofa on the floor of the marble shower and my hand slips below my belly button imagining the weight of Mauro's body over mine. His lips, his hands in exploration of every inch of my skin.

Five minutes later, my body shudders and the glass door rattles under the pressure of my other hand. An emptiness sets in, knowing my imagination and my hand are not going to ever be enough to quench my thirst for Mauro.

I liked it better when I thought he was an ass.

I step out of the shower and begin to dry off when my phone chirps from its position on the counter.

Mauro: I want to apologize for tonight.

I wrap myself in a towel and take my phone over to my bed, sitting down and leaning back against the headboard.

Me: No need. It's really none of my business.

The three dots appear immediately.

Mauro: Should we talk about the kiss?

Me: There was no kiss.

Mauro: I wanted there to be. That's what we need to discuss.

God, I wanted there to be, too, and if he only knew what my mind took the liberty of exploring moments ago in the shower, he'd probably be surprised at how dirty my mind could be.

Me: It was a moment of weakness. Just forget it.

Mauro: I don't think it will be our last.

Me: We need to make sure it is.

Mauro: Madison, I want you.

My nerves tingle and an unbelievable feeling of euphoria fills every cell in my body.

Me: Mauro…

Mauro: Tell me you don't feel the same?

Me: We should talk face-to-face.

Mauro: If we were face-to-face right now there'd be no talking.

I smile like a goon.

Me: We just need to keep a firm line drawn.

Mauro: So that's a no?

Me: No to what?

Mauro: No to you wanting me. You don't
want to jump me?

Me: Maybe like Lauren jumped you a few
times.

Mauro: LOL… I'm serious. I gotta know if I'm
in this alone.

Me: Why do you have to know?

"Who's that?" Lauren walks by in her pajama shorts and cami, her hair still tucked into a towel.

"No one."

"Tell Mauro I can still kick his ass," she says and heads down the stairs.

Mauro: I need to know that if I kiss you, you
won't pull away.

Me: You can't kiss me.

Mauro: That wasn't part of the buying
agreement.

Me: I added the stipulation.

Mauro: We're both adults here. We can
handle it.

Me: Time to think with your other head, Mauro.

Mauro texts a laughing gif.

Mauro: Don't be funny, that only makes me think with the wrong head.

Me: I think it suffices to say this conversation is going in a circle and will never end.

Mauro: It will when you agree to let me kiss you.

Me: I have to go get some sleep. And I believe you have to get up early for a shift.

Mauro: You're gonna leave me hanging like that? I can describe in great detail what it will be like if you want.

The blush encompasses my entire body.

Me: Gotta go now. See you in a couple of days.

Mauro: I'll be counting the minutes.

I shake my head and don't respond because who knows what will spill out of his mouth next.

When we began this partnership, I figured my biggest challenge would be keeping my own attraction to him in check. I didn't consider the fact that he might like me, too.

———

The next night, I'm vegging on the couch after a long day of grabbing samples from textile and paint companies. And when I say vegging I mean carrots, cucumbers, and celery with ranch dip.

I'm flipping through the channels by myself—Vanessa is gone again—and Lauren is out on a date—not with Luca. I breeze by Chicago Fire since that would only remind me of Mauro, but the ticker on the bottom of the screen grabs my attention. It's a breaking news alert and with everything going on in the world today I figure I better read it in case I need to head for cover.

I sit up, squinting to see the small print when the words fire, high-rise, and danger catch my eye. It goes on to say that all available engines have been called because it's out of control and there's a chance the blaze will spread to the high-rise beside it.

All too quickly Chicago Fire disappears from the screen and a news anchor appears, the scene behind her reminds me of a war zone—emergency vehicles everywhere and a fire blazing out of control in the building behind her.

I swear my heart stills inside of my chest and I sit on the edge of my couch, my phone in hand.

One fire truck after another pulls in behind the woman, each raising their ladders up in the air. Some firefighters climb them, others run inside with hoses and masks on. Angry red and yellow flames pour out windows on the one side of the high-rise condo building.

I pick up my cell phone knowing I won't get an answer.

> Me: Mauro, please let me know when you
> get back to the station so I know you're
> okay. I saw the fire on tv.

Is this what it's like to care about someone who works in emergency services? I have more compassion for Cailin now and what she must have gone through every night her husband was on shift and then when she eventually lost him.

I lean back on the couch, trying not to let my worst fears invade my mind.

Hours go by and the news is no longer covering the fire, they've gone back to their regular programming while I pace back and forth. This feeling of helplessness is horrible. The waiting even more so.

I pull out my phone and look up where Engine Fifty-Five is located.

I shouldn't go.

I'll look like a loon.

I don't even have to talk to him. I just need a glimpse of him when the truck pulls in.

I won't sleep until I know.

I grab the keys off the table and race out to my car.

The street the fire station is on is lined with cars. There are some reporters hovering around the red doors, but they're all shut, meaning the firetruck hasn't returned yet. I drive around the block, circling back to see the same scene as before.

I decide to park on a side street. I don't want to chance looking like a stalker around the firehouse, so I sit tight and decide that every ten minutes I'll drive around the block.

And yes, in case you're wondering, I'm fully aware that I am out of my mind.

The thought of something really bad happening to Mauro has me acting like a crazy woman. His friend Hunter died not that long ago in a fire at a commercial building that they didn't know had explosives in it because it had been abandoned. It goes to show that anything can happen.

The sixth time driving around the block the bay doors are open with two firetrucks and an ambulance inside each one. The guys are taking their gear off and cleaning up the trucks.

Double parking for a second, I catch a glimpse of Mauro stepping out of his bunker pants. His face has soot on it and there's a trace of blood from his eyebrow down to his lip, his hair a sweaty mess. But he's alive and to me, he's never looked better.

The tension dissipates from my body and I pull away before he notices my car.

On the ride home, I realize how much trouble I'm in. I've done the one thing I shouldn't have. I've fallen for him, truly fallen for him as a person, and his text messages suggest he has for me as well.

But does he want me for more than one night?

Even if he did, would the novelty wear off after he had me for a while and he figures out I'm still the nerdy girl I was in high school at heart?

Once I'm inside the house, I head to bed, falling into the softness of my mattress. My phone dings an hour later, stirring me from sleep.

> Mauro: I like you checking up on me. Tough one, but I'm okay. Maybe you can show your civil serviceman some gratitude tomorrow with a kiss.

My girly parts go into a full five-alarm fire and I don't respond because right now the only thing I'd be texting him back would be to come straight over when he finishes his shift in the morning.

CHAPTER SEVENTEEN

Mauro

I'm not sure what I expected when I walked into the tile store. Okay, that's bullshit. I expected Madison to run into my arms, clinging to me like a damn Koala bear, thankful I was alive and standing in front of her in one piece. I didn't expect her just to tell me that she picked me up a coffee and ask if we should go with either blue or gray.

"I figure dark stained floors and cream colored cabinets in the kitchen. Since we broke down the wall between the kitchen and dining room, how about we install an island with seating for kids to eat breakfast." She taps her pen to her mouth, contemplating the idea.

"Sounds good."

She glances to the side at me. "I was thinking soapstone for the countertops?"

"Cool." I sip my coffee not looking at the textiles laid in front of me.

"Can you excuse us for a moment, Meadow?" Madison

asks the young woman who's been helping us and sneaking glances my way. She has long blonde hair that matches her long legs. She's attractive and maybe before Madison, I would've liked the looks she's been giving me. But there's only one woman who's been filling my mind this morning and that's the one whose eyes are locked on me right now.

"Certainly. Just holler when you're ready." Her heels click as she walks away.

Madison places her pen down on her pad of paper next to her coffee.

"You know I want your opinion, right? Don't just go along with whatever I suggest. Feel free to challenge me."

Her voice and her eyes are soft and sincere. Just like they always are. Maybe that's why the ache in my chest won't disappear. After her text last night, I thought she'd be more enthusiastic about seeing me this morning and would lower the wall she'd put up between us. Obviously, I was wrong.

"I know, but I'm not really good at this design stuff. Maybe I should go back to the house and get started on the drywall."

"No!" Her hand presses on my arm. "I want us to do this together."

"Okay." I shrug and stuff my hands into the pockets of my jeans, not sure what advice I can really offer.

"According to the budget you gave me, we have..."

She rattles on about square feet and inches, but I really don't care because my mind is still focused on why I give a shit if she cares.

What the fuck am I doing? Sitting here in this textile place not worried about the house anymore but why Madison Kelly who I never knew existed until a month ago doesn't seem to care that I could have lost my life last night. The flames were hot, the fire unpredictable. High-rise fires are always the riskiest when you go up through a stairway. Maybe it was the relief I felt when we were safe back at the station or the grateful look on my crews' faces when the truck pulled into the station. Everyone found their phones to contact their loved ones.

I knew I'd find a text from Ma, but Madison's message surprised me. The elation inside me grew and that's when the light bulb popped on, I want more than a kiss from this woman.

Now to arrive this morning to an all business Madison wounded me when it shouldn't. I told her not to see me as a hero and if she'd have jumped in my arms when I walked in the shop this morning, I'd know she hadn't listened to me. Having her see me as a hero only raises the expectation level and sets us up for failure.

"Honestly, I'm cool with whatever, Madison. I just want clean and streamlined and it seems like you have it handled here."

Meadow returns with more samples of stained wood, holding it up to the backsplash.

"I don't want the bathrooms to look the same as the kitchen, can we do a painted wood on the cabinetry with an epoxy that resembles marble?"

Madison doesn't bother acknowledging my comment, making me sit there through the entire ordeal, shooting me a pissed off look whenever I say cool or okay instead of giving an opinion.

By the time we're readying to leave Meadow slips me her number when Madison goes to the bathroom complaining about too much coffee. A sour feeling takes over my stomach over the fact that I accepted it. Not that I'm going to use it, but I never want to make anyone feel bad by refusing. Still, somehow the piece of paper in my pocket makes me feel dishonest.

"Do you like Meadow?" Madison asks as we stop on the

sidewalk next to our cars. "She worked with me on my last house and manages to get some really great deals. Plus, she really has an eye for modern, trendy and sleek."

"She's okay." I shrug.

Madison rolls her eyes before her fist nails me in the shoulder.

I wrap my hand around the area she hit. "Ooouucchh," I deadpan, confusion laced in my tone.

"What's with you?" She juts her hip out, her papers high in her arms.

"Nothing. Tired I guess."

I use my usual excuse of tiredness to cover up my emotions. The only woman to figure out my M.O. so far is my mom.

"You seemed chipper when you came in."

"Chipper?"

"Yes, like happy," she says.

My muscles tense in annoyance. "I know what chipper means," I bite out.

She throws her hand out. "Whatever. Why don't you go sleep it off for the rest of the day. I'll handle the house." She heads to her car, opening up the passenger side door and tossing her papers in.

"You'd like that, so you can say that I'm not carrying my weight."

I have no idea where this anger is coming from, but the words leave my lips anyway.

She glances over her shoulder, her forehead scrunching up, not understanding. "No, I wouldn't. I know how hard you work at the station. I'm sure last night shook you up a little."

So, she's finally going to acknowledge last night.

"I'm used to it. It's my job."

"I know but still..."

"Don't baby me, Madison. We signed up for this together."

She stares at me, her eyes alit with questions. "I'm not. If you want to go to the house, then go to the damn house." Her voice is raised, causing a man in a business suit to pause briefly behind us on the sidewalk.

"Do you want me to go to the house?" I ask, stepping closer.

She lightly shakes her head, her back falling to the passenger side of her car. "Truth?"

"Always."

"Not if you're going to be the jerk you're being right now." She crosses her arms and the button on her blouse slides, giving me a glimpse of her green lace bra. My mouth waters and my hands tighten into fists.

"Fine."

"Fine? What the hell do you want from me?" she asks. Her voice is low and I can tell she doesn't want to cause a scene by the way she's glancing around us.

What I want is my lips and my body pressed against hers.

"Nothing." I step back, closing my eyes to regain any amount of composure I can muster right now. "I'll see you at the house." I turn around to head to my truck.

"Mauro?" she calls out.

I circle back around, not stopping my feet, walking backward now. "I'm sorry, Madison. I think it's just the stress getting to me."

That's not even a lie. She'll think it's the job and the house, but in truth it's her.

Back in the serenity of my truck, I watch Madison slide into her car and sit for a moment.

I'm such a fucking asshole. Why would I expect her to act like a girlfriend would after last night? She's not my girlfriend and I need to keep reminding myself of that.

There are two people I can call right now and only one will give me solid, serious advice, so I dial Cristian.

"What's up?" he answers.

"You have a minute?"

"I just left the gym. You want to grab something to eat?" I hear him tell someone else it's his brother and he'll see them tomorrow.

"No. I have to be at the house."

"I can pick up some food and head over there. I'm sure you and Maddie need to take a break." My brother's always thinking of others.

I blow out a breath and run my hand through my hair. "Definitely can't talk at the house."

Silence is the only response.

"Cris?"

"You didn't?"

"Didn't what?"

"Have sex with her. Please tell me you didn't give in to the temptation and now you have a house half-finished and you guys can't stand to be in the same room with each other."

Irritation raises its head again.

"What are you, her keeper?"

"You did. Jesus, Mauro, what are you thinking? She's not like your usual girls." His disappointment is clear from his tone.

"I didn't sleep with her," I grind out.

Silence.

"But I want to."

"Do yourself a favor and go out tonight, find one of your other admirers and screw them. Leave Maddie alone."

My hands tighten on the steering wheel, wishing he was in front of me and that we were ten again when I could justify wrestling him to the ground and pounding my fist into his face.

"I don't want to screw anyone else. Hell, I just got a girl's number five minutes ago."

An exasperated breath flows over the line. "Good to know."

"What am I missing here, Cris? Why are you so protective of her and why do you always think the worst of me with her? It's not like you're talking to fucking Luca."

He's quiet for a long time, but I can hear the sounds of the city through the line—horns honking, bells ringing, and muffled conversations coming and going as he walks.

"Let me ask you something...do you really want something with her? Like something more than one night?"

Two days ago I might've said I don't know, but after last night's message and my reaction to it I can't lie to myself any longer.

"I think I do. She's different, you know?"

"I do know and that's why I'm asking because if you cross the line, Mauro, there's no going back. You're business partners and I have a feeling that if you hurt her, she'll be gone forever."

I swear Cristian is talking in code.

"So, you *don't* think us is a horrible idea then?" I look over my shoulder and pull out into traffic.

He chuckles. "No, I think you just need to make sure you'll give this an honest shot otherwise leave her alone."

I drive for a minute not responding and Cristian stays on the line, knowing me well enough to know I'm deep in thought.

"Am I missing something?" I finally ask.

I follow Madison down the street the house is on. Construction crews for the new roof are already hard at work. With the dark clouds looming I'm not sure how long their workday will be.

"What do you mean?" he asks.

"I mean, do you like her or something?"

Even if he did, I'm not sure I could hold back and do the right thing. I never thought a girl could come between my brothers and me, but a possessiveness runs through my veins whenever he and I speak about Madison.

He laughs like I'm a stand-up comedian. "No. I just don't want to see her hurt. I saw... look, just be one hundred percent sure, that's all I'm saying."

"I will, now stop lecturing me." I park a few cars down from Madison. "See you later."

I hang up the phone, hearing Cristian's sarcastic mumble of 'you're welcome asshole' before the line disconnects.

I still can't help but think I'm missing something that makes Cristian put on a big brother persona when it comes to Madison. She wasn't even in his grade. What kind of connection could they have?

Grabbing my tools I head over to Madison where she stands beside her car putting on her ball cap. She turns to me. "I think we need to talk."

My feet come to a sudden stop. There's no smile on her face, no reassuring tone, nothing in her body language that implies that everything will be fine.

Fuck, now I've done it.

CHAPTER EIGHTEEN

Madison

On the way to the house, I tried to figure out why Mauro was so angry. What had set him off? The last contact we had was a flirtatious text and I let it go because I just don't know if we should cross that line.

But one thing is for sure, we can't let any unresolved issues remain between us or it'll ruin this project. When I saw his truck parked a few cars behind me, and I made the decision to stop him before we went into the house so we could talk and leave all our toxic issues outside.

"I think we need to talk." I tuck my hair into my ball cap, flipping my ponytail out.

He drops his tool bag, the stress lined in the creases around his eyes. "I'm sorry, I can't even explain why I acted like that..."

I hold my hand for him to stop. "You know what I think?"

A smile tugs on the corner of his lips and the tension plaguing his face loosens. "What?"

"That I've done something to upset you and you didn't

think I wanted your opinion on textiles. I tried to go back through everything since this morning, but I can't figure out where I might've not treated you as an equal. It's important that we keep an open line of communication between us, so just tell me. I promise I'm a big girl and can handle it." I stand up straighter like I'm proving how tough I am.

He stands there, his head tilted like I'm a mathematical equation he's having trouble trying to figure out.

"It's okay, give it to me." I close my eyes tight waiting for him to rip the Band-Aid off.

"Give it to you?" he asks and it's true that you can hear a smile in someone's voice. "Open your eyes," he almost whispers.

I do and his blue eyes are right in front of me, a smirk on his face.

"Did you think I was going to sucker punch you?" He steps back and I miss his nearness immediately.

"No. It's stupid. Something Lauren and I do when we have to tell the other person something bad. Like if you don't see how pained their face is for having to tell you it helps you cope better."

He looks as confused as I am as to why I'm telling him this. Embarrassment heats my face.

The roofers are pounding nails into place and we're standing outside the car making spectacles of ourselves. At least I am.

"I'm not upset with anything to do with the house," he says.

Oh phew. That's a load off. I'd thought I was being fair, but of course the person writing the lists always thinks everything's split down the middle.

"You're working too hard. You're exhausted. I get it and really, I don't mind being here longer hours. I don't think..."

He laughs, shaking his head.

Now this is the us I love. Not that version back at the tile place. My sixteen-year-old self is impressed by the way I've been able to develop this growing friendship with Mauro.

"No?" I ask, taking the hint that my statement isn't correct.

"No." He shakes his head.

"What could it be then? Last night? Did the fire bring up bad memories of Hunter? Do you want to talk about it? I know we've never really talked about anything too deep, but I'm a good listener. Just ask Lauren and Van." He places his fingers over my lips, stepping forward and caging me against the car. He really likes this domineering role of having his body hovering over mine. Let's face it, I kinda like it, too.

"Close your eyes, Madison," he whispers.

One hand lands on the roof of my car and then the other one next to my head.

When my eyes are still open a few seconds later, he repeats his earlier statement. "Close your eyes." His voice is soft and sultry and could probably make me strip down for him right now if we weren't in public.

My eyelids flutter shut but pop back open. "You're not going to kiss me, are you?"

His head falls forward in defeat, his body language saying I ruined the moment.

"Well?" I prod.

His hands fall back to his sides leaving me free to escape. "Yes, Madison, I was going to kiss you."

I'm not stupid but what I just did was stupid. I effectively took the damn hose and doused the fire between us. Maybe that's a good thing. I don't even know anymore.

"I'm sorry."

He shakes his head. "Of course you are." Picking up his tool bag, he waits for me to walk up the sidewalk first.

"Wait," I say. He turns in my direction. "You still haven't explained what made you so angry earlier."

He looks up to the sky as though the answers are up there somewhere. "I think this is a longer conversation than we can have right now."

Just as I'm about to suggest we head inside to talk, Emmanuel, the contractor doing our roof, calls out to Mauro from the ladder.

"Saved by the contractor." Mauro winks and heads up the walkway.

They talk while I bundle the samples in my arms that Meadow gave us. I've almost reached them when Emmanuel climbs back up the ladder with some tarps in his hand.

Mauro approaches me before I reach him. "Bad news. Rain is coming so they're covering up and heading out for the day."

I look up at the sky, the dark clouds fast approaching. "This is what those spare days I put into the schedule are for. No worries." I slide by him to go into the house.

His tools jiggle in the box so I know he's two steps behind me.

"Just me and you today," he says once we're both in the house.

"I'm going to tackle the basement."

"I was going to start the drywall, but maybe I should go down there with you."

I laugh. "I can handle it myself."

I head through the large living room to the dining room and kitchen. We'll need to pick our paint colors soon. There is supposed to be a crew in here over the next few days to lay whatever drywall Mauro doesn't get done. He's been amazing at arranging the help. His men work all day with the strongest work ethic I've ever seen, never cutting a corner.

Compared to my other projects, this one is going a thousand times smoother.

The wooden steps creak on my way down to the basement and I remind myself for not the first time that old houses make strange noises. Nothing to freak out about.

Grabbing my sketchpad to figure out how we'll configure the basement, the fact that Mauro said he was going to kiss me outside lingers in the forefront of my mind.

I still don't understand why he was so angry earlier, but maybe it's better to just let it go unexplained.

An hour later, I've got my plans to go over with Mauro. When I step onto the top of the landing of the staircase I see that the sky appears even darker and angrier than earlier.

"A storm is definitely on its way." I shut the back door, the cool rush of air igniting a cascade of goose bumps along my skin.

I turn to find Mauro there, his shirt stripped off, long forgotten on his toolbox. Sweat glistens off the curves and crevices of his muscular body.

Did I say I was cold? It's suddenly like an oven in here. His hat is on backward which I've realized he only seems to wear when he's working. It reminds me of the high school version of himself.

It takes me a second, but I realize that Snow Patrol is playing through a small Bluetooth speaker to his right.

The night from forever ago rushes back to me. This was the song playing on the radio when I drove him home.

I sit down on the dining room table we didn't have the heart to remove and watch his corded forearms strain as he lifts a sheet of drywall. He really is a man's man. So different than any other man I've dated. They were all good with their heads. Engineers, professors, accountants. Mauro holds more sex appeal than all of them put together.

His looks are what drew me in all those years ago. The cocky quarterback every girl wanted. An Adonis of a guy that all the girls dreamed of taming. Now years later, after getting to know him better, it's clear that I never really knew him back then.

That night under the stars on that baseball field that I saw as a moment of bonding and trust on his part wasn't. The man that's standing in front of me now isn't an unsure boy taking an opportunity when it presented itself. He's so much more than a handsome face. He's smart, considerate, and hard-working. I need to get my expectations back in check.

"The storm is going to be here any minute." Mauro talks directly to the wall. "I'm trying to just finish this wall then we can head out."

I pull my legs up to my chest and let a contented sigh out. This view coupled with the promise of being unable to do anything but lay in bed listening to the rain. Or reading a book. I love these lazy days.

"Do you like thunderstorms?" I ask, never letting an opportunity pass where I can get to know him.

He shrugs. "Yeah, I guess. More just the steady rain than the thunder and lightning." His answer is nonchalant so I don't offer my own opinion and he doesn't ask.

Finishing up the wall, he drops the X-acto knife in the bin and studies his work. "The crew I hired should be able to finish over the next few days. We're really making progress."

Whereas I've always done days of framing, followed by days of drywalling, followed by days of mudding and taping, Mauro decided on a different plan of attack. One where one group immediately follows the first and so on. I think it's going to work well and it'll definitely reduce our turnaround time on the house.

"You do good work, Bianco." I nod at the wall.

He grabs his t-shirt drying the sweat from his face and tucking it into the waistband of his jeans. God, he's gorgeous. Not a stray hair anywhere on his chest and I can't help but want to run my tongue over the planes of his rippled abdomen.

"Can I ask you a question?" He takes a sip of his water.

"Sure."

"Have you hooked up with my brother before?"

"Luca?" My mouth hangs open for a second before I begin laughing. "Absolutely not, no."

Mauro doesn't laugh nor does he smile. "Cristian?"

My mood sobers a bit with the realization that he's serious. "No. Why would you ask me that?"

He tries to shrug it off, but I'm not letting this go. Is this the reason for his earlier anger?

"Mauro?"

"It's stupid, but he seems almost protective of you when I talk about you to him." He lifts the hat off his head with one hand and the fingers on his other, thread through his hair. "He's really worried about me hurting you. When I asked him if I was stepping on his toes, he said no, but I know my brother well enough to know I'm missing something."

His eyes bore into mine, asking me to clarify his brother's reaction. My initial reaction is an inward celebration that he's been talking to his brother about me. It's all clapping and jumping around and happy times inside. But my head makes its way into the conversation and I know that now is the time. I need to fill in some of the blanks for him.

I pat the table next to me. "It's time we had that talk."

He slides up beside me on the table. As embarrassing as this is going to be, he has to know the truth before anything happens between us. His reaction will solidify whether I risk taking a chance on him or not.

CHAPTER NINETEEN

Mauro

I slide up on the oak table I plan on redoing as a gift to whoever buys the house. The table deserves to have its beauty revealed. I think it's Amish made which explains how it was able to stay in decent shape since its owners beat the shit out of their house.

Madison's fidgeting scares me and I'm crossing my fingers that she didn't have a one-night stand with my brother. Or some secret crush on him. Not that I think she did, but the two of them are definitely keeping something from me.

"So, you know how you've been hinting at us kissing?" she starts.

Her tone is back to heavy and somber. I hate it. Loathe it is more like it. I can easily figure out that whatever she has to tell me, she's unsure how I'll receive the news.

"Our first kiss would have been over and done with had you let me kiss you at the car." I smile down at her, teasing, trying to purge the tension from the room.

She shoots me a soft smile and her cheeks color pink. I

love pulling that reaction out of her and I can't wait to have the opportunity to see her entire body flush in that same shade.

"That's the thing," she continues.

Her eyes focus in on her entwined hands. Just as I can't stand the wait any longer, she swivels her body to face me. Her gaze shifts from her hands to my face. Gorgeous blue eyes filled with adoration pierce mine.

"We already had our first kiss."

"What?" I scrunch my forehead in confusion.

"Back in high school."

I wave my hand in the air to stop her before she continues. "Is this some joke you're helping my brothers pull off?" It would be just like them to talk Madison into messing with my head just for a laugh.

She shakes her head, her teeth biting down on her lower lip like she does when she's nervous.

"No?" I ask, stunned.

"No."

"How could I not remember kissing you?" I slide forward, taking her hands in mine.

Rain starts beating down on the house, and light inside is dim now from the dark and stormy skies. I can't help but relate the storm to whatever story I'm about to hear because seconds ago I would've said I had a better chance of being struck by lightning than not remembering that I'd already kissed Madison at some point in my life.

"You were drunk," she says.

"Were you?"

Please tell me she was and that maybe, just maybe she was able to remember it a little but not fully because if I kissed her when I was drunk, it probably means I did a piss poor job of it.

She shakes her head.

My eyes roll into the back of my head and I look anywhere but at her. Here I've been flirting with her based on the idea that we'd never been together in any way and now I find out that we've already kissed.

"Okay, give it to me. How much of an ass did I make of myself?" I squeeze her hands and her eyes find mine once more.

"You were a senior. I was a sophomore. It was at a bonfire party." She pauses for a second and I think she's testing me to see if I remember anything at all, but my memory is still a black hole.

With my silence, she continues.

She tells me about the party, finding me in the woods, driving me home, "Chasing Cars" by Snow Patrol playing on the radio, the slide in the park across the street from my parents' house. Lastly, the outfield of the park I played Little League in.

"You were asking about God's plan. Talking about how you wanted the trifecta. The career, the family, and the house. It was sweet. Then you asked if you could kiss me."

A wistfulness fills her eyes as she recollects how she expected to see a shooting star. I wonder how many times her mind has drifted back to this memory of us? The same memory that was erased from mine because of alcohol. I feel an aching loss inside because of that that I can't comprehend.

Her soft smile leaves her face and her shoulders tense. "My braces cut you." She cringes, and for the first time her gaze shifts away from mine. "You were bleeding."

Oh Jesus, what I could have said? It was high school, so I probably reacted like a rude asshole. Did I yell at her for cutting my lip? For all that is holy, please tell me no.

"You didn't seem to care. You just touched your lip and told me like it was a fact."

Thank God I wasn't a complete jerk off. I'd better get to church on Sunday and ask for forgiveness.

"Then we stood up and you asked me if I wanted to swing." She shrugs, but her eyes are welling with tears.

"Madison." I sigh, my hand sliding up her arm, past her elbow, bypassing her shoulder, molding to her cheek. "I'm sorry I don't remember."

My heart squeezes over the fact that a moment that clearly meant so much to her wasn't even a blip on my screen.

"Cristian showed up right after, you threw up in the trashcan, and he took you home." A tear slips down her cheek. "As embarrassing as retelling this story is, you had to know before we move forward because we already had our first kiss, but I was the only one who remembered."

"And Cristian, he knows?"

She shrugs. "I think he suspected. I actually think he thought we had sex at first."

I hate that I have to ask her this question, but I need to know. "We didn't though, right?"

Her face is beet red and she slides out from my hold, her feet hitting the floor. "No. I wasn't that pathetic." She begins throwing stuff into her bag. "Telling you was a really bad idea. I need to go. We should've kept this platonic. It's not too late though. We just need to shift gears and forget all of this emotional stuff. Keep things uncomplicated."

I hop off the table. Coming up behind her, I still her hand with mine and she pauses. "I didn't mean the question as a bad thing. I hate the fact I don't remember and I had to know what I'm up against." I dip my head down into the crook of her neck, the strawberry scent of her shampoo intoxicating and arousing. "So I know what I need to do to make this right. Madison, I don't want to go back to being just business partners. Not by a long shot."

Her body loses the tension of a stretched rubber band.

"It's mortifying that I admired you from afar and you had no idea who I was."

I ease her around to face me, but her eyes focus in on my chest. Placing my finger under her chin, I nudge her to look up into my eyes. The second our gazes lock, her shoulders relax and I swear she sinks into my body. "I'm sorry that I didn't notice you in high school. All I can say is that I was a self-centered jerk, but I see you now Madison Kelly. In fact, you're all I see."

Both my hands cup her face and as badly as I want to lean in and kiss her right now, our second kiss needs to be special.

"Kiss me," she asks, her chest heaving with breath, the hard points of her nipples pressing into my chest.

My head fights my heart as I wonder if there's ever going to be a perfect time for us. She's just put her heart out there for me. Trusting me for a second time and I don't want to take advantage. I want her to know I'm in this.

My cock strains in my pants as our eyes swim together in a mix of hazy lust and need. I lick my lip in anticipation and when I can't stand the building tension between us anymore, I lose all control of my body and my head dips, my heart winning the war.

She licks her lips, her fingers wrapping around my shoulders, rising on her tiptoes. Our eyes fall closed, our lips nearing one another and I can feel her breath on my face.

The tornado sirens blare outside and like a snap of the fingers, our moment is over.

Her eyes widen in fear. "Mauro," she says my name with a soft plea.

"Basement." I grab her hand and lead her through the kitchen, down the stairs.

Large hail pounds atop the half-completed roof.

We race downstairs, turning on the lights, but I know

with the way the power lines in Chicago are, electricity will be the first thing to go.

"I'll be right back." I run back up the stairs.

"Hurry, Mauro."

Grabbing the candles she had lit before, I find the one flashlight I have in my toolbox. Shutting the front door, I run back into the basement where Madison's arms are crossed as her teeth nibble on her bottom lip.

"It's okay. We'll be fine." I wrap her in my arms.

"I just hate storms like this."

The sirens are still blaring. I don't even remember the last time I heard them sound here. I was probably a young boy.

"It will pass. Tornados don't hit Chicago." I rub my hands over her chilled arms.

As we stand in the middle of the basement, her in my arms, her story from a decade ago runs through my mind while I try to gain a flicker of recollection, but nothing surfaces.

"I'm so sorry, Madison," I whisper and she turns her head to peer up at me with those sweet blue eyes that could make me do just about anything for her.

Her hand caresses my cheek. "I made peace with it a long time ago."

"Still. I just...I had you ten years ago and let you go."

A smile plays on her lips. "Who said you had me?" Turning in my arms, she winds her arms around my neck. "Maybe I let you go."

"You're way too nice. You should be kicking me in the nuts right now."

She laughs and her forehead falls to my chest. "Then I guess you're lucky that I'm a people pleaser."

The lights flicker once, twice before blackness surrounds us. "Hold on." I turn on the flashlight and hand it to Madison.

Lighting the candles, I place them around the space and we sit down on a tarp that Madison had down here when she was working.

"Tell me about your parents." I try to do anything to get her mind off of the storm looming overhead.

She looks off over my shoulder. "They're divorced. My dad lives in Florida. My mom's in Oregon. This is where everything fell apart." She glances up at the ceiling. "My dad left and my mom lost herself for a year or so."

I reach out for her knee, my thumb rubbing back and forth. I've never experienced the repercussion of divorce, but I've heard enough stories from friends to know how bad it can mess up someone's belief in love after seeing their parents' happily ever after fall apart.

"It was so many years ago and if you didn't think I was a loser before, wait until you hear why I bought this house." She lets a self-deprecating chuckle escape her lips.

"Hey, let's get one thing clear, I never thought you were a loser."

She smiles like she doesn't really believe me. I mentally mark that down to prove her wrong.

"Reserve your judgment for a moment."

She reaches out and rubs my shoulder. It's a casual move, but one she's never done before. And I enjoyed it way too much.

"I bought the house so that someone could build a happy life here. I wanted a family to love one another and for some other little girl to get the dream I didn't."

Nothing could've blown me away more than the words that just left her mouth. I'd actually been thinking she wanted revenge of some kind on the place, but it's the opposite of that. And her reason speaks way too much for who she is. How thoughtful and kind she is right down to why she rehabs houses.

"What about the other houses?" I lean in and my arm rests behind her back. I want that kiss more than anything right now.

She locks eyes with me. "Same." Her unsure voice continues. "I just want to build a place for families to love each other in, one that reflects on the outside, the love you can find inside. A home is so much more than wood and glass, carpet and stairs. It shelters and protects the people you love most in this world."

"Madison?" I raise my hand to her cheek.

"Yeah?"

"I'm going to kiss you now."

CHAPTER TWENTY

Madison

He's slow to start, deliberate in his actions, wanting to make this a kiss to remember. Just like that night ten years ago, my body hums and heats under his soft lips. But it's different this time. It's not Mauro kissing me, it's us kissing each other. Another small piece of my heart floats out of my chest and nestles into his.

His tongue sweeps across my lips, asking without words if it's okay. Opening my mouth, my skin ignites in a wave of goose bumps when his tongue slides across mine. We entwine ourselves in one another slowly until I don't know where I stop and he begins.

I give Mauro credit, he's as patient as the saint his mama probably prays to every night. Pressing my body to his, I'm the one who deepens the kiss. His arms tighten around my back and the feel of his powerful chest against my own makes my nipples taut.

Somewhere between the butterflies roaring into an uncontrollable flutter in my stomach and all my sensory alarms flashing overload, we sink into one another. Our mouths colliding one second, gentle the next. One of his hands runs up the length of my spine until his fingers reach my hair and he manipulates my ponytail holder, my hair spilling down across my shoulders.

His dark hair is smooth as my hands run up the back of his head, trying desperately to cling to anything. My legs beg to wind around his waist, but I force myself to stay grounded. Never have I ever felt so much from one kiss.

I'm not even sure which of us slows down, but long after our lips have stopped moving, our bodies are still entangled like wild vines.

"Let's pretend that was our first kiss." He smiles down at me.

"Not a chance."

"That was a pretty spectacular kiss." He presses his lips to mine one more time. "Definitely top ten." His smirk says he's joking. I lightly punch him in the stomach. "You sure you don't want to forget that first one?"

"I'm positive, but I'll take another kiss like this one anytime."

"If you're not going to pretend that was our first kiss then I have no choice but to try to erase it from your memory." His head descends and again, the feel of his lips on mine catapult me back to euphoria.

We come up for air minutes later and I'm surprised and if I'm honest maybe a little disappointed. Mauro didn't even try to cop a feel. His hands ventured down to my ass, but he stopped short. The only part of the kiss that was NC17 was his erection pressed into my stomach.

The lights flicker back on, the soft glow of the candles disappearing.

"If this place wasn't so disgusting, I'd never want to leave,"

Mauro murmurs, his lips pressed to my temple. "I'll go check on the storm."

It's only now that I realize the sirens have stopped wailing outside.

He releases me and I miss being in his arms immediately. His footsteps pound up the stairs and I hear the back door opening.

"We're good," he calls out before he comes back down the stairs.

The first thing he does is extinguish the candles with a lick of his fingers and a press to the wick. I can't help but smile at that.

"I'm starved. You want to go somewhere for dinner?" he asks.

"Sure."

We each have an armful of candles as we head upstairs.

After walking around the house to make sure none of the windows are broken, Mauro suggests we drop off my car so he can drive us to dinner.

Right before I pull away from the curb, I let the image of the house sink into my memory. I'd never want to take back our first kiss, but this one was so much better.

———

I turn down the alley while Mauro parks on the street in front of the house. Lauren's yellow Fiat is in the garage and my stomach drops, wondering what she'll say if she answers the door when Mauro reaches it.

So, I do what any normal girl would do to protect the guy she's falling for from her friend's wrath—I race inside through the back door, sprinting to the front door and swinging it open.

Mauro draws back, but I press on his shoulders to turn him back down the stairs he just climbed. "What's going on?"

"Nothing, just my stomach was rumbling the entire way over here. I need food."

Mauro smiles over his shoulder.

"Whoa, whoa, whoa!" Lauren's voice at my back is like the squealing of tires locking up on dry pavement.

You know when you hear that noise followed by the sound of piercing metal crashing two seconds later?

"Taking our girl out without talking to the friends? I would have thought your mama taught you better than that, Mauro Bianco."

We both turn to find her standing on the porch, hands on her hips. She's wearing a pair of yoga pants and a baggy sweatshirt that's printed with the words *Physical Therapist - I'm here to fix your ass not kiss it.*

Mauro chuckles to himself. "Lauren Hunt, hello. I guess I should be grateful that you didn't jump on my back this time." He jogs up the steps and puts his hand out. "I heard you're going on a date with Luca. Good luck with that."

Lauren shakes his hand and rolls her eyes at the same time. "That's never going to happen."

"I'm kidding. He's a good guy. Deep down."

Lauren leans back and yells into the house. "Van! We've got company." She steps back and opens the door wider. "Come on in, Mauro."

"We were just leaving," I say from the bottom of the stairs.

Lauren peers around Mauro as he's circling around, clearly confused as to why I'm still standing at the bottom of the stairs.

"You can wait five minutes. Vanessa's never met Mauro." Lauren smiles. The one that's conniving and means she's up to trouble. "We can order pizza."

"Five minutes, Lauren." I run up the stairs, grabbing Mauro's hand and pulling him in behind me.

His eyes scour the inside of the house.

"Nice, right? Maddie redid this place." Lauren leads us to the family room and sits down on the couch, patting the cushion next to her. "Come, sit, Mauro."

His eyes veer to mine, but he sits, albeit hesitantly. "What've you been up to, Lauren?" He falls back onto the sofa, resting his ankle on his knee.

"I'm a physical therapist." She points to her sweatshirt. "But I'm much more interested in knowing how this whole partnership thing is going from your perspective?" She waggles her finger between Mauro on the couch and where I stand.

"It's going great, right Madison?" Mauro's eyes find mine, a smirk on his lips.

"Yep."

Lauren narrows her eyes, trying to dissect my inner thoughts.

"What's going on? I'm about to head out." The echo of Vanessa's heels sound down the stairs before she appears in the room wearing a skin-tight dress that ends right below her ass.

Suddenly, I feel frumpy and boring.

Mauro stands up from the couch, crossing the room, his hand already out before Vanessa has even looked up from her phone.

"If this is about your vibrator, I'm going to say it again, Lauren, I didn't take it. That's not something you borrow from someone."

"Van," I say and knock her elbow. She glances up at me, smiles. "Hey, did you get caught in that storm?"

I shift my eyes and she follows the direction of my gaze.

"Oh, shit, have you been standing there for longer than one second?"

"Well, I don't think Maddie twitched her nose and he appeared." Lauren laughs. "I didn't say you borrowed my vibrator, I was simply asking if you saw it when it was delivered. Do you ever even listen to us anymore?" Lauren blows at a hair that's fallen down onto her forehead.

Ignoring Lauren, I introduce Vanessa and Mauro. "Vanessa this is Mauro, Mauro this is Vanessa, our third roommate."

Mauro shakes her hand. "Nice to meet you. Your dad is the commander of the eighteenth district?"

Vanessa's smile falters. "He is."

"My brother Cristian says he's a good man."

Vanessa drops his hand, her focus back on her phone. "He can be."

Vanessa's a master at hiding her true feelings, but I've known her long enough to know that she's giving Mauro the answer he expects.

Mauro's eyes find mine, a smile on his lips. I hate that for a second I feared that Mauro would be attracted to Vanessa. She was definitely his type in high school. I loathe the part of me that refuses to let go of all my baggage from that time in my life.

"Have a seat, Vanessa, we're going to put Mauro through the wringer about his intentions with our girl."

"No, you're not. Mauro and I are going to get something to eat," I say.

Lauren tilts her head. "Surely, he doesn't care. You don't have anything to hide, do you?"

This is getting annoying. Does she think if he's using me he's going to divulge that to her right here and now? She acts like she's some ace detective on *Law & Order* who can squeeze a confession out of a person of interest with just a few pointed questions.

"Enough with the protective dad act," I say.

Vanessa is still buried in her phone, her fingers going a mile a minute. "One question from me and then I'm out." She surprises all of us by joining the conversation.

"No girls, we aren't going to do this." I shake my head.

Mauro puts his arm around my shoulder. "No, Mad, it's fine." He shifts his attention to Vanessa.

"Do you like our girl?" she asks.

"Yes."

"Then I'm good. I think it goes without saying that if you hurt her, you can expect a visit on your doorstep from me. And Lauren." She nods to where Lauren still sits on the couch. "Oh, and do me a favor and tell your brother to stop fucking calling me. I'm not going to go out with him." She turns and walks toward the back of the house, probably to catch another ride in a black town car.

"Are you dating someone? Is that why you won't date him?" Mauro calls out and Vanessa stops walking, slowly turning around.

Lauren and I are silent, waiting for her to answer.

"No, but I don't date people who work under my dad. That's a bad situation for all involved."

Then she's gone through the back door.

One down, one to go. Unfortunately, it's the piranha that's still circling.

"You get one question, Lauren." I turn to face her, but Mauro sits down in the chair across from her.

"Three is more than fair," she says.

"Two," I negotiate and she wiggles in her seat and rubs her hands together.

"First question. Was it a coincidence that you showed up to bid on the same property as Madison?"

Seems like a waste of a question to me. Obviously, it was a coincidence. But I'm happy that's what she asked because it could have been so much worse.

"Yes." He gives a sharp nod of his head.

"Question two. You're not using her to screw her over in the future, are you?"

"No."

"Question three—"

"No, Lauren that's it." I hold my hand out for Mauro to take. He doesn't accept it.

"It's fine. I'll answer as many questions as you want." He sits up, resting his forearms on his thighs. "But before you ask, I'll just save us each a bit of time."

Lauren sits back, crossing her arms over her chest in a way that suggests he'll never win her over, but she'll let him try and fail.

"First off, thank you for bidding on me at the bachelor auction. Though our first date didn't go as well as I'd have hoped, it put Madison on my radar. The property thing was a complete coincidence, but I'd like to think it was fate stepping in. Now, she told me what an asshole I was in high school. Don't worry, I'm still trying to figure out how I could have possibly forgotten the first time I kissed her."

Lauren's eyebrows scrunch and she glances my way.

Shut up, Mauro.

"But I plan on making that up to her. I like Madison. A helluva lot more than a friend. This is new to both of us and we have to tread carefully with the business partnership and all, but I guarantee you, my intentions are pure." He leans back into the chair, his hand out for me to take it. "Any more questions?"

"Just one." She holds up her finger. "What the hell is he talking about a kiss in high school?" She glares my way.

"Nothing."

Now both of them are looking at me. I throw my hands up in the air.

"That night of the bonfire when I drove him home..."

Please don't make me retell this story.

Her eyes narrow. I silently slice my finger across my throat. She takes my hint and gives me a quick nod.

"Oh, that time when Mauro was drunk and all over you because he wanted you so bad? I completely forgot about that time," she says.

Be jealous girls, she's all mine.

The light in Mauro's eyes dims again with that pitiful puppy look, staring up at me.

"She's kidding, Mauro." I place my hand on his arm.

Jeez does he do push-ups every night?

Lauren shakes her head and Mauro shifts his attention to her. The two share a look of 'she's way too nice.'

"What? You love me just the way I am." I stand, looking at Lauren, whose eyes move to Mauro.

My cheeks flush because now Mauro took that as I think he loves me.

Lauren busts out laughing.

"Go you two. Try to screw the niceness out of her will you, Mauro?" She grabs the remote and the television lights up.

Even Mauro's red now. Lauren has that effect on people.

"You'd rather sit at home and watch television than go out with my brother?" Mauro asks, grabbing my hand in his to lead us out of the room.

"Yes." She points to Mauro. "And what does that say about your brother?"

Mauro chuckles. "So, I have your permission to take Madison out to dinner, Warden Hunt?" He raises our hands.

"I suppose so. But, if you screw her any other way then doggie style, missionary, or reverse cowgirl, then I suggest you walk around with a jock cup permanently in place because I'll be coming for you."

Mauro gives me a look like 'is she fucking serious?'

"You've been warned," I whisper.

"Night Lauren," he says and I give her a quick wave too which she responds with two thumbs up and a million dollar smile behind his back.

I try to ignore the warm feeling in my chest once we're back outside and he's leading me to his truck.

I'm going out with Mauro Bianco, someone pinch me.

He opens his car door and I slide in. "Tough girl. But I like it that she's around to look out for you."

The door shuts and I watch him round the front of his truck.

Okay, I'll admit, I pinched myself. I had to see if this was real or not.

CHAPTER TWENTY-ONE

Mauro

"I'm sorry about Lauren," Madison mumbles when I climb into the driver's seat.

I wait to start the truck, my hand gripping hers first. "I would've answered as many questions as she had. I understand her concern, and I meant what I said, I'm glad she's there to protect you."

When I think she's appeased, I insert the keys in the ignition and start the engine.

"Now, where do you want to eat?" I ask.

Pulling away from the curb, Madison waves to her neighbors standing on their porch watching a little girl and boy jump in puddles on the sidewalk.

"That's the ADA I was telling you about, Reed Warner," she says as the kids wave and scream Maddie's name when we drive away.

"Oh yeah, and that's his family?"

She nods. "Well, his fiancée and her daughter. The little

boy is around a lot so I'm not really sure if he's just a friend or a relation. They're cute though, right?"

The look of longing on her face says she wants what they have. I'd be lying if I said I didn't either, but wanting and getting are two different things.

"Very cute."

She settles in the seat, crossing her legs. "I'm not really dressed for a nice dinner, so how about Portillos?"

"Sure." I flick on my turn signal.

Once we have a destination, silence looms in the car.

"What about you? Do you want a family? I mean, I'm not implying..."

I laugh and she stops her rambling. Reaching over, I grip her hand again, entwining our fingers like the real couple we're becoming.

"I'm Italian, I'm not really sure I have a choice if I want a family." I chuckle and give her hand a squeeze. "My ma is already down all our throats for grandchildren. The Catholic guilt might crush Cristian, but not me or Luca. We'll take that step when we're ready."

My words are the truth, but I'm failing to mention one thing. That trusting someone is hard for me and after Jenna, even harder. Since that's a key component of promising yourself to someone forever, I'm not sure when I'll be ready for that huge step.

"I'd rather have that than your parents just assuming you'll never get married or have kids. My mom thinks my independence scares off men. My dad still sees me as the ugly duckling I was in high school."

"Don't say that about yourself." I let her hand go so I can put my signal on and turn a corner.

Agitation bursts through me hot and angry. We sit in silence for a minute before we pull into the parking lot of Portillos and I slam the truck into park, turning to face her.

"Beauty isn't just something you find on the outside. Besides, you weren't that bad in high school."

She raises her eyebrows at me in challenge.

"Listen, the inside of someone can make them ugly, too. Someone can be attractive and present themselves with a perfect bow on top, but if when you get to know them, they're mean and callous with your heart, you no longer see their beauty. I understand that you have your hang-ups from high school, but I noticed you the night of the auction. I'm going to lay myself on the line here." I inhale a deep breath and squeeze the steering wheel in my hands.

"When someone pointed you out as the winner of a date with me, my breath caught in my throat. Mentally I already had us in every sexual position possible, my lips on every inch of your skin as I buried myself inside of you over and over again."

She flushes and looks away, but I use my other hand to rest under her chin, bringing her eyes back on me.

"But it's these last few weeks...the beauty inside of you that has drawn me to you even more. I know I ridiculed you for being a people pleaser, but I was wrong. You genuinely care for people and how they're feeling. The way you bring water for the crew. Tell someone to take a break when you noticed they're bagged. The fact you know more than me about the guys I've been working side by side with for years. You remember their wives and kids names and ask how their little league game went the day before. How you trust me and you see the person I am inside of me. Madison, you've come to consume my thoughts, my heart, hell my life in a matter of weeks."

She smiles, beams really, her cheek leaning into the palm of my hand, the strands of her hair tickling my forearm. I lean over the center console, pressing my lips to hers. As much as I want to deepen our kiss, her stomach growls from hunger, so I pull away with a chuckle.

"Too many interruptions." She fists my shirt and pulls me closer, our lips colliding, our tongues each trying to claim dominance.

I want to slide my seat back, pull her over onto my lap, kiss her neck and nibble on her earlobe. I'd do just about anything to feel her heart beating against my chest. Who am I kidding? I want to take her home and lock her in my room for an eternity.

Slowing our kiss, our chests both heave for a breath and I rest my forehead on hers. "I'm going to feed you and then take you to your place before we lose control."

I want nothing more than to bury myself deep inside her, but I don't want to screw this up by pushing her too fast.

She giggles. "Who said I wanted to go home?" She climbs out of the truck before I have a chance to open the door, rounding the front and waiting for me.

I hop out of the driver's side, adjust my half-erect dick and quickly grab her hand when I reach her. "You're going to have to learn to wait for me to open the door for you."

She places a hand on my bicep and leans her head on my shoulder. "Oh, Mauro, I enjoy chivalry, but I don't need help in and out of the car."

"It's not about you needing help, it's gentlemanly."

"Well, when we go on a real date, I promise to wait."

I stop us before entering the rotating door to the place. "I wanted to ask you. Will you go out with me on Thursday? Me, you, and a fancy restaurant?"

Her eyes light up and she smiles so wide it encompasses her entire face. "I'd love to."

We head inside where I buy her a hot dog and fries. We talk a bit about everything including what it was like for me to grow up in a large Italian family and how much they mean to me. She actually seems excited when I talk about our Sunday dinners.

With any luck, she'll find out soon enough that they're much more than spaghetti and meatballs.

CHAPTER TWENTY-TWO

Madison

"Wear this. No this." Vanessa's throwing clothes out of her closet. "Do you want my fake eyelashes? I have the perfect shade of nude lipstick that will pull all the shades of your coloring out."

"She doesn't need all this shit. Mauro's already smitten with her." Lauren smiles at me through the mirror of Vanessa's vanity.

"Smitten?" I ask and she shrugs.

"I have to admit, I gave him a green check mark after his speech the other night." Lauren sits on the bed, leaning against the headboard pretending to relax, but I can tell her eyes are secretly taking in Vanessa's space, looking for clues.

"What speech?" Vanessa comes back out of her closet holding a simple pink dress with a beaded belt and neckline. I like that it flares at the waist so it will hide my thighs.

I stand up and grab it.

"Well, if you didn't have to run off to a mystery location

you would've been here to hear it. He basically declared that he'd take her off our hands."

I roll my eyes.

A purse hits my head. I turn and stare back at the culprit, Lauren.

"It's true, Maddie, he likes you. So, don't go all glam for him. Just be yourself."

Lauren will forever be the 'I am who I am and if you don't like it then so be it' kinda girl. She could feel sexy in a track-suit, but I don't think there's anything wrong with putting in a little effort and I can't wait to see Mauro's eyes when he sees me out of my overalls and baseball cap.

"Thank you, but I want to dress up to feel sexy for him." I take a seat on the bed. Vanessa stands on the other side, after months of being absent, she's really here, present in this moment with us. "I'm not worried about not being good enough for him."

Lauren purses her lips and crosses her arms over her chest.

"Okay, not like I once was. But this dress and that makeup will show everyone that I belong with him."

Lauren stares at me for a moment and Vanessa's hand lands on my thigh. "You don't need other people to think you belong with him. You're more than worthy of Mauro. You know that, right Mad?"

Vanessa glances at Lauren, the two of them on the same line of thinking.

"I do."

Lauren slides up to me and wraps the three of us in a hug. "Close your eyes, Madison," she whispers.

"No. Not tonight, Lauren." I try to get out of their circle of truth, but they tighten their hold.

"Close them," Vanessa orders.

I do as they say, my heart pounding, waiting for what they're going to tell me.

"You are perfect. You have no reason to feel insecure when you're with him." Lauren speaks first.

"You're gorgeous. Though I do wish you'd wear a tighter dress and show off that ass."

The three of us laugh at Vanessa's comment.

I love these girls.

They release me from their hold and my gaze veers to the clock on Vanessa's nightstand.

Shit, it's almost time for him to pick me up.

I collapse on the mattress, my hand on my stomach. "I can't believe I'm going out with Mauro Bianco and it's not some sick joke. Pinch me, girls." I hold out my arms.

They both grab pillows and smack me on the head.

"Hey," I say, standing up.

"It's not a dream and he should be the one pinching himself." Lauren smiles and Vanessa takes the dress off the hanger.

"Come on, let's get you ready. He'll be here soon." Vanessa holds it out for me.

I take a deep breath and grab it from her hands.

Unlike when I was sixteen, or our time at the café, this date feels like it means something and I'm surprised to find that anticipation and excitement are at the forefront of my emotions, not anxiety or nerves.

That has to mean something good, right?

CHAPTER TWENTY-THREE

Mauro

"You need to leave." I grab one of Luca's friends by the shoulders and push him toward the door. "Luca, the gang needs to leave."

Cristian comes in fresh off shift, his uniform still on.

"Shit the cops are here." Luca pretends to weave like he's about to run.

Cristian tosses his keys on the side table. "Funny asshole. I'm beat."

"Great, then get changed and head to Mom's. I need the apartment tonight." I grab the empty beer bottles off the coffee table.

"Hell no. I want my bed." He walks down the hall.

"All of you." I circle my finger to the guys. "Out." I point to the door.

Luca laughs. "Are you bringing a girl home?"

I give him my fuck off expression. It's one he knows well by now.

"Go ahead, guys. We'll have to watch the fight at the bar," Luca says to his pack of followers.

His friends whine and complain in response, but I don't give one shit.

"Here's an idea, why don't all of you get your own apartments." I toss the beer bottles and put the dirty dishes in the dishwasher. Seriously, Cristian usually does all this shit. He plans the night before I'm taking Madison out to act like a slob.

One of Luca's friends flips me off and the other one makes a comment about how I used to be fun and then they shut the door behind themselves.

"I'm not joking, Luca, this has got to stop. This place is not a frat house."

"I agree." Cristian reappears in a pair of athletic pants and a t-shirt that says, *I'm no hero, but I've walked beside a few*. He buries his head in the fridge, pulling out a Vitamin water. "I'm done with this shit. You made a huge-ass mess last night."

Luca holds up his hands in the air. "What is this 'pick on Luca day?'"

Cristian blows out an exasperated breath. "This is 'stop using our damn apartment' day. We kicked you out because of your parties, why are you bringing them to us?"

"Jeez, can't a guy miss his brothers." He flops down on the couch and props his feet up on the table. "Let's talk about Mauro wanting the apartment to himself. Do I hear bells?" He inches his head toward the window like an idiot.

I smack him on the back of the head as I pass.

He holds it like I really hurt him. "Hey, that spot is exclusive for Ma." He rubs at it like the baby brother he is.

"Is all this for Maddie?" Cristian peers into the brown paper bag with a box of condoms in it that I left on the counter.

I walk over and snatch it away. "Just go so I can set up, shower and get ready for her."

"Oh, are you doing the deed tonight? Man, you move fast," Luca says, who's now relaxed with his hands behind his head and his feet on our coffee table.

"Right. Should I use your timetable? Wait two grinding songs and four shots?"

Cristian smiles over his bottle. "So, things are good if you're going to this much trouble." He checks out the apartment. It's cleaner than I've ever made it.

Luca jumps over the back of the couch. "Oh, I bet he's planning some kinky—" I run over, but Luca gets the fridge open before I can. "Someone's planning on making breakfast in the morning. Cut up fruit, eggs, bacon. I think those *are* bells I'm hearing."

I shut the fridge door. "Stop with the wedding bells shit."

He claps me on the shoulder. "It's not wedding bells, it's warning bells. They're trying to warn you this path you're headed down is the wrong way."

"Stop being such a commitment-phobe." Cristian hits Luca in the head with the top of the bottle.

"I am not. I'm a realist. One who says I'm much too young and much too attractive to settle down with one woman yet."

Cristian rolls his eyes. "Whatever. Anyway, you're really going to sleep with Madison tonight?" he asks me.

I look around and glance at my watch. "Did I just warp back to two thousand and eight where I would actually discuss my sex life with you?" I deadpan.

The two of them share a look and shrug.

A smile forms on Cristian's face. "That means he's serious about her." He gulps down the rest of his water.

"None of your fucking business. Now leave so I can set up."

"Where are you taking her for dinner?" Luca leans back, snagging a chip before I can take the bag away.

"Eddie V's."

"Pulling out the big guns." Luca chomps down on his chip. "You're willing to max out your credit card for her. Mama's going to be so proud when you pop the question." He claps me on the shoulder and steps closer to Cristian. "I'm just going to head over here because I don't want whatever you caught rubbing off on me."

"You're an asshole."

Cristian glances at Luca and then to me. "I think it's awesome. I'll go pack a bag and get out of your way."

"Seriously, you're not going to give him hell for this?" Luca calls out to Cristian's back. "You guys should thank your stars that Ma and Pa had me because otherwise your lives would be boring as hell."

"You do know you were a mistake, right?" Cristian calls down the hall.

Luca's face pales slightly, Cristian having hit his Achille's heel.

This is really a topic no one knows the answer to for sure because my parents would never admit it, but who plans to have three kids back to back? I'll let you ponder that for a minute while I razz my brother.

"I was not. If anyone was, you were." He points to Cristian's bedroom.

"Keep telling yourself that," I say.

"Either that or you were so ugly, Mom and Dad didn't want to take any more chances," Cristian says, popping his head out from his bedroom door.

Luca narrows his eyes. "Mama loves me the most anyways."

"Everyone knows I'm her favorite. Firstborn." I thumb at myself.

"I'm the baby. I'm the favorite. She hugs me tighter."

"Whatever, I'm the one who goes over there and checks on her all the time," Cristian says. "I go to the deli almost every day for lunch."

"Sorry, but I'm not sitting on my ass in a car my entire shift. I'm busy saving lives, not ruining people's days."

I purse my lips because Luca's got a point, but Cristian is doing me a solid by leaving so willingly so I don't say that out loud.

"You know who her favorite will be?" I say instead.

They both stare over at me.

"The one who gives her the first grandchild." I hold up my brown paper bag. "I'm a lot closer than either of you, so feel free to invest in a plaque with my name on it."

"Shit, you're going to make Luca take a redeye to Vegas and marry the first girl who says she's ovulating." Cristian laughs as he comes back down the hall, swinging his duffle bag over his shoulder.

"Fuck that. You can have the title then." Luca grabs his coat off the back of the couch. Standing by the door he pretends to rub his eyes. "It's just so hard, our boy is growing up." He opens the door, smiles and leaves.

"He's so competitive, I hope he doesn't take it as a challenge," I say.

We both laugh. I don't think either of us will be surprised if in nine months the first Bianco grandchild to be introduced to the world belongs to Luca.

"Let's hope it's the first time he can let a challenge go." Cristian's eyes find the bag in my hands. "I'll leave you to it. I'm on shift tomorrow so I won't be home until dinner. If for some reason you need more time, text me."

"Nah, I'm sure we'll be heading to the house in the morning. Thanks for staying with Mom and Dad for the night. I owe you one."

He heads to the front door. "Who said I'm staying at their house?" He waggles his eyebrows.

I tilt my head in confusion, I didn't think he was seeing anyone. "Then I don't owe you one."

He laughs and leaves but before the door can shut I hear him say hello to Mrs. Peterson. He just got stuck in that hallway for at least fifteen minutes.

Not wasting any time, I get everything set up for when I bring Madison back here tonight, then quickly shower and get ready.

This is the first time I've been really nervous for a date. This revelation should probably concern me, but instead it makes the smile on my face grow wider.

And just like that, I realize that I'm all in.

CHAPTER TWENTY-FOUR

Madison

The doorbell rings and the inside of my stomach feels like a bunch of monkeys climbing around a jungle gym.

Lauren and Vanessa each smile at me from where they sit on the bed.

"Do you want me to do the whole I answer and we make him wait thing?" Lauren slides off the mattress to stand.

"No, but thanks for the offer."

I leave Vanessa's room, descending the stairs while staring at the outline of Mauro in the small window next to the door.

"Stop staring you two. Go do something."

I don't turn around, but I don't have to in order to know that they don't move from their positions at the top of the stairs.

When I open the door, I almost can't believe what's waiting there for me.

Mauro's hair is gelled into a tousle of loose waves. He

wears a pair of dark jeans, a light sweater, and a jacket over top. Delectable doesn't even do him justice.

His gaze slowly roams up and down my body, his smile growing as his attention travels past the hem of my dress to my exposed legs. When he meets my eyes again, a calmness settles over me.

"You look breathtaking, Madison." He steps up, wrapping his arm around my back, pressing his lips to mine. "I want you to know that you absolutely take my breath away."

The scent of his cologne that I've only had the pleasure of smelling that one night at the game café, sends a zing of awareness to my lady parts and I clench my thighs.

"You don't look so bad yourself."

He smiles, not releasing me. "Thank you." He kisses my temple and his fingers run up and down my spine before settling on the small of my back.

We take each other's presence in for another moment until we head down my walkway to his truck. As promised, I wait for him to open up my door. When he slides in the driver's side he leans over and kisses me, teasing me with a swipe of his tongue. "I'm not sure I'm going to make it through dinner."

"We can skip dinner if you prefer." I wink, teasing him because I'm more than ready to feel him between my legs.

"Nope. I'm feeding you first. You're going to need your energy for what I have in mind."

All the papers and empty cups that usually fill Mauro's car are gone and the warm sensation in my chest reappears over the fact that he cleaned his truck for me.

"Where are we headed?" I ask once he's driving downtown.

"Eddie V's. Are you okay with seafood?"

"Definitely, but Mauro, that place is so expensive."

We're talking four dollar signs expensive. He doesn't need to spend that much money to impress me.

"It's where I *want* to take you." His fingers strum on the steering wheel as we wind through the traffic of downtown.

I watch him as he drives, casual and in control.

"Have you ever not been sure of yourself?" I ask, curious.

He glances over for a second. "You mean whether I could accomplish something?"

"Yeah, I guess. You always seem so confident in everything you do."

He shakes his head, almost to himself and stops at a red light. Turning to look right at me, I'm transfixed by him, those blue eyes are alive and bright tonight. My favorite shade.

"I wasn't confident with you. I mean I doubted myself when it came to the house at first, but I still felt comfortable that I'd finish it well. But with you...I don't know if it's because I have no control over your feelings or what, but the idea of me screwing up what's happening between us keeps me up at night."

The light turns green and without warning wetness coats my eyes.

You will not cry on your first date with him.

"Mauro," I sigh, my brain unable to process everything as my beating heart floats out of my chest and places itself in his lap, flopping around, begging to be his. I never knew a man like Mauro could be so sentimental and sweet, too.

"Jesus, I'm just full of cheesy shit lately. I could act arrogant and say how I don't care what you think, but it'd be a lie. I don't want to play games with you."

I reach over and touch his thigh, the roughness of the denim like light sandpaper on my palm. "I don't want to play games with you either."

He glances to the side at me and smiles. "I'm glad."

His hand comes down over top of mine and he webs our fingers together. We sit in the truck, letting the moment soak in. We just might be creating something worth fighting our demons for. If only those demons weren't so big and scary.

Stop it. I will not ruin this for myself.

Moments later, he pulls onto a street that's clearly marked permit parking only. Finding a spot, he puts a ballcap with CFD embroidered on the bill on the dashboard.

He eyes me for a second. "Remember the deal?"

I move my hand away from the handle of the door. "Yep." I act as though I wasn't about to push the door open and hop out.

He smirks and rounds the front of his truck until he reaches my door, opening it and offering me a hand.

As elegantly as someone can, I climb out of the large truck and he shuts the door behind me.

"So that works? The hat?" I ask.

He shrugs. "If it doesn't, Cristian will try to work his magic. One perk of being a civil serviceman." His hand finds mine again and we walk side by side on the sidewalk toward Rush street.

"I need one of those."

He chuckles. "You get a parking ticket and I'll handle it." His tone is all macho and I only find it utterly charming.

We arrive at the restaurant and are seated along the windows. After he orders steak and scallops, and I order tilapia, we laugh and enjoy each other's company as our legs brush along one another's and heated glances are exchanged over the rims of our wine glasses by candlelight. Mauro's ability to carry a conversation and also be a great listener shines through the entire meal. We opt to take a slice of cheesecake to go, both of us anxious to leave.

Once we're outside his apartment door, he pauses before inserting his key.

"I'm not being too presumptuous, am I?" he asks.

Who is he kidding? We've been working our way up to this all night and we both know it.

I slide my arm through his, snuggling into the warmth of his big body. "Not at all."

He smiles and inserts his key, pushing the door open for me.

"Is Cris..." The name dies on my lips when the line of small tea light candles that lead to his bathroom come into view.

The door shuts and his hands land on my arms, his lips coming down to my shoulder. "He's gone for the night."

My hand covers his and I fall back into his chest, taking in the scene of what I thought at first glance were real candles but I now see are actually those battery operated ones. Bending down I pick one up and laugh.

"I'm a firefighter." He shrugs and a flush of embarrassment washes over his face.

I place the faux candle back down and stand on my tiptoes, reaching up to rest my hand behind his neck. "I love it. Thank you so much." Pressing my lips to his, I let my body follow suit, needing the feel of him more than my next breath.

"You're worth it." He circles me around. "Follow the path."

I kick off my shoes leaving them at the door and follow the lighted path he made for me, past a bedroom and a bathroom to the end of the hall. The flickering of faux candlelight dies and I'm overcome by the vision of a million stars glowing all over his bedroom from a tiny projector he's set up in the corner.

"This is virgin worthy," I say in awe.

My heart beats a mile a minute as I take in his queen size bed in the middle of the room with a dark comforter slung over. A dresser and television are placed along the wall. The space is very minimalistic, but it suits him.

I circle around and he's staring at me, waiting for my reaction. "I absolutely love it, Mauro. You didn't have to do this all for me."

"Don't you see? I want you to know how much you mean to me. I don't want to just sleep with you, I want to make love to you."

I close my eyes, wondering if I'll ever not feel like this is all a dream. My hand runs along his cheek, and I meet his gaze, letting myself get lost in him. My other hand slides around my back, finding the zipper of my dress and pulling it down. The dress falls off my shoulders and cascades to the floor. I step out of it, leaving me in my black bra and panty set.

"What are you waiting for?" I ask in a soft voice.

His gaze dips and a low growl escapes his throat. "Damn, Madison. You are so fucking hot."

I smile at the compliment knowing he probably didn't want it to come out that way. Gorgeous and beautiful are amazing words, but the fact he couldn't control himself is so much better.

He pushes the hair off my neck, his eyes still taking me in. "I think you need to pinch me." He chuckles, bringing his lips to my neck as his hands slide up and down my back before resting on my hips.

I pinch him and he chuckles into my skin.

"You're still here," he murmurs, his teeth scraping along my collarbone.

"I am." Tightening my arms around him, I close my eyes at the feeling of his hands and mouth worshiping me.

He steps us back until the back of my legs hit the mattress and he stops, shrugging out of his jacket and tossing it into the corner of the room. Kicking off his shoes, he pulls his sweater off, revealing abs I'd like to explore for days before coming up for air. Mesmerized by the indentations, it's not until his jeans fall to the ground that I realize he's now in front of me in only his boxer briefs.

No one would blame me if I passed out right now because he really is the perfect specimen of a man, right down to his heart of gold.

His eyes land on mine, keeping contact as he inches toward me, his hands taking my face in them, making sure I'm where he wants me once his lips reach mine. Our tongues tangle and he nudges my body to move onto the mattress.

I lower myself to the bed and he follows. We climb up until my head hits the pillow. The space between my thighs throbs when the weight of his body finally rests on top of mine. Our legs tangle and our hands explore, both of us surrendering to the desire ebbing and flowing between us.

His mouth is hot and sinful, and a moan escapes my throat when his steel length grinds into my core. My pelvis rises, desperate to feel the result of his desire for me again. His fingers thread into my hair, our mouths now frantic. Never in my life have I lost myself in a man so quickly.

A thrill shoots through my body when his fingers pull down the straps of my bra, his lips following the path of his hands so they don't miss an inch of my bare flesh. My fingers scrape at his back and my hips continue to rise and fall.

At this rate, I won't make it to the finish line. This man, the boy I dreamed of when I was a teen, is worshiping my body like I'm his favorite dessert—tasting and savoring until he's licking the bowl for one last morsel.

"I'm never going to get enough of you, Madison." His voice is a throaty whisper and I dig my fingernails into his back.

My other bra strap falls off my shoulder and his hands reach around my back to undo the clasp. Picking up the fabric, he tosses it aside and his hands cup my breasts, his thumbs running over my nipples while he licks his lips.

"Mauro." My fingers tighten on his strong shoulders as they flex with his movements.

His mouth covers my nipple and he sucks and twirls his tongue around the hard bud. Need consumes me. Wrapping my legs around his torso, he looks up at me, a smile teasing his lips as he moves to my other nipple.

Just when I think I'm going to lose all control, he flips over on his back, rolling me over on top of him. His hands burrow under my panties and grab at the delicate flesh of my ass.

I grind against his thick cock, my just-out-of-reach orgasm pulsating between my legs, begging for more.

"I want you over and over again tonight." My lips crash against his and his hands squeeze my ass cheeks, pushing me down harder into him.

"Not a problem." He stops the kiss for a moment, his eyes finding mine. "Tonight is ours."

I can have him over and over again.

The realization coils the need inside of me like a tight elastic band on the verge of breaking.

"Take me now, Mauro," I beg, our lips devouring one another again.

His fingers slide my panties down my legs and I help by kicking them off. He reaches over to the side, taking a condom from the nightstand.

Flipping me back over, his palms slide over my legs, forcing them wide and his face nestles between my legs.

"Mauro," I plead.

"There's no way I'm not tasting you first." That cocky smirk that once drew my attention to him spreads across his face.

Dipping down, his tongue slides along my slit, teasing my

clit and then sucking the greedy flesh into his mouth. His hands slide up my bare stomach, each palm taking control of a breast, tweaking my nipple while his mouth works me into sheer bliss.

Pushing all thoughts away, my hands burrow into his hair, gripping tight as my orgasm crests then spirals out of control.

I scream out, all the tension in my body falling away as I melt into the bed, melt into him. I open my eyes to the sound of foil ripping. Mauro's removed his boxer briefs and has positioned himself between my legs.

I don't want to stare or anything, but this is the first chance I've had to look at his cock. I have to say—no complaints.

Tentatively, his body lowers to mine, inching his way into my depths as he kisses me senseless until he's fully inside me, filling me completely.

"Mad, you feel so fucking good." He rocks a little and I pull my knees up, my toes curling from the euphoria of his hard length rocking into me.

"So do you."

Our bodies move as one as the pressure of our release threads through our veins, tugging at our nerve endings in a desperate attempt to erupt. His heated body on top of me, the light stubble on his face running along my jaw, the sinful moans falling from his lips the deeper and harder he claims me—all of it makes my head spin as I lose myself in pleasure with him once again.

"Ohhhh, Mauro!" The thread that Mauro wound so tight inside of me snaps and my toes curl on top of his comforter.

He stares down, watching while I lose myself. His breathing labors for a second and he props himself up on his elbows, his gaze locking with mine.

"Trust me, Mad. I know we can make it. Just stick with me."

I reach up and grab his face between my hands, smashing our mouths together until he thrusts and then stills inside of me on a groan I catch with my lips.

Both of us spent, Mauro falls on top of me and slides off, his fingers grazing down my glistening skin, kissing me slowly and sweetly.

There's no chance I haven't already fallen hopelessly for this man. Not when the reality is even better than what I'd conjured up in my imagination all those years ago.

CHAPTER TWENTY-FIVE

Mauro

I'm still wrapping my brain around our first time together. Never have I felt that close to someone during the act. Like I wanted to crawl inside of her and make myself a home so I could stay there forever.

My hands wouldn't move fast enough, my mouth unable to get enough of exploring every inch of her skin. There's so much more that I want to discover about what makes her cry out, what makes her whimper, even better, what makes her beg.

"Cheesecake?" I ask, throwing on a pair of sweats as I return from the bathroom.

"Perfect." She moves to get up, holding the sheet tight against her body.

Modest now, huh? An hour ago she was the one who stripped her dress off.

"Here." I grab a t-shirt out of my drawer and place it over her head.

She looks down at it and smiles. "Where do you guys get

these?" She holds the cotton away from her chest and reads it out loud. "Firemen do it with a big hose?" She quirks an eyebrow at me.

"My mom bought it. I don't think she understood what hose was referring to."

She laughs. "She doesn't seem like the kind of woman who would let you walk around like that."

I put my hand out in front of me and help her up from the bed.

Damn. I like how she looks in my shirt way too much.

Cute as hell with the neck draping over and almost exposing her shoulder while the length of it reaches down to her knees.

I could get used to this.

I usher her forward down the hall, letting the faux candles stay lit because I'm way too lazy at the moment to turn off one hundred tea lights.

"She gets them for us every Christmas. My brothers and I each get one for our career. Half the time we're cracking up and she has no idea why we think they're so funny." I grab the cheesecake I left abandoned in the takeout bag on the end table before following her down the hallway.

With two forks, I meet her at the counter. Forking off a bite, I place it in front of her lips.

She opens her mouth and allows me to feed her. I didn't realize this would be so damn hot that I'd have a chub again after only five minutes.

"You know what this needs, right?" she asks after swallowing down her bite.

"Tastes pretty good as it is. Not as good as you though." I wink at her and like I knew she would, she blushes.

She walks toward her purse. "Chocolate. Always chocolate." Opening a smaller purse than I usually see her carrying around, she pulls out a bag of half eaten M&Ms.

With dedication and precision, she presses them into the top of the cheesecake, pops one in her mouth and then opens her mouth for me to give her another bite.

I do as requested because I'd be an idiot if I didn't. A moan that would put me at full salute escapes her and her eyes close.

Fuck me right now.

"So good." She grabs an M&M and holds it up in front of my mouth.

I open and she places it gently on my tongue. Without any hesitation, she takes the fork from my hands and this time she feeds me. She's right, it needed the chocolate.

I've been eating cheesecake my entire life plain without knowing what I was missing.

Reminds me of my life pre-Madison.

"Should I ask why you carry around a half-eaten bag of M&Ms in your purse?" I pick her up by her hips and prop her up on the kitchen counter and then find my spot right between her legs, picking up the fork to continue feeding her.

If this was my life, I'd die a happy man.

"Well, I have a bit of a chocolate addiction so when I have a hankering for something sweet or I'm stressed out, I grab a handful."

"Why not eat the entire bag at one time?"

She tilts her head and for the first time ever she looks at me like I'm stupid. Except this is Madison, so it somehow looks like a polite gesture coming from her. "Did you see my high school yearbook picture?"

I set the cheesecake down on the counter, reaching my hands behind her, pulling her center toward my stomach. My fingers delve under my t-shirt to cup her ass.

"What's your point?"

Again with the head tilt. I'm a smart enough man not to

fight this issue with her, so I'll let it go, but I'll make it my mission to let her know I'll take her however she comes.

"How perfect that we have a candy made after us." I nod at the package. "M&Ms. Mauro and Madison."

She giggles. "I think it would be Madison and Mauro."

"You do, do you?" My fingers skim up the t-shirt to tickle her ribs.

She squirms and her arms are rigid at her sides, trying to free herself from my torturous hands, all the while her sweet and melodic laugh echoes through my apartment.

Unable to stop myself, I allow my hands to run up the length of her torso, forgetting the tickling and cupping her breasts.

"You play dirty," she says in a breathy voice as she stops fighting me.

"You complaining?" My mouth salivates I want to taste her again so bad.

"Never." Her arms loop around my shoulders and her thighs tighten around my stomach. "You can tease me whenever you like, as long as you finish what you start."

"Hmm...I like the sound of that." I dip my mouth to her neck, licking up her jaw to her earlobe. "I'm going to run to my room, wait here until I get back."

"Why?" she asks when I dislodge from her hold.

"Condom. We're doing it right where you are."

A soft smile crosses her lips. "But there's some right there." She points to a box of condoms with a bow on them at the edge of the kitchen counter.

How did I miss those?

I pick up the box and sure enough, there's a sticky note attached that says, 'Be safe, Love Ma's favorite.'

I rip the box open and take out one of the foil wrappers. "Luca," I sigh as I eliminate the distance between us.

"They're Luca's?" she asks, stopping me from opening the foil packet.

"No, he bought them for us."

A horrified look crosses her face. "Maybe you guys are too close."

"No, no. It's not like that. We were talking about who was my mom's favorite and a comment was made about grandchildren." The hell if I'm going to tell her that comment was made by me. "This is his way of trying to secure his spot as number one son."

"Oh." She still looks surprised and a little worried that I'm going to rate her performance with my brother's tomorrow.

Ten plus if you're wondering.

"Hey." I place my hand on her cheek. "We don't talk about women like conquests or judging our partners or anything like that. It's literally his joke."

She smiles and I lean forward biting lightly on her bottom lip with my teeth. Once I'm there I figure I need to seduce her all over again, so I keep the kiss going until the worrying that's occupying her retreats and I'm all she's thinking about.

Her arms wind around my shoulders again and I slide her forward more, needing her as close to me as I can have her. Our tongues tangle and slide as one, eliciting moans from each of us.

I grab the hem of the t-shirt pulling it off her. A shiver runs through her body, but her feet press on the waistband of my sweats and I take my hands off her ass for a moment to help. I slide the condom down my length and wrap my arms around her again.

"Jesus, Mad, you're everything and more. So much more than I dreamed of." Holding her up, I swing us around so her back is pressed against the wall. Keeping her in place with my thigh, I position myself at her entrance and sink into her again with a groan.

Her fingers dig into my shoulder blades and her teeth tug on my ear as I fill her up. Never will I get enough of her. Making love to her in my bed was something, but under the kitchen lights when I can watch myself moving in and out of her is making me lose control. Her tits bounce in my face and shatter my small reserve of self-control.

Her blue eyes are laced with arousal and need for me and it's my undoing. I slam into her over and over again, claiming her as mine.

"Mauro." My name slips from her lips like a plea to never stop and as much as I'd love that, I'm close to blowing my load right now.

Rotating my hips, sweat trickles down my face dripping between our bodies and I thrust into her again and again, switching between watching her expressions and where we're joined.

"Mauro!" she screams, her fingernails digging into my flesh, her slick heat convulsing around my shaft.

Her sweet cries and the sound of me sliding in and out of her body throws me over the edge I was teetering on. Inaudible words ring out between the two of us as I spill into the condom and she crashes in my arms, spent and exhausted.

"You want to go to bed?" I ask after I've regained my ability to form a complete thought.

She nods, holding on to me.

Carrying her to my bedroom along the lit path, her breathing slow and steady against me, might be the highlight of my night. I lay her down on my bed, slide the covers out and tuck her in.

"I'll be right back." I kiss her forehead and disappear into my bathroom to dispose of the condom.

When I return to the room, she's wide-eyed and watching me. Joining her under the covers, I waste no time in pulling her into my arms.

After what we just shared, I know it's time for me to explain to her my hesitation to get close to anyone. Even though I've let her in, and I'll hurt no matter what happens to us, I need her to know. I just pray she doesn't judge me for the decisions I've made.

"You tire me out." She kisses my chest, placing her hand over where she kissed like she's sealing her affection into my skin. Little does she know, but she's already branded me. Not in a way that anyone else can see, but in a way that only I can feel.

I brush my knuckles down her arm. "Do you ever wonder why I'm scared of love?"

She rests her chin on my chest, staring up at me. "I knew you had reservations, but I didn't think you were scared."

I tuck a strand of her long hair behind her ear, memorizing the different shades of blue in her eyes. "I need you to know something about me before we move forward and I'm hoping that it doesn't change anything."

She bolts up, pulling the sheet with her, effectively leaving me exposed and naked.

"Calm down." I loosen the grip of her hands on the sheets and they fall back in place, as does she. "It's not like I murdered someone."

"Do you have a kid?" she asks.

"Remember the whole conversation before I took you up against the wall?" I raise an eyebrow.

She laughs. "Oh yeah. Okay just tell me. Is this something I should close my eyes for?"

"No, baby, no."

The affectionate pet name falls from my lips unexpectedly and I'm as surprised as she looks. She doesn't say anything, just smiles, and I take that to mean that it's okay to use it from this point forward.

Inhaling a deep breath, I decide to let it all out. Tell her the truth and wait for her judgment. "My buddy Hunter, the one who died in the fire...the one I was going to partner up with?"

She nods.

"After he passed, I was tasked with cleaning out his locker so that Cailin wouldn't have to do it. She was already falling deeper and deeper into a depression as each day passed. The surprise of his death was too much for her to take. I mean there's always the worry in the back of your mind, but you don't let that fear stop you from living your life. Anyway..."

She's silent in my arms, her hands running up the side of my stomach. Back and forth like she's assuring me that she's here.

"He had a cell phone in there. One I'd never seen him use before. I didn't think much of it because it didn't turn on right away, so I figured maybe it was an old one and he was going to trade it in or donate it to the battered women's shelter. I took it home and charged it up to make sure it worked. Other than the phone there was just his personal stuff, some notes from Cailin, the card we put on his locker after Devin was born. I packed it all in a box and took it over to their house."

"So, I'm guessing the cell phone wasn't what you thought, but I'm unsure what this has to do with you." She slides up closer to look me in the eye.

"Remember I mentioned that I had an ex-girlfriend named Jenna?"

She nods.

"We broke up six months ago."

She nods.

"Hunter died six months ago."

"I know." Her sweet, innocent eyes look on at me, not getting where I'm going with this.

"Put those two things together and add the cell phone."

"You're making me solve a case to figure out the answer. Wouldn't that be Cris—" She abruptly stops talking. "Oh my God, Mauro." She covers her mouth. "No way!"

This time it's me nodding. "Yeah. They'd been having an affair for months before he died. The text messages were excruciating to read. I'm thinking he'd gotten the phone well after their first night had started, but there were sexts and shit talking about me and Cailin on there."

She rests her body on top me, squeezing me in her arms. "I'm so sorry, that's like the ultimate betrayal."

I love the fact she's trying to make me feel better. "I'm good now, Mad, thanks though."

She falls back to her side. "I see why you'd have trouble trusting people."

"You've helped me get over that. There's something about you...I know you'd never purposely hurt me. But that's not why I told you all this." Again, I tuck a strand of hair behind her ear, delaying the inevitable. "Cailin doesn't know."

"What?" Her head rears back, judgment clear in her tone.

"I couldn't hurt her and Devin that way. Destroy the man he was to them for what? It wouldn't change anything—he was dead. There were no text messages about him wanting to desert his family for Jenna. He's gone and Cailin doesn't need that baggage to deal with on top of everything else it will take for her to move on with her life."

"But..."

"I'm not changing my mind. All I need to know is if that changes the way you see me."

She sits up, straddling me, her hands on my cheeks. "I understand. I do. Did you think I wouldn't?"

"The only person who knows besides you is my mom. When we were at the deli, that's what we were arguing about. She thinks Cailin needs to know because she believes all women know when their husbands stray and it would confirm what she believes Cailin already knows deep down. But Cailin's never mentioned any suspicions to me so I'm not going there. Other than you and my mom, I've told no one and I want to keep it that way."

She nods. "Okay."

"You're really not going to argue with me?"

She shakes her head. "No. It's your decision, but what *I* need to know, is whether that experience makes you distrust not only the women you date but your other co-workers? I need to know that you're safe on the job." She runs a hand through my hair as she waits for me to answer.

"I can't say it doesn't fuck with my head a little, but you'll never do that to me, right?"

She collapses on top of me, her hair a veil on either side of my head. "Never," she says with conviction.

I roll us over and spread her legs, ready for round three before we find sleep. She happily obliges and after tonight, I know I'll never be prepared to give her up.

CHAPTER TWENTY-SIX

Madison

With a few weeks of bliss between me and Mauro, fall has rolled into Chicago, bringing the changing colors of the leaves, cooler weather, and stores full of items in preparation for Halloween and Thanksgiving.

The house is ready for the interiors to be installed and I'm practically giddy. This is my favorite part of any flip—when things start to look pretty.

"This house needs some color," Mauro comments, grabbing my ass on his way to the kitchen.

I pull the paint roller away from the wall. "It's neutral. Neutral sells."

"How about red? Red hot just like you babe."

"Spare us, please," Luca groans walking into the house with a sub in his hand.

"You don't see enough heart attacks that you decide to witness your own after eating all that processed meat?" I bring the roller back to the wall, running the cool gray color on the surface.

"Yeah, Ma's not gonna like you. This is the Italian." He holds up his sub. "You keep lecturing people about deli meat and you'll drive them out of business. Then Mauro will be on the black list. Actually." He pauses to think. "Go ahead and put up a sign in the front window saying how bad deli meat is for your health."

Mauro comes back into the room, pushing him with his shoulder and then wrapping his arms around my waist, lifting my feet from the ground. I let the roller drop in the paint tray and his lips find mine as they often do these days.

"Get a room." Luca disappears and Mauro quickly carries me to the half of bath that's yet to be finished.

He cradles me in the corner where the sink and cabinet will go, his hands making quick work of my overalls, letting them fall to my waist.

"Hold up cowboy, we've got a house full of people," I say with a smile.

This isn't to say we haven't already made quick work of most of the rooms in this house. The dining room table has been our favorite spot this week.

"So what? Like none of them have sex." His lips are exploring my neck, his hands halfway up my chest, prepped and ready to cup me.

"Ew! Come on guys," Cristian says as he walks in the room with his uniform on.

If Mauro had closed the door, there's a good chance he would have had this way with me. You snooze, you lose.

Mauro glances behind him quickly and his hands might fall to my hips, but his lips are still traveling over my neck. "Aren't you out of district?"

"I just got off, but if this is why you need my help tonight, then I'm out. If you'd keep your hands off each other, the house would probably be done by now."

Mauro stops and puts me all back together, fastening my

overalls back in place and kissing me on the forehead. "We'll continue this later."

Leading me out first, I go back to painting the wall. "Hi, Cristian. Thanks for helping."

"Yeah, yeah. You owe me. Your friend is still giving me the cold shoulder and her dad keeps asking when I'm going to make good on our date. I'd lie, but I think he's having me tailed." Cristian sits on the dining room table.

Mauro and I share a look that has me biting my lip remembering how he took me from behind last night right where Cristian is sitting.

"Jesus." Cristian hops off the table. "Is there anywhere I can sit in here?"

Mauro and I laugh uncontrollably. "Not really." Mauro shrugs like it's no big deal, while my face heats with embarrassment.

"I have to hear you screaming my brother's name like he's God all fucking night and now you drag me to a place where I have to imagine the two of you fucking in every corner?"

"Tell me about it. He grabs her ass every time he passes her." Luca joins the party, crumpling up the sub wrapper in his hands. "It's disgusting. These innocent eyes cannot unsee what these two do."

We all laugh because Luca's eyes have probably seen more than all of us combined.

"Come to the backyard. I need your help with this fountain." Mauro winks at me. "Be right back."

I place the roller down in the tray, not willing to let them handle this huge-ass fountain alone. It could very well land on all three of them. I linger by the window looking from afar to make it seem like I think they're macho, but I'm ready to lend a hand at any second.

They each evaluate the situation and offer their take on how to move it. Cristian even looks like he's doing a little diagram with his hands, directing the other two. Luca and Mauro squint their eyes and lift the edge, quickly putting it down. I told Mauro we should hire a service but he swears him and his brothers can handle this.

The statue isn't even lifted off the base yet and they're arguing.

"You bringing Maddie to dinner on Sunday?" Cristian asks, pretending to see what's under the fountain.

They're all delaying the inevitable.

"Yeah."

"Big step." Luca chimes in.

He's right, it is. And though I'm looking forward to it, I am a bit nervous still.

"Ma's already met her. I had her at the sandwich shop, she loved her, told me she saw our future together. I'm not shaking in my boots." Mauro's confidence shines through and I can only hope he's right.

"What about the firehouse? You take her there yet?" Luca asks.

Mauro's already shaking his head. "Not yet." The sureness of his tone evaporates like sun beating down on a puddle.

"She knows you're a firefighter, what could you possibly be afraid of?" Cristian asks.

I hate that I'm eavesdropping. Especially since I've shifted so that I'm not right in front of the window anymore, proving how badly I still feel like I need reassurance that he likes me.

"Let's just move this fucking monstrosity, okay? You're always jabbering on like a bunch of chicks." If I wasn't supposed to hear their conversation, I'd scold him for his depiction of women. Besides, I know what he's afraid of and they don't.

I give it to the three of them, they somehow get the fountain moved to the outside of the yard where the service is supposed to pick it up tomorrow.

The three of them walk toward the house and I run back to my roller, trying to lather on some layers.

"Let's order pizza," Luca says, finding his spot on the table, watching me paint.

The rest of the crew is packing up for the day and we all wave and say goodbye.

"You just ate," I say, not turning around.

"I'm a growing boy, Maddie."

"I can't eat all that cheese, it'll upset my stomach. I'll get a salad," Cristian says.

"Pussy," Mauro coughs out.

Cristian comes up to my side and grabs the edger, stepping up on the ladder and helping out. He's changed out of his uniform now and is in a tapered pair of athletic pants and a t-shirt that says *Cop-A-Feel* and an arrow pointing down. For some reason, he's still wearing his belt with his gun on it.

"There's something about a police officer out of uniform with his gun still on his belt painting a wall. Where's a camera when you need it?" Luca pretends to snap a picture.

"I'm not going to lay this thing down just anywhere. Besides, it's better than the two of you idiots watching her work."

Mauro comes up behind me, his hand covering mine on the roller handle, moving it up and down the wall as he grinds against me. "Here, I'll help."

I slide my ass out, effectively moving him away. "That's not helping."

He laughs, pulling his phone out. "Gino's or Lou's?"

"Gino's," we all agree.

"Damn, we're all Gino's?" Luca asks, disbelief in his tone.

"I told you, she's already like a Bianco," Mauro says and I

try not to let my heart leap out my chest, purposely ignoring his comment.

Madison Bianco.

I already knew when I was sixteen years old writing it on my binders that it had a nice ring to it.

CHAPTER TWENTY-SEVEN

Mauro

This is a first for me. I've never brought a girl to my parents' for Sunday dinner. Not even Jenna. Ma never really cared for Jenna. Women's intuition I think.

Opening the door to my parents' place, the aromas that still make my mouth water hit me full force. I still feel the anticipation of sitting down for a meal that will stuff me full for days. Okay, I'll eat the leftovers she sends us home with later tonight.

Madison's hand is clammy in my own. I squeeze it to tell her not to worry, but her teeth are still nibbling at her bottom lip like they did most of the drive over here.

I purposely got here before Luca and Cristian. It's a rarity that we'll all be present for the dinner—usually one or two of us are on shift.

My dad comes out of the kitchen, his apron already stained red but sadly not enough to cover up the writing on it.

Madison giggles but tries to hide her response when she sees the words, *If you like my meatballs you should taste my sausage*. I'm not sure my mom understands the humor in the English language sometimes.

"Madison, the smarty pants. Welcome." He extends his arms, gripping her by the shoulders and pressing a kiss on each cheek. "Mauro." He ruffles my hair and kisses me on each cheek as well. "Come. Come." He disappears through the archway of the kitchen, where I know Mama will be found.

Our house is small, a typical Chicago bungalow with three bedrooms. Each room smaller than the next. My bedroom moved to the basement as soon as I could escape Cristian at fourteen.

I'm eager to give her the tour, wanting more alone time with her even though we just got here.

In the kitchen, my mom is breading and frying chicken breasts while gravy simmers on the stove. She has all the salad preparations for Cristian on the small butcher block.

"Ma," I say, coming up behind her and pressing my lips to her cheek. She pats my hand on her shoulder. The one she's not currently using to hold the chicken.

"Mauro," she says my name like she usually does, with love pouring out of every syllable, like I've done something to make her proud just by saying hello.

"Madison is here," I whisper and she must've momentarily forgotten because she seems a little alarmed.

"Oh." She whips around, chicken dripping down to the floor. "Hi. Hold on." She hems and haws on what to do so I take the chicken from her hands and place it on the plate.

Rushing to the sink, she thoroughly washes her hands for thirty-seconds—as always—singing the happy birthday song in Italian. Madison probably already thinks we're a bunch of nut cases.

"Hi Madison, right?" she asks before greeting her much the way my father did except she pulls her into her arms catching Madison by surprise.

"Maddie is fine. Thank you for having me."

"I'm so happy you came. You're welcome anytime." Her eyes find mine across the room and she smiles her proudest grin, the one that says I did good, like when I joined the Chicago Fire Department.

I wash my hands at the sink, drying them on a towel.

"Can I help?" Madison asks like the good guest I knew she'd be.

"No. You go sit and enjoy yourself with Mauro." She shoos us out of the kitchen as usual. It's her domain.

We leave my parents much to Maddie's argument about helping and earning her meal.

"Come on, I'll show you where I slept in high school. Your fantasy come to life."

She swats me in the stomach and I corner her before the basement stairs, caging her into the wall like I love to do. "Tell me no part of you wants to know where I slept in high school. Did you ever imagine it for yourself?"

Her cheeks redden. "Keep it up and you'll be using your hand like you did in high school instead of my mouth," she whispers in my ear.

My head falls back in laughter. "This is me backing off." I hold up my hands in the air and nod to the basement stairs.

She follows behind me down to the wood-paneled basement. The smell down here is the same as I remember it and it makes me a little nostalgic for a time when this house was crawling with so much testosterone I thought it'd bust the walls down.

My parents haven't changed the space at all. My bed still sits in the corner, a small table next to it with an alarm clock. The guitar I pretended to play to impress girls in the corner.

The chair I played my video games in sitting front and center of the television.

I drop down to the bed. "This is where it all went down. Lube, my hand and a lot of dirty magazines lost their lives here."

She sits down in the chair, watching me like I'm a different person than the one she walked in with.

"Come." I pat the spot next to me. "I promise I don't bite."

She laughs, standing and coming over to my side. "I kind of like it when you do."

Rolling her over, I kiss her lips, nibbling at her bottom lip. "You know I aim to please." I gently bite all over her neck and jaw.

She swats me away. "We are not doing this in your parents' house."

I slide my hands up her sweater, finding a camisole that's fitted to her body. "Double wrapped? Not cool. I'm supposed to have easy access all the time." I let my thumbs trace over her breasts, finding two peaked nipples hungrily looking for attention. "Maybe I'm wrong."

"Maybe you should reserve judgment until you've investigated the situation." She eyes me, smiling over the fact she's not wearing a bra under her camisole.

Great. Now I'm hard.

"You going commando on me, too?" I fiddle with the button and zipper of her jeans.

"You'll have to wait to find that out." Her hand lands on mine, stopping me.

"You expect me to go all day without knowing?"

She slides out from under me. "This is my first time in your parents' house. I'm not about to let you get to third base." As she stands at the side of my bed, footsteps start to sound from overhead. Seconds later they're joined by loud Italians talking.

Madison winks and unbuttons her jeans and pries the edges open. A simple pair of red panties greet me that say, *Hose Connection Here* with an arrow pointing down.

"Come." I wave her over, sitting on the edge of my bed now, adjusting my hard-on.

Surprisingly she obliges and stands in front of me as I pull down her jeans a little bit.

"I love them." I press my lips right below her belly button.

She doesn't fight me, so I take the opportunity to slide my finger under the crotch of her panties, feeling how wet she already is.

"Hey." She backs up, zipping up her jeans, my obsession quickly covered up.

"What did I do to you that you're punishing me so?" I haul her onto my lap and she winds her arms around my neck.

"Gotta keep you on your toes." She kisses my cheek and the scent of her perfume overwhelms me in the best way possible.

I will never get enough of this, of us.

Small feet scurry down the stairs and she bolts up off my lap.

"Uncle Mauro! Uncle Mauro!" Devin runs across the room right into my arms.

I'm surprised to see him, but I hug him back. "What's up Little Man? I didn't know you were coming today." I ruffle his blonde locks and hold my hand up for a high five. "This is Madison, my girlfriend."

He stares her down and turns back to me without saying hello.

Another set of footsteps come down the stairs, a voice calling for Devin and my entire body tenses.

Cailin turns the corner and her head rears back in shock for a second.

I know things are about to get complicated when I hear Madison's sigh.

CHAPTER TWENTY-EIGHT

Madison

"Hey, Cailin." Mauro stands, holding her son, Devin, in his arms.

"Hi. We were at the sandwich shop and your mom invited me to dinner. I hope it's okay that we came."

Mauro glances at me, letting Devin slide down to the floor. He runs to his mother as Mauro settles at my side. "You remember Madison?"

Cailin's eyes set on Mauro's hand on my hip and then raises to meet my eyes. "I do. Nice to see you."

"You as well." I slide an inch closer to Mauro.

Jealousy? Maybe.

As if the uncomfortable static suffocating the room wasn't enough, two more footsteps sound on the stairs and Luca stops at the bottom, a piece of bread in his hand.

His gaze investigates the scene, his eyes shifting in each of our directions.

"What's up guys?" He steps farther into the room, leaning

toward Cailin and placing a kiss on her cheek. "Ma said you were coming today. How are you doing?"

Cailin kisses his cheek back and the sad expression that crosses her face has me feeling bad for feeling possessive over Mauro. She's grieving and here I am thinking she wants to steal my boyfriend. She just needs support from someone who understands what she's going through.

"What's up, Maddie?" Luca greets me with the same kiss on the cheek. "Mauro." He nods.

"Hey." Devin tugs on Luca's Bears jersey.

Luca pretends to circle around completely missing Devin. Cailin smiles watching the scene unfold as Devin runs to the other side of Luca, but he turns around the other direction.

"Here!" Devin yells, his hands reaching up in the air.

Luca finally glances down with a surprised look on his face. "Oh. I didn't see you down there." He picks him up and flies him around the room like he's an airplane, complete with zooming noises.

Devin laughs uncontrollably, drool falling from his mouth. "Let's go steal a meatball," Luca whispers and the two fly upstairs.

Leaving the tension to suffocate us again.

"I'm going to go insist that your mom let me help in the kitchen." I kiss Mauro on the cheek, his hand firm on my hip in a gesture that tells me he doesn't want me to leave. But I can't handle this tension and if Mauro can trust me after what Jenna did to him, I can surely trust him.

"She never lets anyone help her," Cailin comments as I pass her by to reach the stairs. "I've tried and she always pushes me out of the kitchen."

I didn't really need her opinion. I mean, I'm doing this to be nice so she can have some alone time with Mauro. I'd much rather be here in the basement making out with my boyfriend than cutting up lettuce.

"I'll give it a shot. I think she's just used to having boys around. Maybe with a woman coming around now, she'll appreciate the help."

"And that woman is you?" A hollow laugh leaks out of her. "Slow down there, *Madison*, you two aren't married."

"Cailin," Mauro warns, his eyes shooting me a look of apology.

"What? I was just saying you guys have been dating for like two days..."

Mauro removes his attention from her causing her gaze to fall at her feet.

"Madison, I'm sure my mom would love the help. I'll be right up to join you."

I walk up the steps wondering what their conversation will consist of now.

"I thought we were clear about this," Mauro says to Cailin before I'm out of earshot.

"I know you said you like her, but come on, Mauro, you just broke up with Jenna. She's a rebound and she's acting like—"

"Enough, Cailin. I'm not sure where you think you get any say in the person I decide to spend time with."

Not really interested in hearing any more from Cailin's mouth, I wind my way back to the kitchen. I will busy myself with whatever task Mrs. Bianco deems me worthy of.

I wasn't expecting the small space to be packed full of people, all speaking Italian with their hands moving around like rapid fire. There are mostly women, but a few men are sprinkled around the table, eating the samples the women are shoving in their faces.

"Welcome to Italian life." Cristian's voice from behind surprises me and I jump. He grins. "Where's Mauro?"

"He's downstairs with Cailin," I say.

His lips draw straight, but he smiles to try and cover it up.

Yeah, I feel the same.

For the next three minutes, Cristian introduces me to his aunts and uncles, cousins and family friends who don't have family nearby. Everyone seems confused as to why if I belong to Mauro, Cristian is the one introducing me. I ignore the ache in the pit of my stomach as I wonder whether Cailin might always be a problem for us.

Quickly, I refute my assumptions. She lost her husband, I can't be that heartless to not have empathy for what she's going through. Finding comfort with the man closest to her husband doesn't seem that strange. Even if her husband was a piece of shit, but she doesn't know that.

Mrs. Bianco sits me at the table, placing lettuce on a cutting board. "Salad?" she asks like this is the only thing I could really help her with.

"Got it."

She smiles, her palm rubbing on my shoulders before she walks away.

I'm busy cutting the lettuce and the tomatoes up while running through the possibilities of what could be going on downstairs. Eventually Mauro appears in the doorway.

At this point I've worked myself up so much I'm not sure I can even look at him. All those doubts from ten years ago have resurfaced. Cailin is the tall, curvy blonde that someone like him belongs with.

"Mauro!" an uncle hollers and pulls him into his arms. He smacks his cheek, says something in Italian and both their eyes wander to me.

Mauro's lips tip down and he nods to his uncle, responding in Italian. An aunt smacks him on the back of the head on his way over to me, but then grabs his head and kisses him on the cheek. The entire way, Mauro ignores the pats, hugs, and kisses from his family as his gaze stays glued on me.

Once he reaches me, I'm a ball of nerves, trying to cut up a cucumber nonchalantly. I don't even know how that's supposed to look, but I don't want him to know all the messed up things that have been going through my head.

Bending down, he kisses my cheek. "Sorry about that," he whispers and sits down next to me. The air between us crackles with electricity like it usually does when we're less than six feet apart.

I shrug, continuing my job of making the salad.

"So Ma gave you a job?" He smiles, watching me.

"I think this might be the only thing she trusted me with, but it's something."

His arm stretches across the back of my chair, his lips landing right below my ear. "I want you so bad right now," he says softly.

The heat he stirs in my body rises up to my cheeks. "Sure, elbow deep in lettuce? That's your turn on?" I whisper.

He slides his chair closer to me, his knee pressing against mine, his hand finding my thigh. Way too high on my thigh I may add.

"I want you every second of every day, but the fact that my mom trusted you to make anything says how much you already fit in here. My uncles scorned me for leaving you alone. Said I'm lucky my uncle Mikey isn't here. He'd kick my ass. Or hit on you." He winks and I can't help but smile. "They're right. I shouldn't have left you alone." His teeth snatch my earlobe and when he pulls, shudders travel all the way down to my clit.

I hope this phase of never getting enough of one another never dies. Though I know in the back of my head that I'm bound to lose my shine as far as Mauro is concerned at some point.

"Mama!" Cristian yells and Mauro bolts up out of his chair.

I turn to find Mrs. Bianco's hand on the counter as though she's holding herself up. Cristian grabs her by the waist and she lets him hold her until Mr. Bianco comes over and takes the place of his son.

"Maria. Maria," he says her name like it's a prayer.

"LUCA!" Mauro yells. Everyone else is looking around for the paramedic in the family.

"A fire again? That's Mauro's department…" His voice dips seeing his mom in the arms of his dad, pale and tired. "What's going on?" He rushes to her side, his fingers already on her neck. "Ma?"

She shakes her head, speaking in Italian and shooing all of them away from her.

"No. Let me grab my bag."

"I'll get it." Mauro claps him on the shoulder and then weaves through the throes of people.

"It's too hot, that's all," his mom says. "Everyone give me some space."

The aunts and uncles yell at one another or what sounds like they are since it's all in Italian and I'm quickly figuring out that if I want to come to more of these dinners, I really need to learn the language.

I join the family in the dining room right as Mauro comes back in with his brother's backpack. He shoots me a look of worry, but I try to reassure him with my eyes that she'll be fine.

"I'm sorry, Madison," Cailin says, coming to stand next to me as I wait along the wall.

I give her a small smile. She seems sincere and I have no choice but to give her the benefit of the doubt.

"It's just his last girlfriend treated him so poorly. Always making him do everything, making him take her to the latest restaurants and shows. He spent so much money on her it was ridiculous. I mean firemen don't make a ton of money, I'm sure you know that."

"It seems unfair since the job they do puts their lives at risk."

She nods, looking behind her to find Devin playing with Legos with one of the aunts.

"Exactly. She liked him for the title he had, not that man he is."

I desperately want to ask who she thinks that man is, but that would be wrong. If I want Mauro to be part of my life, Cailin and Devin come with him, so I need to learn to play nice.

"Well, I assure you that's not me. If anything, his profession scares the crap out of me."

Her lips dip to a frown.

"I'm so sorry, Cailin. I'm an idiot. I shouldn't have…"

"No, you're right. The danger is there every time they leave the house. I think I took the years of safe returns for granted. It becomes a part of your life. I wish I would've hugged him hard every day he came home. Instead, I usually handed him Devin and said he's yours for twenty-four hours now."

My hand finds her shoulder and I let her vent as long as she needs to.

"I'm sorry."

It's now that I understand Mauro's decision to not tell her about Jenna and Hunter. She already holds enough guilt, and although she shouldn't hold any guilt that he cheated on her, let's be real, she would dissect their relationship from beginning to its end.

Mauro comes out of the kitchen and the two of us approach him at the same time. I'm not sure I'll ever get used to that.

"She said she just felt faint and that her heart was racing, but Luca said she seems good right now. He'll make a doctor's appointment for her. I guess it could have just been the heat in the kitchen." Mauro doesn't seem completely convinced and if I had to guess, he's realizing that his parents are growing older.

I hug him. "I'm sure she's fine. I was sweating in there. It is really hot."

Mauro glances down at me a small smile in place. "I like you sweaty," he says.

"And that's my cue to leave." Cailin turns around as Mauro's lips descend down on mine.

For the entire meal, everyone's eyes stay on Mrs. Bianco instead of their overfilled plates. The aunts don't let her clean up one dish even though she seems okay by that point.

Thankfully, Cailin and Devin leave right after dinner which gives me some time with his family without the awkwardness of feeling like she's watching my every move.

When we leave his parents' house, I'm so exhausted I fall asleep in his truck, content and happy.

CHAPTER TWENTY-NINE

Mauro

"Lunch delivery?" I ask Madison as she hands me a bag of food.

"Well, I want to see where you work." She steps into the garage. "You do eat lunch, right?"

"I do." I smile down at her.

"So, are you going to show me all your cool tools?"

She's covered up today, thank God. Jeans, ankle boots, and a jacket. Perfect to keep what's mine from being seen around here.

I wrap my arms around her waist. "I think you've become well acquainted with my biggest and best tool."

She giggles, her forehead falling to my chest. "True." I love the blush my comments pull out of her.

"Do you want me to put on the sirens?" I ask, holding my arm out for her to enter the truck.

She takes no time at all to hoist herself up and pretend she's driving the truck.

"Press the button right there." She follows the direction

my finger is pointing and the sirens blare. She quickly retracts her finger and covers her mouth with her hand, eyes wide.

A few guys head into the garage, seeing her in the truck.

"Bianco, you hiding gorgeous women from us today?" Lloyd calls out.

I roll my eyes. "I'm hiding my girlfriend."

Madison climbs out and I catch her in my arms as she slides down my body before her feet land on the cement floor.

"You make it impossible not to hold onto my hero complex. Just an FYI." She kisses me briefly and then walks over to my buddies. "Hi, I'm Madison."

The guys each shake her hand in turn.

"Jack."

"Lloyd."

"Trevor."

The three youngest members of our squad blatantly appraise her and I'd like to gouge their eyes out of their sockets.

"You dating this guy?" Lloyd asks, running his hand through his short blonde hair.

Madison looks at me, smiling widely. "I am."

"How did he manage to get you?" Jack asks.

Madison scrunches her eyebrows. "I think you mean, how did I get him?"

Trevor bends over laughing. "You're a ten and he's like a six."

I wrap my arms around her, my hands resting on her stomach. "Even so, she's mine and don't you forget it. We're going to eat. The three of you, make sure everything's ready to go in case we get a call."

The three probies walk past us and I grab my girl's hand, leading her into the firehouse.

"I agree with their line of thinking but..."

I cage her against the wall, swallowing her doubt with a kiss. Her hands never miss a chance to thread into my hair and she does just that as she grinds against me, lifting one leg to wrap around my thigh.

"Every night away from you is excruciating," I mumble along her lips, closing our kiss.

"I know, but the good news is that the countertops are coming in today."

I draw back. "Here I am laying my feelings out there and you're thinking countertops?"

We walk up the stairs and I drop the bag of Portillo's on the table and take a seat. Patel isn't on shift tonight so I expect dinner will be nothing special.

"Well, you or the countertops." She pretends to weigh the options with her hands teetering up and down like a scale.

"I don't think countertops can make you scream like I do." I wink at her.

She pretends to look at the ceiling, nibbling on her lip. The one move that drives me batshit crazy. "I might scream when they get installed. I'm really excited about them."

Standing from my chair, it falls down to the linoleum floor and I take her head in my hands, kissing her feverishly until her head spins. By the time I release her, her eyes are dilated and dark with arousal. Exactly what I was going for.

"Okay, one point for Bianco." She swipes an imaginary line in the air.

I pick up my chair and unwrap the food she brought me.

"Why is there nothing in here for you?" I ask, taking a second glance in the now empty bag.

"I already ate." She sits down and crosses her legs, placing her phone on the table.

"What? A granola bar?"

She cocks her head to the side. "I'm sorry, are you judging me?"

I unwrap my beef sandwich. "I'm just saying you need to eat more. I hate that you watch everything that goes into your mouth."

She digs into her purse and wiggles the bag of M&Ms in her hand until some fall out, like that's proving a fact.

"Case in point. You don't even eat the entire bag. You eat five in a sitting."

"Hey now, don't ruin my M&Ms for me," she warns.

The conversation is turning to where it might not go the way I want it to.

"One bite of my beef and I'll leave you alone." I smile at her.

"You act like I have an eating disorder. I don't."

I blow out a breath. There's no turning back from this conversation.

"I don't think you do. I just hate that you worry so much about it. I'll like you no matter what."

"You didn't even notice me when I was 'Fatty Maddy' with braces and glasses, Mauro, let's be realistic."

Anger boils inside of me. She just doesn't get that I might not have noticed her back then, but that doesn't mean it was right. That right now, in this moment, it's not her beauty that has me, it's her heart, her mind, her personality. I could list twenty things about her that I've fallen for but it feels like she'll always see the most important of them as her beauty.

"That's so unfair." I slide out my chair, patting my leg, needing to feel her body because I do not want us to spend a night apart in a fucking fight over how much she eats.

"No." She crosses her arms over her chest.

"Come here, you know you want to." I hold out my arms, inviting her.

"No."

Stubborn, one quality that I haven't fallen for. Yet.

"I'm sorry, I just want you to see why I'm with you and how it has nothing to do with your perky tits and great ass."

A slight smile forms at the corner of her lips.

"I need to feel you."

She looks around, stands and then sits on my lap.

Moving her hair off her shoulder, my lips find the spot right under her earlobe that gives her goose bumps. She wiggles in my lap, stirring my dick in my pants.

"I'm sorry, baby, but I need you to know that I don't care about your body. You're so much more than just a beautiful woman and I want you to see that when you look in the mirror."

She nods, but I know she doesn't believe me.

I turn her face toward me and capture her lips with my own.

My tongue slides through the part of her lips and the anxiety in my chest brought on by our fight diminishes. I know it won't always be this easy to end our fights, but I'll take what I can get tonight.

My fingers push through her hair, the silky strands wrapping around my hand. I swallow her moan and my hand slides up the side of her ribcage.

The bell goes off and I blink my eyes open to see Madison's eyes shifting in every direction as men from all different areas in the house head in one general direction.

She jumps up from my lap.

"I gotta go, babe. Grab your things."

She frantically gets her cell phone, puts it in her purse and positions it crossways over her body.

Some guys are heading down the pole and others the stairs. Madison runs down the stairs trying to stay out of everyone's way before I even see that she's left. I slide down the pole, then get my gear on. All the guys pile into the truck.

I spot her off to the side so I race over to her.

"Like I said…hero complex." She smiles as I kiss her one last time.

"This is just my job."

The horn honks on the truck, the sirens blaring.

"Go." She shoves me but I slide my tongue into her mouth one last time, my body not wanting to leave her.

"BIANCO!" someone shouts.

"Gotta go. Remember, no hero." I shake my head.

"Call me after?" she hollers out as the truck starts to leave and I grab on to the handle and climb into my seat.

"I will." I wink and she watches the truck race out of the station.

I'm always concerned about returning whenever we leave on a call. But watching the look on her face as I race toward danger makes coming back feel that much more important.

CHAPTER THIRTY

Madison

I was torn whether to be worried or horny watching Mauro hop on that truck as it was pulling out of the station. It was like a scene from a movie and he was the heartthrob hero.

Pulling into my own garage, I climb out of my car and for the first time in a long time, I'm home at a decent hour. Walking the path from the detached garage to the back door I see my neighbors out in their yard.

"Maddie," the little girl says, jumping up and heading to the fence line.

"Hey, Jade." I see she's holding a cute white puppy in her arms. "You got a puppy?"

Her eyes light up, a smile so big I can see why Reed finally caved. Jade's been begging for a dog for months.

I pet the dog's head, and it leans in already too used to getting a lot of attention.

"I named him Snowball." Jade holds him up in her arms.

"He's adorable." I continue petting him thinking maybe a

dog would be a good idea if I stayed in a house for any length of time.

"I know. I can't believe my mom and Reed agreed. My daddy brought him as a good luck in school gift this past weekend."

I cringe inwardly, wondering how pissed off Reed must have been.

Speaking of the man, he walks out of their house and over to us in jeans and long sleeve t-shirt. He's definitely an attractive man and talk about a potentially dangerous job. Assistant DA isn't exactly a cakewalk either.

"Hey Maddie, I see you met our new addition." He drinks from his cup, staring down at the furball in Jade's arms.

"I did. Snowball is a cutie."

"Not so cute when he can't figure out that he needs to pee and poop outside," he says.

"Not much of a dog person, huh?"

"Reed says Snowball is going to ruin our house so he's stopped all renovations until he's potty trained," Jade says.

Reed shakes his head with a smile.

"It's a nice gift," I offer.

"From a person who doesn't have to deal with it, of course." He raises an eyebrow.

Jade drops Snowball to the ground, following the puppy as it wanders around their small yard.

"Sorry, ex-husbands, huh?"

He shrugs. "Did you see her smile though? How can I argue with that?"

"And Victoria?"

"She's the same as me. Jade's got us wrapped around her finger. She's wanted it and we'd thought about it. Pete just beat us to it."

Pete must be Jade's father and if memory serves he lives in California. From what I can tell, they all get along pretty well.

"I'm glad I ran into you, I've been meaning to talk to you about something." Reed glances behind him to make sure Jade isn't within earshot. Which is hard in our small yards but she's so consumed with Snowball, I don't think we have to worry.

"What's going on? If it's about the sale, I'm waiting for another project to be finished and then I'll be putting this house on the market. I'll let you know what I list it at."

He waves off my concern. Usually I don't know the neighbors of the houses I rehab, but Reed, Victoria, and Jade are outgoing and it's summer so we've had more interaction than I normally would.

"No, I saw a black truck picking you up and dropping you off a few times. Is that a new boyfriend?" I can tell he's uncomfortable asking me.

"He is."

"A firefighter? I saw the sticker in the back window." He sips from his cup again, his eyes looking over his shoulder one more time.

"Yes. Engine Fifty-Five."

"The one with Hunter Zaxby?"

"Cut to the chase, Reed. I feel like you're about to ruin my day."

He chuckles. "I'm not. The case is pretty clear-cut—it was arson that killed Hunter. I'm not sure if your boyfriend knows that yet. The case is finalized tomorrow, but I have some concerns, off the record."

He takes a deep breath. "I don't think this was the owner of an abandoned building wanting his problems to burn up. Just tell your boyfriend and his buddies to be careful. We're having another look at some other fires that were originally ruled as accidents, but his job might be a lot more dangerous than usual if an arsonist is using ingredients to make fires uncontrollable and unpredictable."

"Why would anyone purposely go after the fire department?" My stomach churns and my chest is tight thinking about someone trying to harm innocent workers who lay their lives on the line.

"I don't know, but I intend to find out. It could be anything from a disgruntled former employee to a psychopath. There's just too much coincidence in what I'm seeing. I wondered if he'd be willing to sit down and talk at some point."

My hands grip the fence. Mauro's in even more danger than he normally is?

"I'll ask him. Hunter was a good friend of his so I'm sure he'd do anything to help you figure this out."

"Reed, Snowball just threw up," Jade calls out.

Reed rolls his eyes. "Remind me to thank Pete again."

I laugh.

"You can give him my number or if he'd rather you're there, the two of you are welcome over anytime. I just really want to pick his brain." He walks away from the fence line, placing his cup down and unwinding the hose.

"I'll ask him tonight and get back to you."

"Thanks, Maddie."

"Anytime."

The house is empty, which I already suspected since Lauren's Fiat isn't in the garage. I dig through my purse for my M&Ms and flip on the television to see if there's any news about the fire Mauro had to run off to. Reed's fears become my own that he'll have the same fate as Hunter if there's some crazy person out there setting fires to harm firefighters.

There's nothing on the news about it except what Reed already said about the announcement tomorrow morning on the fire that took the life of a firefighter. No mention of arson yet. Once that's decided they'll start the investigation.

I can't help but worry about how this will all affect Mauro.

Will it churn up feelings of anger toward someone he considered a best friend and betrayed him? One thing is for sure, our easy road of lovemaking and small disagreements is about to be turned on its head.

I hope we're strong enough to get through it.

CHAPTER THIRTY-ONE

Mauro

"Your girlfriend seems nice," Trevor says on our way back to the firehouse.

The small kitchen fire wasn't anything much, and it sucks that what one person could have easily taken care of stole me away from my lunch date with Madison.

"She is and you can stop thinking about her right now."

He rumbles with laughter. The kid is overzealous to say the least. Always at a ten.

"You worried I'm going to steal her away?" He moves his eyebrows up and down.

"No. Because you wouldn't stand a chance with her."

"I never said I wanted her. All I said was she was nice." He holds up his left hand with a ring attached.

Well, I've been fooled before. That piece of metal means nothing.

"And I'm just confirming that she's mine."

"Jeez, lay off the testosterone."

We sit in silence for the rest of the ride. I know I'm being a jealous prick. I've seen Trevor and his wife, Ariel. They're much like me and Madison where they can't keep their hands off each other. She's all bright eyes and huge smiles, bouncing around next to Trevor when she comes in. That's one thing Cailin and Hunter never had. They never did seem that happy, but they were married and in my opinion that held more weight than the affection they shared.

The truck is about to turn into the station, a few passersby watching us as always. A little boy waves and Big Gus honks the horn. The kid's face lights up.

I'll be thankful to get back to the station, call Madison and if I'm lucky, get each other off with some dirty talk.

"Engine Fifty-Five," a dispatcher comes in over the radio.

Big Gus pulls the radio down to his mouth, pressing the button.

"Another call. A warehouse on..." My mind drifts with the word warehouse.

Trevor pales across from me, his eyes finding no serenity at the kid jumping up and down on the sidewalk. He was there that night. Being a newbie, he was only able to assist in hose preparation. Tonight, he'll be in on the action.

My LT turns to us from the front, his eyes finding mine.

"They're calling in other engines for back up. It's a big one boys."

As we back up onto the streets of Chicago, another set of guys head to the ladder truck, climbing in. The ladder truck hasn't been used since that night and all of us in the cab of this truck know it.

Fuck, uneasiness unsettles my stomach as the truck sirens blare down the street. It's a bad omen when you have to go into a call with a monkey on your back like this. I try to shake it off as we whip through traffic, but it's impossible.

Ten minutes later, the thick, dark smoke billows out into the blue sky and we've arrived at our destination. The ladder truck goes first, positioning itself to spray down into the structure.

At three stories, this one is bigger than the one six months ago.

My lieutenant jumps out, as we all do, the physical aspects of the job second nature by now. It's putting the mental mind fuck aside to function as the team we're trained to, that's the challenge.

A car is parked in front of the fire hydrant, so Trevor breaks one window and I the other as I pass him the hose to hook up. The car alarm joins the chorus of fire trucks approaching the scene.

"Bianco!" Lieutenant waves me over. "You and Conley handle hose."

I nod to Trevor Conley who looks like he's about to puke in the middle of the street.

I grab the hose, put on my helmet and button my jacket up.

We head up the sidewalk, following the other fighters with axes to break down anything that blocks our way.

All that's on my mind is Madison. The way her eyelashes flutter when I kiss her good morning. How her body seeks mine, her arms and legs anchoring my body down in bed like she's afraid I'll disappear.

The heat of the flames hits my face, and I switch the hose on, cementing my legs to keep control of the water, spraying down the uncontrollable rager in front of me. I'm fighting the fire physically but my mind wanders to her.

I remember two mornings ago when I woke up to her hands sliding down the waistband of my boxer briefs.

How her heated gaze stayed on me while her tongue licked up my length and she settled between my legs.

Her soft hair wrapped around my fingers as I rocked into

her mouth. The tension that stiffened my legs as my balls drew up while her soft hands massaged them.

The name Madison falling from my lips while the morning light flowed into my bedroom.

The warmth of her body as she slides up to meet me.

The way I tasted on her tongue.

Her giggle as I flipped her over and returned her good morning wake-up call.

I never wanted to leave that room.

"BIANCO!" Trevor yells and I wake up from my daydream to hit the flames about to melt our boots on the floor. "It's everywhere, man!" Fear laces every word.

It takes us a while but when the front room is clear, we head upstairs while another team covers the first floor.

"Just keep the hose firm in your grip. It will be over before you know it." I say to him.

"Second floor is practically nonexistent," another firefighter says over our line. "Need another hose ASAP."

"Coming," I say, increasing my speed.

Trevor keeps up and we find two guys outside a door, one with an axe in his hand.

"One, two, three." The guy beats it down and we all stay on the side to see what kind of flames will emerge.

When it's clear, me and Trevor head in, spraying down the rapid rupture of flames climbing the walls. Again, as I extinguish the hungry beast, Madison enters my mind once again.

Last week when she went over to my mom's and they discussed options to expand their kitchen. A ventilation system that would ensure it did not get so hot. She even suggested a double oven. The call from my mom after her visit, proud that I found such a keeper.

That's exactly what she is, a keeper and I have to make sure she doesn't slip away.

From room to room, we combat the fire, making ground

and all I want is for this to be over so I can see Madison. I'll call her as soon as I get back and ask her to come to the station just so I can hold her in my arms.

We break down another door, waiting for the flames to emerge before we spray it down and enter. We've already done this more times than I can count but based on the other rooms I wasn't prepared for the flames to cover every surface like an out of control vein on steroids. Within seconds, every surface around us was covered.

"What do we do?" Trevor asks as I try to spray each corner, only to have it covered by fire again immediately. The flames aren't going out and panic starts to bubble in my throat. "It's closing in on us, Mauro. What do we do?" Trevor is in a full panic.

"Conley! Bianco! You need to get out. It's way too dangerous. We're going to have to fight it from the outside only!" the lieutenant shouts in my ear.

I turn around for a second to signal to Conley for us to find some way out of this, but he's as baffled as me. "We've got nowhere to go. We're caged."

"Find a way, goddamn it. Find a fucking way, Bianco!"

My eyes search, spraying the hose in all different directions trying to get enough control of the fire to allow us a moment to escape. It feels hopeless as I watch the water-sprayed wood feed the fire down the path we came.

"We have no choice. We have to go forward to get out."

"We'll never survive," Trevor says behind me.

"Look behind you, Conley, we'll never survive that way. We have no choice." Moving forward, the heat becomes almost unbearable.

"If you live and I die, tell Ariel I love her. Tell her I'm there with her when the baby is born. There's a letter in my locker, in case anything like this happens. Give it to her."

I don't want to hear this shit because I've never told the

woman I love that I love her. I've been too chicken shit in case she doesn't feel the same way about me yet.

"I will, but we're getting out of here, you hear me?"

"Watch out!" Conley yells and a wall falls down to the right of us, sending embers in all directions.

I have to get it together, but visions of Madison at my funeral plague me as we search for escape. Visions of the flag draped over my coffin and her walking behind the truck assault my mind as each room brightens with more intense flames.

She'd never know how much I love her. If I get out this, I'm telling her, to hell with the consequences.

"BIANCO!" Conley bellows and this time I have no time to react.

CHAPTER THIRTY-TWO

Madison

"A firefighter from Engine Fifty-Five has been taken to hospital," the anchor on the news channel says.

I stare at my phone, wishing, pleading, praying that it will ring.

"The fire is finally out, but it took a lot of resources and crews to accomplish. Many in charge are comparing it to the fire six months ago that took the life of Firefighter Hunter Zaxby."

Nope. I'm not waiting.

I grab my purse and my keys, not caring that I'm in my pajamas.

Racing over to the fire station is scarier than when I checked up on Mauro the first time. I'm so much more invested in our future now. Which I'm not sure I realized until this moment. It always takes something big like this, right? How fucking stupid.

Pulling up, I park on a side street and head up the sidewalk, with each footstep unsure of my decision, but he's my boyfriend, and I need to know he's okay.

I round the corner and the truck pulls in, some of the guys hopping out, hugging the women waiting for them. Mumblings of I love you and I was so worried can be heard coming from the women while the men give them assurances of how they were safe and had the fire beat the entire time.

I smile at the man with soot all over his face, cradling his wife's stomach, relief etched in his face.

"They were trapped and couldn't get out," one man says to his wife. "The ambulance took him before I saw anything. They called his brother."

My heart stops beating and blood rushes in my ears.

Oh my God, it was Mauro. They called Cristian or Luca, I know it.

Why would they not call me?

Because they don't have my number.

"Excuse me?" I approach the man, needing to know. "The injured firefighter?"

The big man raises his eyebrows and purses his lips like he's not going to tell me shit.

"Do you know if Mauro Bianco is back yet?" I ask.

"MAURO!" a woman's voice screeches from behind me.

I turn to see Cailin running across two lanes of traffic, not stopping, heading right to the other side of the truck.

"He's right there, ma'am," the guy says to my back and then continues his conversation about whoever the injured firefighter is.

My eyes are glued to the end of the truck, watching Mauro emerge and drop his gear, opening his arms to Cailin. Burrowing his head into her neck, he picks her up like a man coming home from war.

My mouth hangs open and tears prick my eyes.

Mauro places her back on her feet and she looks into his

eyes, her hands on his face, his shoulders, like she's trying to make sure he's real. It's like I'm having an out of body experience or peering into an intimate moment between lovers.

Nausea rumbles in my stomach.

She raises on her tiptoes, keeping his head firmly between her hands.

I watch the scene unfold and I can't look away even though it's torture and I know I'll never be able to clear the visual out of my head.

Their lips meet and I close my eyes, tears spilling down my cheeks. The roller coaster of emotions my body went through in the last five minutes too much to deal with.

Turning around, I walk away.

"Hey, Madison, right?" One of the guys from earlier today reaches out to me. "Your guy was quite the hero today. He saved my ass."

I nod. His pregnant wife looks at me with sympathy, probably because I'm crying and walking away from the scene. She obviously sees something her husband doesn't.

"I'm glad you're safe," I say and step away.

"Wait. I'm sure he'll want to see you." His hand lands on my forearm, but his wife hits his arm and he turns to see what she's talking about. "Oh."

Sympathy that matches his wife's tells me I don't need a second look.

Instead, I round the corner of the street and when I get into the safety of my car, I down the entire bag of M&Ms in my purse, before ripping the wrapper into small pieces. I never want to see those initials again.

CHAPTER THIRTY-THREE

Mauro

"Cailin!" I push her shoulders and remove her hands from my cheeks. "What are you doing?"

She falls back to her heels, her cheeks red with embarrassment.

"I'm just so happy you're okay and in one piece. They kept comparing it to the fire, and Hunter's name and picture were all over the news again. I had to make sure you were okay."

I blow out a breath.

"We need to talk." I shake my head, staring down at the ground.

"Maybe I got too carried away, but I'm just so relieved." She heaves for breath and her mascara is trailing in waves down her cheeks.

"I get that, but you know I'm with Madison."

The other guys with their significant others are lingering around and my eyes do a quick scan of the area. No sign of Madison. I'd hoped she'd see the news and come.

"I know," Cailin says in a small voice.

"Do you?" I take her by the hand, pulling her to the side of the building away from prying eyes.

"I do," she says with her back against the wall.

"I think you're transferring your feelings for Hunter on to me or something."

She shakes her head and rubs her face with her hands. "I just don't want to be alone. It's so hard, Mauro. Raising Devin, going to bed alone every night."

I hug her. "I know. But I'm not going to take his place. My heart isn't up for grabs."

She nods into the crook of my neck, sobs wracking her body.

As I'm consoling her, I look off onto the road and spot Madison's car parked down the street. It can't be her, can it?

"Hold on. I'll be right back."

Cailin keeps her head down, tears continuing down her face as I jog down the street.

Approaching the small SUV, I figure it's a car similar to, but not hers, because if she's here, why isn't she in my arms?

When I bend over and look through the window, her head is on the steering wheel, the keys in her hands, resting in her lap.

"Fuck," I murmur, looking back at Cailin and then at my girl.

She came. I smile at the fact that she came to make sure I was okay.

My knock on her window startles her and she straightens her back.

"Madison, what's wrong?" I ask.

She doesn't take time to wipe her own tears but puts the keys in the ignition.

My hand tries to open up the passenger door, but it's

locked. She quickly puts the car in reverse to get out of the parallel parking spot. I bang on the window. "Madison!"

She ignores me, her eyes set on her task of getting the fuck away from me.

Realization makes my gut clench and panic tightens my throat.

"It's not what it looks like. Let me explain. Don't leave!" I bang on the window again.

She reverses again, the asshole in front of her way too close to give her any room. Of course, I'm thanking that asshole as I round the hood of her car and plead through the window.

"Come on Madison. I promise you it isn't what you're assuming. Hear me out." Our eyes meet and she stills.

"What are you doing, Mauro?" Cailin approaches the car.

I place my hand up in the air. "Stop."

"Is that Maddie?" she asks, continuing to walk toward us.

Hasn't she caused enough trouble tonight?

Madison catches me looking away and turns her head, looking out her side mirror.

A fresh set of tears fall and she moves not caring if she hits me or not.

"FUCK!" I yell as she pulls out of the spot and her taillights round the corner.

"Did she see us?" Cailin asks.

"No, she always drives away from me like that. What do you think?"

From the tone of my voice anyone else would know to leave me the fuck alone, but Cailin follows me as I jog back to the firehouse.

"I'm sick and going home," I say to my lieutenant passing him by.

"No, you're not. We have to unpack the truck, get it ready

in case we're going back out. You're on shift until the morning." He follows me. "Oh, hello, Cailin."

She stops him long enough for me to strip out of my gear and head upstairs to grab my keys and phone.

"Bianco, you can't leave," the lieutenant says.

"Then fire me."

I run out of the fire station down the street with Cailin yelling my name behind me.

I don't give a shit about any of it. I just need Madison to understand.

I call her, not surprised when it goes to voicemail over and over again. I leave pleading messages for her to listen to me and explain that it was a one-way kiss.

What seems like a lifetime later, my tires squeal to a stop outside her house and I jog up the steps, ringing the doorbell over and over again until it finally swings open.

I instinctively cover my nuts.

"Lauren."

No smile this time around which means Madison is home.

"You are such an asshole. I trusted you and here you're having an affair with your partner's widow? You sick motherfucker. Do you enjoy torturing Madison?" She steps out onto the porch and my gaze flickers past her, wondering how I can get around her.

"It's all a misunderstanding."

"Were your lips on hers?" she asks, her hands on her hips, eyebrows raised in question.

"For a millisecond until I threw her off me. Where is she? I need to speak with her." I look into the house again and still see no sign of Madison.

"Nope. You're not going near her again. I gave you the benefit of the doubt, Bianco and you fucked it up." She turns her back to me, but I slide by her, shutting and locking the door behind me.

She is going to have my nuts, I know that as I hear her banging and yelling my name, but I'll deal with that later.

Madison isn't in the family room, or the kitchen, so I run upstairs, finding her bedroom door shut. I knock.

"Just give me tonight, Lauren, okay? We can talk in the morning."

I try the knob and it's locked. Fuck.

"I'm serious, I just can't tonight. Please understand."

No fucking way I'm letting her go a whole night thinking I'd hurt her like that.

I reach up on top of the door and retrieve the key she was adamant about us keeping on the ledges of all the doorframes at our flip house.

Trying to be quiet so she can't put a dresser in front of the door, I insert the key into the lock and turn until the click sounds.

The pounding on the outside door and ringing doorbell sounds below, Lauren voicing all the ways she's going to torture me when she gets her hands on me.

When I open the door, Madison is on her bed, a pillow tucked in her lap.

"Madison?" I ask, walking in and shutting and locking the door just in case Lauren gets into the house.

"If you're here, who's knocking?" she asks, startled to see me.

"I might have outplayed Lauren at a game of chicken."

She doesn't find it as funny as I do and this isn't the moment for me to be raising my fist in victory. We'll laugh tomorrow morning when all this behind us.

"Cailin kissed me and I pushed her away immediately. I told her I'm with you." I sit on the edge of the bed, wanting this fight to be over so we can go back to being us.

"I believe you. It took me a minute to process, but I knew

you wouldn't do that to me because it was done to you." She wipes at the tears on her cheeks.

Relief fills my insides.

"Never. I'd never do that to you." I reach for her, needing to feel her, but she leans away from me.

"But it made me realize something, Mauro." She leans over and grabs a Kleenex from her nightstand and blows her nose while all the relief I was feeling a moment ago flees.

"For a moment I felt like that girl again…the nerd in high school and she was like the cheerleader. I think I'm always going to be screwed up like this. It's not fair to you. You shouldn't have to reassure me all the time and feel like you have to prove that it's me you want." A tear trickles down her cheek, but she swipes it away.

"I don't feel like that and I'm happy to tell you every morning we wake up together and every night before we go to bed. As long as I have you, I don't care about any of that." I slide closer, but she moves back, keeping the same distance between us.

"This is never going to work. I'll forever be that girl at the bonfire staring at you while you're thinking of someone else. At least in my own head. We tried and I thought maybe it could work, but I see now that girl will always live on inside of me. She's not going anywhere."

"This is ridiculous. As I was fighting that fire tonight, do you know what I was thinking about?"

I want her to know that I love her, but at the same time I can't tell her right now. I'm afraid I'll scare her away and she'll think I'm just saying it to make her feel better.

"What?"

"How much I wanted to be with you. I wanted you wrapped in my arms. It was scary there for a second and I fought to get out of that building just to hold you. That's what got me through. Madison, don't do this. It's all high school bullshit that doesn't matter. Who cares if I was the jock and you were the nerd, we're here now. And what we have, few people get."

"Ha! You asshole, get the fuck out." Lauren storms into the room, a key in hand.

"I'm not going anywhere without her." I look between the two of them, determined to make this right.

"First of all, you're stinking up our entire house with the smell of smoke. Second, she doesn't want you here."

Madison's gaze shifts to her friend and then back down to her lap.

Maybe it's good that her friend is here.

"Tell her, Lauren," I beg. "Tell her how good we are together. I'm with her because of the person she is inside. That I was a blind bastard ten years ago and I'll spend the rest of my life making it up to her."

Lauren's rigid stance falters and her gaze lands on Madison who is busy sniffling and wiping away tears again.

"I thought he cheated on you?" Lauren asks.

Madison says nothing.

"She caught my buddy's widow kissing me. I pushed her away, told her I didn't want her and I was with Madison. But now she's saying we'll never work because we're too different."

Lauren's head falls back in what appears to be exasperation, like this isn't the first time she's dealt with this issue when it comes to Madison.

"Maddie." She makes her way across the room and when she reaches her friend, she wraps her arm around her shoulders. They sit there in silence for a minute, Lauren must see something I don't because she moves off the bed and nods for me to meet her in the hall.

Is she crazy? I'm not leaving without making this right.

Lauren grabs my shirt and pulls me out into the hall, shutting the door behind her.

"Just give her tonight to be by herself and process her thoughts. I'm sure she'll come to her senses tomorrow," Lauren says.

"You're kidding me, right?" I take one step toward the door and Lauren's hand presses into my chest. "I'm not leaving. She needs to know I'm not going anywhere when things get tough."

"I understand, but you won't get through to her tonight. Trust me, I've known her my whole life. Her wounds are deep, Mauro, and I wish she didn't see herself as that girl in high school, but the rejection she felt during those years still lingers. She never even told me about whatever happened between the two of you at the bonfire party. I'm her best friend, and she didn't think she could tell me which means it hurt bad. So bad she chose to pretend it never happened. Now here you are, telling her you want her. It's hard for her to believe that deep down. That the one thing she wished for every night for years before bed is coming true. When it comes to you, she feels second best."

Lauren's words make me realize how deeply I hurt her and how far I'll have to go to make it up to her.

I push my hands through my hair. "I still don't want to leave."

Lauren gives me a small smile. "Listen, Maddie is a thinker. Always has been. Let her sort this out a bit in her head and you can try to talk some sense into her again."

"I need to come up with a plan to make her realize."

"Good luck with that." Lauren pats my back like she pities me because whatever I come up with will never work.

She obviously doesn't understand my competitive drive. Madison Kelly is mine and I intend to keep it that way.

CHAPTER THIRTY-FOUR

Madison

*L*ucky for me, Mauro is stuck in an interview today about last night's fire, so I don't have to worry about him coming to the house. The only reason I know this is because he texted me since I'm still not answering the phone.

He's upset and doesn't understand why I'm pushing him away. I'm not sure why he doesn't see how this will never work out between us. We're nothing alike and sooner or later he's going to realize I'm not worthy of him.

Tonight killed me when he showed up at my house smelling of smoke, the soot still lining his jaw and forehead. The urge to wrap my arms around him because he was okay nearly catapulted me off that bed, but what good would that do? Just delay the inevitable.

As I'm walking around the house, writing out a list of everything that needs to be finished before we can put the place on the market, I hear a car pull up outside. I sigh, worried that he got out of the interview early and has decided to plead his case again.

It's not even just him. Somehow, he's won Lauren over because she left me a note on my dresser about not wasting true love. Who knew she was such a romantic?

Even Vanessa sat me down earlier today telling me that I had to put the past behind me and live for the present. That I was giving up something special not many people share. Easy for the beauty queen to say.

"Hello?" a feminine voice calls out into the house.

"Yes?" I walk down the stairs, stopping mid-flight when I see Cailin.

The vision of her lips on Mauro's is still vivid in my mind.

"He's not here," I say, walking down the rest of the way, rounding the bottom stairway and heading to the kitchen.

She holds up a thermos and two cups. "I'm here to see you."

Her blonde hair is pulled back into a high ponytail, no makeup on her face.

"I'm not sure why? I'm out of your way now. He's all yours." I cock my hip and stare her down.

"Even if you broke up with him, we both know he's not mine. He's still yours." She sets the thermos on the dining room table that has somehow become a staple of this home.

"Sometimes things just don't work out. He'll find someone else. Someone more suitable."

She places the two cups she brought and fills them up with tea from the thermos. I take a few tentative steps over toward the table.

"I need to apologize, I was an evil witch and I deserve it if you want me to have no contact with Mauro, but don't take what I did out on him. He didn't want that kiss. I convinced myself he did, hell that I did, for that matter, but I was just trying to replace what I'd lost."

She slides the cup my way.

Dropping the pad of paper on the table, I sip the tea, crossing my fingers it's not poisoned.

"When Hunter died, we weren't the happiest of couples. We fought a lot. About money and his schedule and the new business venture he was going into with Mauro. We argued about parenting, sleeping times, me not wanting sex enough. In my head, I thought that was just marriage....we had a young child and this is what happens with couples at that stage of life. There were times it felt like we were headed for divorce, but he'd always come home with a bouquet of flowers, telling me how much he loved me. We'd make love and we'd be back in our happy place until the next fight."

If she only knew what he was doing behind her back.

"After he died, I propped him up on this pedestal as a man who could do no wrong. A man who fought fires and saved lives. A man who gave up his own life helping others."

A tear slips down her cheek and I can't help the compassion I feel for her, much as I'd prefer it weren't there.

"I morphed him into the perfect father, the perfect husband in my head. And I believed it for a minute there because I hated that I ever thought ill of him now that he was gone. But you know what? Everyone has their flaws. Look what I did...treated you terribly. Kissed your boyfriend. Tried to steal him away from you. I know you don't know me, but that's not me. I never would have done that six months ago."

I swallow down the revelation I want to give her about Hunter.

"I don't know why you and Mauro broke up but if it's because of the kiss, don't. He didn't even reciprocate. He told me you held his heart, Madison. I'm sorry that I was so lonely and wounded that I tried to ruin what you two have."

The pained look on her face has me telling her that I

accept her apology. And I do. She seems sincere and I do feel awful for what she's going through. But it doesn't change the fact that at some point Mauro is going to come to his senses.

"You're the one for him, Madison. Mauro told me that you went to high school together, but he didn't know you at the time. He was over one evening to fix my garbage disposal and he stayed for a drink after Devin went to bed."

I really don't want to hear this.

"He went on and on about you. How he wished he did know you. That it felt like he'd wasted these past ten years because the woman he's meant to be with, he'd already met years prior."

She smiles like that should appease me in some way.

It kind of does.

I clear my throat. "Nice of him to say."

She laughs in an exasperated way that asks 'how much more convincing do I need to give you?' "I don't know who brought Hunter into my life, but he was there for a purpose. He gave me Devin and for that I'm grateful. People come in and out of our lives, some return, some you never see again. I like to think there's a reason that this is your time with Mauro. Maybe back then it wasn't the right timing. Do you really want to take the chance that the paths you're on don't meet again?"

I sip the tea and allow her words to soak in.

"We don't know each other well, but I *do* know Mauro. He and Hunter were close since the academy. I've seen women come and go in and out of his life and none of them have had anything like what you two do." Her hand covers mine and I see she still wears her wedding band. "I promise you, his feelings are genuine and true."

With a squeeze on my hand, she turns around and leaves as I lower myself to the wood floor wondering what the hell I'm doing. My eyes shift around the room, taking in what we built together. This house was a bid away from being bulldozed and now it's a bright and happy home, ready for a family to build memories, a life in.

Cailin's right. Something brought Mauro into my life. We could've had that date and then never saw each other again, but he showed up at that auction.

Regret and determination fill me and I stand up, finding my phone and calling his number.

No answer.

I hammer out a text message for him to call me as soon as he's out of the interview.

Locking all the doors and shutting all the windows, I run out to my car, peeling away from the curb to wait for him outside his apartment.

I have to make this right. I just hope it's not too late and my issues haven't scared him away.

CHAPTER THIRTY-FIVE

Mauro

"Just get as many people there as possible. I don't care who they are. Did you leave the outfit on her bed?" I ask Lauren, who thankfully has moved over to Team Mauro.

Our agendas match—make Madison see she's deserving of love. I have no doubt that if I pull this off, she'll be back to giving me hell tomorrow.

"It's all set, but she hasn't returned home yet," she says.

"I drove by after my interview and her car wasn't there."

I pace around the grass, wondering where the hell she could be.

"What's up, man?" One of my buddies arrives to help me set this entire thing up.

"Hey." I nod toward the area where the other guys are lingering.

"Did you call her?" she asks.

"I texted her. I'll call her now." Lauren hangs up and I see that there's a text message from Cristian waiting for me.

Cris: She's outside the apartment waiting for
you. I just woke up from my double shift.

Fuck. She's come to talk to me and I can't even make it
to her.

Me: Tell her to go home. That I'm not there.

Cris: Pretty sure she's going to stick around
and wait.

Me: Do whatever you have to do, just get her
home so Lauren can do what she needs
to do.

Cris: I'll try.

I pull up Lauren's contact and send her a message so she'll
know what's going on.

Me: She's at my apartment. Cristian is going
to try to get her to go home. Did you get a
hold of her?

I pace a path from one side to the other. I need to pull
this off.

Lauren: She said she's an idiot and she's
going to wait for you until you come home. I
don't think she's budging on this.

Damn it. I thread my fingers through my hair.

Me: Okay. She had texted me so I'm going
to tell her to meet me at your house.

Lauren: Then I'll kidnap her. Perfect.

Starting a new thread, I pull up her earlier text that I was going to ignore until she got here.

> Me: I can't talk right now but let's meet at your house in a half hour?

The three dots appear immediately.

> Madison: I'm at your apartment. Just come here. Your brother just left. I don't want to talk in front of Vanessa or Lauren.

I stare up at the sky silently asking why this woman is determined to be so stubborn.

> Me: I'll get to your place quicker. We can go somewhere and talk.

That's the best I have before begging her to go home.

> Madison: Okay, I'll head over there now.

Finally. I pull my thread with Lauren back up on my phone.

> Me: She's heading home now. Make sure you get her in that dress before you bring her.

> Lauren: On it.

I spend the next hour preparing a scene going off someone else's memory. It's time to redo history.

CHAPTER THIRTY-SIX

Madison

I walk into my bedroom, Lauren on my heels from the moment I opened the front door.

"I know I've been stupid so you can stop your lectures. I'm apologizing and I'm going to try and put all the past behind us..." I trail off as I spot a dress I've never seen before laid out on my bed with a small note placed on it.

I glance back to Lauren, who's smiling.

Come back to two thousand and eight and let's start fresh. Put on the dress and have Lauren drive you to me.

Love,

Mauro

"I'll let you change." She shuts the door behind her and I have the passing thought that I now realize she's wearing a pair of baggy pants and a tight t-shirt that shows a sliver of her stomach.

Puzzled but hopeful, I strip out of my jeans and sweatshirt, putting on a dress very similar to the one I wore ten years ago. The one that ended up drenched in beer. I'm tying my shoes when my bedroom door opens and there stands Vanessa and Lauren.

Vanessa's decked out in a gold headband and a babydoll top.

"Are you ready, Maddie?" she asks. "I heard there's a bonfire going down tonight and Mauro Bianco is going to be there." She flutters her eyes. "He's so dreamy."

Lauren knocks her shoulder. "Two thousand and eight, not nineteen sixty-eight."

Vanessa laughs.

"I'm ready."

Hope feels like it's filling my chest from the inside out, expanding my chest with every breath. I stare in the mirror for a moment reflecting on the differences between the person I was a decade ago and the one that stands here now, not just in appearance, but personality, too.

A decade ago I never would have been able to hold a conversation with Mauro. Kissing him just about made me mute, never mind sleeping with him. I would have agreed with everything he said because that's what I thought you were supposed to do with boys. Now I fight for what I believe in. I didn't know what I wanted out of life back then, but I do now.

And I can't let my fears and insecurities stop me from having them. Mauro is a good man and if he says that he cares for me, I have to trust in that. The same way he was trusting me not to hurt him.

I realize now that there are no guarantees in life. The best any of us can do is try. And if we fail, well…at least we had our moment in the sun. It's better than withering away to nothing in the shadows.

The three of us head out of the house to the garage where Lauren's Fiat awaits.

"Your parents are so great to buy you this car, Lauren." Apparently, Vanessa is still pretending we're in high school. "My dad told me no car until I'm eighteen. I'll get him to cave though."

The three of us continue to make jokes like we really are sixteen again and living with our parents.

"Did you know that all the Bianco brothers are going to be there tonight?" I ask because now that I've figured out what's going on, the outfit I saw Cristian in earlier at his apartment makes more sense. He was wearing his jeans halfway down his ass with a brown belt and plaid shirt. Totally ten years ago.

"Whatever. The only one worth anyone's time is Mauro. You should totally talk to him tonight, Mad." Vanessa nudges my shoulder.

"I don't know, I think they all have their own redeeming qualities," I say.

"Luca can suck my tit. He'll never have a chance with me. He's so cocky and thinks he's great at everything he does," Lauren says.

I raise my eyebrows at her.

Finally, we arrive at the same place high school bonfires were held ten years prior and Lauren parks on the grass.

There's a bonfire roaring in the middle of the field between two sets of trees. People are scattered over the grass, Solo cups in hand, laughing and having a good time.

"Party time!" Vanessa hollers. She wasn't there originally

when I begged Lauren to go home, but I wish now that she were.

We all file out and I'm not sure how he managed it, but everyone acts like they don't know why we're there, barely giving us a glance. Searching the area, I spot Mauro talking to a group of guys.

A smile crosses his lips, his eyes flowing over my body like it's the first time he's seen me.

I blush, of course I do, and shake my head at the absurdity of this entire situation.

He's wearing what he wore that night minus the backward hat which I'm kind of happy about because I love his hair so much. Oh and he's added his letterman jacket, though it's a little snug now with all his muscles.

"Come on, let's get a drink." Lauren tugs me the other way.

We head into the woods where the conversations we pass consist of topics like kids, date nights, and save the dates rather than SATs, parents, and midterms.

Lauren fills her cup but makes me leave mine empty. I'm surprised Lauren remembers or maybe she's going off of what I told Mauro about that night.

Regardless, I end up on a log in front of the fire. As I watch the flames, I assume he'll appear across from me and our eyes will meet.

"Do you mind?" his voice says from next to me and my body hums with the awareness of him.

I look up and his smile is so wide I'm ready to throw myself into his arms, begging him to forgive me for my stupidity and take me back to his apartment. I just want to go back to where we were.

"No," I say, playing my part although he's changed the script.

He sits down and sips his beer. "I'm Mauro." He holds out his hand.

"Madison."

"Nice to meet you." He stares ahead. "I saw you earlier with your friends."

"Yeah, we're sophomores. You're a senior right?" I can't help but smirk at him.

He nods. "I am. You want some M&Ms?" He pulls a bag out of his letterman jacket.

I smile wide. "My favorite, how did you know?"

He pours some in my hand. "I didn't. They're my favorite, too. Kind of cool the way they're our initials huh?" He pops a few into his mouth. "I heard they're great with cheesecake." He winks at me.

"Really? I'll have to try that sometime." I bump his shoulder with my own.

"Maybe we can try it together?" His thigh presses to mine and the cage to the butterflies in my stomach is opened. How can he still have this effect on me?

"Are you not drinking?" he asks, noticing me flipping my Solo cup around.

"No, I'm the driver."

"Great, I've had a few, not too many but I shouldn't drive. Do you mind giving me a ride? You can drive my truck." He pulls his keys out of his jacket.

"Sure, let me find my friends to let them know."

"Cool. I'll wait by the truck. It's over there." He points off into the distance.

We both stand and he steps closer to me, tucking a strand of hair behind my ear. "Thanks for this."

"You're welcome," I croak out because I'm torn on wanting to finish this scene to see what else he has planned and jumping him right now.

"Hurry, okay?"

I nod and he steps back until he disappears into the darkness.

God, I miss him already.

Turning around, I survey the crowd to find Vanessa and Lauren. At first, I spot no one and I'm about to tell Luca who's pretending to arm wrestle someone to fill Lauren in for me. Then I see she's the one standing behind Luca's competitor screaming at him to kick Bianco's ass.

I head over to her and tap her on the shoulder. "Hey, can you get a ride home? Mauro just asked me if I could drive him home."

"Um, no you agreed to be my DD. The hell if you're going off with that shithead."

Luca stands up. "That *shithead* would be my brother."

"Okay, funny guys. This didn't actually happen so I'm driving Mauro home. Lauren you have your car and I played the game, so...thanks."

They both smile at me but quickly narrow their eyes at each other again.

"I was kidding." She hugs me. "Go get him, Mad," she whispers in my ear before releasing me.

Luca places his hand on my shoulder. "Give him hell and I mean it. Don't make it easy on him."

I smack his hand and walk away from them, looking around for Vanessa, but when I don't see her, I figure Lauren will tell her and so I head toward the truck, walking faster the closer I get.

Just like that night ten years ago, he's leaning on the passenger side waiting for me. This time he isn't swaying or looking like he might throw up.

"Thanks for this, Madison." He hands me the keys.

"Mauro," I say being done with the game, but he places his fingers on my lips.

"We need to play the song." He leans forward, his hands on either side of my face and he closes his eyes. "Just listen to the lyrics of the song, okay? It says everything I want to on this night." He kisses my forehead and then releases me.

I climb into the driver's seat, a little intimidated by the size of his truck. Once we're on the road the song, "Chasing Cars" by Snow Patrol starts to play. The lyrics speak so much to my heart and the two of us. The irony that it played ten years ago when we were strangers to one another isn't lost on me.

By the time I'm pulling up to his parents' house, tears are falling down my face.

"I'm so sorry, Mauro," I choke out.

He takes the keys out of the ignition, gets out of his car and then opens my door.

"Come on. Let's go to the park."

He entwines our hands, his callused palms giving me comfort and letting me know that he's already accepted my apology.

We walk across the street. The park equipment is newer now and a locked fence surrounds the outfield.

"Well, we'll have to do this a little differently this time around." Mauro releases my hand and climbs the fence. "Come on." He waits for me as I do my best to get over the fence without flashing him. Not that he hasn't already seen all of me.

"We'll pretend the fence wasn't there." He laughs, taking my hand again and guiding me to centerfield.

He sits down first and pats the grass next to him. I silently oblige and we both lay back in the grass.

"Do you know what you want to be?" he asks, staring at a sky that's littered with stars to wish on tonight.

"I'm not sure. What about you?"

He rolls on his side. "I want the trifecta—the house, the family, and the career. Hopefully one day I get it."

"I'm sure you will. You're a pretty great guy."

He slides closer, his hand touching my cheek. "I have a vision that in ten years I'm going to meet a woman who will change my life forever."

"Really? A vision?"

He chuckles. "Yeah, I think she'll look a lot like you."

"Weird, I had the same vision of you."

Our eyes lock, blue on blue, and the feelings that pass between us without words feel more powerful in this moment than anything the world can throw at us.

"Can I kiss you?" he whispers.

I nod, swallowing down my excitement, my joy of finally being able to kiss him.

He's hesitant at first like he was the first time our lips met, but the fire, the time apart quickly consume us and he rolls me onto my back. His thigh separates my legs as our mouths claim one another.

Finally, I'm back to where I feel like I fit—with Mauro.

Peace travels through my body even as my arousal pulsates out of control.

"Man, that's some kiss. Will you come to my bedroom?"

I smack his shoulder. "A little forward don't you think?"

He nibbles at my neck. "What I want to do to you can't be done in public."

I place my hands on either side of his face and pull him away from my neck so that he's looking at me. "Take me home, Mauro."

"I love those four words," he says, springing to his feet and hauling me up with him.

We rush to get back to the truck, him driving this time instead of me. I'm so busy staring at him the entire ride I don't even pay attention to the time it's taking to get to his apartment.

"You didn't have to do all that," I say, my hand in his as the song plays on repeat.

"I did. It's how that night should have gone." He stops at a light and he bends over to kiss me. "I'll forever regret those ten years I missed out on with you, but I'm not going to dwell on that if I'm lucky enough to have an entire future with you."

The light turns green and he accelerates and I'm still unable to take my eyes off of him.

"We're home," he says, parking by the curb.

I move to open my door.

"Hey, that's my job." He quickly takes the keys out of the ignition and exits his truck, and I look out the window.

We're not at my house and we're not at his apartment, we're at the flip house.

He opens my door, asking for my hand then leading halfway up the walkway and taking both my hands in his.

"Why are we here?" I ask.

"Because this is where I want to start our life together. We gutted this place and pieced it back together at the same time as our love for one another grew. I only want to stay here and build a life with you until this house is overflowing with kids, pets, and grandkids."

"You want to move in together?" I can barely push the words past the growing lump in my throat.

"This is *our* home. It's not just a house, it's what brought us together, Madison, and I want to finally give you the happily ever after you deserve here. What do you say?"

I stare up at the house that reminds me a lot of myself—good bones, a little disastrous at first, but now with some love and attention, the best parts of it are clear to see—inside and out.

"I say...yes!" I jump up in his arms and he catches me, circling me around.

"I love you, Madison."

"I love you."

"M and M forever," he says and leans in to kiss me like a seal to all my wishes coming true.

EPILOGUE

Mauro

*I*t's been three weeks since we moved into our home. I love the sound of that—*our* home.

Next week is Thanksgiving and we thought about hosting —strike that—Madison wanted to host, but that isn't going to happen. My ma likes to cook and I'm not having my family, aka Luca, mess up our new home.

We've been looking for another property to rehab together, one that will hopefully be on the cheap since we didn't end up pulling our money out of this one, but in the end, it was worth it. We built this home together.

Madison's car pulls up along the curb since we've yet to get the detached garage we weren't thinking about adding when it was a flip property. Lucky for us the parking isn't terrible on this street.

I hide behind the doorway of the bathroom and hear her turn the key in the lock. She enters and flips the light switch that doesn't work.

"Damn it, we couldn't have blown a fuse. Where is he when I'm stuck in the dark?"

I flip on the switch of twinkle lights, the same ones I used the first time we made love. I'm hoping she'll see the rose petals lining a pathway for her to follow and take the hint. I peek around the corner.

"Mauro," she sighs, her hand covering her mouth.

I'll never grow tired of my name falling from her lips.

She walks down the pink rose petal path, dropping her purse, jacket, and bag of groceries on a chair as she goes.

Stopping at the dining room table, I see tears prick her eyes from the glow of the real candles I've set along the table, illuminating the words I've spelled out with custom-made M&Ms.

The message is short. Two simple words that hold the key to my happiness.

Marry me?

I emerge from the bathroom and she looks at me, her eyes pouring with love. I already know what she's going to say.

"It's so quick..."

"No, it's not." I round the dining room table I ended up refinishing for us. "I don't want to waste any more time. I want us to be married. I want you to have my name. I want to see your belly swell and watch our kids grow alongside you. I want the bath time, the goodnight stories, the scraped knees. The learning to ride a bike, building a snowman."

"I'd love to be Mrs. Mauro Bianco." She smiles and I grab her, swinging her around, my lips finding hers.

"You've made me so happy."

Her feet fall to the floor as I lower her.

"How did you do this in M&Ms?" she asks, placing one on her tongue.

"Hey, you can't eat the ones I used to ask you to marry

me." She laughs into my chest. "I had to use M&Ms, they're our candy."

I pick up one from the bowl I set beside my question, holding it up for her.

"Maddie and Mauro." She sighs again and I put it in my mouth. She steps closer and wraps her arms around my neck. "You're too romantic, you know that, right? How will you ever top this one?"

I kiss her, and unlock her hands from around my waist, falling down onto my knees and grabbing the ring box from the chair on the table. Taking out the one-carat diamond with white gold band, I present it to her, sliding it on her left hand.

"It's perfect," she says, gazing down at her hand.

"It was a hard decision, but I thought simple and classic like my girl, worked best."

She presses her lips together and I think she's trying not to cry.

"The best part is that now everyone knows you're mine."

She falls to her knees, her hands cradling my cheeks. "I've always been yours."

"And I'll always be yours," I promise.

I brush my lips along hers.

"Pinch me, Mauro?" she asks once I have her laying down on our hardwood floors.

"I'll do more than pinch you, baby."

"I mean it. Tell me this is real?" Her fingers massage the back of my head.

"It's real. We're in love and we're going to live happily ever after."

"I couldn't love you more," she whispers like it's a secret between the two of us.

I lay on top of her, kissing her neck. "Words I'll never grow tired of hearing. But just so you know, I love you more."

Then before she can object, I crash my lips down on hers, swallowing down her moans.

What fun is marriage without a couple fights over who loves who more?

———

Later that night, I'm eating a row of M&Ms off my fiancée's stomach, when my phone rings.

I'm not on call so I won't be answering it. Whoever it is, has lousy timing.

The ringing stops and starts right back up.

"It must be important," Madison says, sitting up and ruining what I had planned once I passed her belly button.

"Stay there." I point to her and she giggles, falling back down to the mattress, three lonely M&Ms right above her small patch of hair.

I reach for my phone, seeing Cristian's name.

"This better be important because I'm…"

Madison's knee nudges my ribcage and I stop talking. She's still shy about giving my brothers any confirmation that we're sleeping together. Pretty sure they've figured it out.

"A call came through," he says.

"Another warehouse fire?" I ask and Madison sits up, the M&Ms falling off her body.

There are still no leads on who is setting the fires, but the one that almost took my life was found to be arson as well.

"No."

"Okay, Cris, stop fucking around so I can go back to eating M&Ms off my fiancée."

"First off, way too much information. Second, congratulations. She decided to ruin her life and accept your proposal?"

"Did you call me to piss me off?"

"No, like I said, a call came in tonight. It was Mom and

Pop's house." I jump up from the bed, throwing Madison's clothes at her as I try to locate my own from the pile on the floor.

"Ma?" I ask.

"She passed out and she's on her way to the hospital. I'm on my way over from the station, said I had to leave for a family emergency. Luca's doing the same. I'm sorry to ruin your night with Maddie. We tried to wait and see, but when the paramedics decided she needed to be checked out at the hospital, we had to call you."

"Cris, you call me ASAP always. Madison will understand."

"She's heading to Mercy," he says.

I click the phone off without saying goodbye and Madison is already pulling up her pants.

"What happened?"

"Ma's being transported to Mercy. She passed out." I finally find my boxers and pull them on.

Madison comes over, pulling me into a hug, calming my nerves a bit. "It's going to be okay, Mauro. They'll figure it out."

I hold her a little tighter, hoping and praying she's right.

Whatever happens, at least I'll have her by my side.

The End

COCKAMAMIE UNICORN RAMBLINGS

We hope you enjoyed Maddie and Mauro! We feel like we introduced Mauro to you ages ago (for any new readers, he premiered in our Bedroom Games series last February. And then we sprinkled the brothers in through the Charity Case Series, just to tease you some more. #sorrynotsorry

The original idea for the setting of a family run Italian deli came from a place Piper visits for lunch sometimes. It's cute, been in town forever and the family that runs it is always warm and welcoming. From there we decided that we'd love to do a series about three Italian brothers, each of whom work as a different emergency services provider. (When you try to integrate characters throughout series as much as we do, you have to plan ahead!)

When we plot out a new series, we try to give you a storyline that we haven't wrote before. Flirting with Fire falls under the classic troupe, 'Ugly Duckling'—where the girl who wasn't pretty in high school suddenly loses the glasses and braces and drops a few dress sizes, transforming her into a swan. We didn't much care for the name of this trope for obvious reasons and were happy to find that the trope has been renamed 'Beautiful All Along'.

Although neither one of us liked going back to high school, it was enjoyable to write a story where the characters each have so much growth. Proving again, high school doesn't define who you are and who you will become.

Maddie was a beautiful woman inside and out all along,

but she had to find it within herself to really understand that. Her outward appearance wasn't what Mauro fell in love with, he fell for the person she is. And once she saw herself the way he did, they could have their HEA.

Vanessa and Cristian's story is coming up next in Crushing On The Cop...we have some ideas up our sleeve and although it's a 'Boss's Daughter' trope, there's SOOO much more to their story.

Now let's put our hands together for our awesome team!

The cover is awesome thanks to Letitia from RBA Designs and we appreciate her hard work but Colton Bensen did give her a pretty gorgeous face to work with. Are we right?

Wander Aguiar for his top-notch photography skills making Colton our Mauro.

Ellie from Love N Books for line editing. We're still working on giving you a manuscript with more notice (thanks for always being so accommodating and constantly getting it back to us on time).

Shawna from Behind the Writer for being ready when we are, offering not only her eagle eye but story development, too.

Dani Sanchez and the whole Inkslinger PR gang for their organization and planning to get Flirting with Fire out there to the bloggers and readers.

All the bloggers who carve out time to read and review our books. We know there's a lot of books out there and your reading time is precious. Thank you! xo

All our early ARC readers, first for wanting to read our stuff early and for posting their reviews.

And of course, all our unicorns. <3 What can we say that we've haven't in prior CUR's? Without sounding like a cheesy romance novel you keep us going. Without our faithful group who love our characters as much as we do, we wouldn't be inspired to develop more heroes and heroines for you to enjoy!

xo,
Piper & Rayne

ABOUT PIPER & RAYNE

Piper Rayne is a USA Today Bestselling Author duo who write "heartwarming humor with a side of sizzle" about families, whether that be blood or found. They both have e-readers full of one-clickable books, they're married to husbands who drive them to drink, and they're both chauffeurs to their kids. Most of all, they love hot heroes and quirky heroines who make them laugh, and they hope you do, too!

ALSO BY PIPER RAYNE

Blue Collar Brothers

Flirting with Fire

Crushing on the Cop

Engaged to the EMT

White Collar Brothers

Sexy Filthy Boss

Dirty Flirty Enemy

Wild Steamy Hook-up

The Modern Love World

Charmed by the Bartender

Hooked by the Boxer

Mad about the Banker

The Single Dad's Club

Real Deal

Dirty Talker

Sexy Beast

Hollywood Hearts

Mister Mom

Animal Attraction

Domestic Bliss

Bedroom Games

Cold as Ice

On Thin Ice

Break the Ice

Box Set

Chicago Law

Smitten with the Best Man

Tempted by my Ex-Husband

Seduced by my Ex's Divorce Attorney

The Rooftop Crew

My Bestie's Ex

A Royal Mistake

The Rival Roomies

Our Star-Crossed Kiss

The Do-Over

A Co-Workers Crush

The Baileys

Lessons from a One-Night Stand

Advice from a Jilted Bride

Birth of a Baby Daddy

Operation Bailey Wedding (Novella)

Falling for My Brother's Best Friend

Demise of a Self-Centered Playboy

Confessions of a Naughty Nanny

Operation Bailey Babies (Novella)

Secrets of the World's Worst Matchmaker

Winning My Best Friend's Girl

Rules for Dating your Ex

Operation Bailey Birthday (Novella)

The Greene Family

My Twist of Fortune

My Beautiful Neighbor

My Almost Ex

My Vegas Groom

A Greene Family Summer Bash

My Sister's Flirty Friend

My Unexpected Surprise

My Famous Frenemy

A Greene Family Vacation

My Scorned Best Friend

My Fake Fiancé

My Brother's Forbidden Friend

A Greene Family Christmas

Lake Starlight

The Problem with Second Chances

The Issue with Bad Boy Roommates

The Trouble with Runaway Brides

Hockey Hotties

My Lucky #13

The Trouble with #9

Faking it with #41

Sneaking around with #34

Second Shot with #76

Offside with #55

Kingsmen Football Stars

You Had Your Chance, Lee Burrows

You Can't Kiss the Nanny, Brady Banks

Over My Brother's Dead Body, Chase Andrews

Chicago Grizzlies

Something like Hate

Something like Lust

Something like Love

Standalones

Single and Ready to Jingle

Claus & Effect

www.ingramcontent.com/pod-product-compliance
Lightning Source LLC
Chambersburg PA
CBHW020125310726
48970CB00006B/1725